THICKER THAN BLOOD

THICKER THAN BLOOD
DRAGON'S DAUGHTER™ BOOK 3

KEVIN MCLAUGHLIN
MICHAEL ANDERLE

This book is a work of fiction. All of the characters, organizations, and events portrayed in this novel are either products of the author's imagination or are used fictitiously. Sometimes both.

Copyright © 2021 LMBPN Publishing
Cover Art by Jake @ J Caleb Design
http://jcalebdesign.com / jcalebdesign@gmail.com
Cover copyright © LMBPN Publishing
A Michael Anderle Production

LMBPN Publishing supports the right to free expression and the value of copyright. The purpose of copyright is to encourage writers and artists to produce the creative works that enrich our culture.

The distribution of this book without permission is a theft of the author's intellectual property. If you would like permission to use material from the book (other than for review purposes), please contact support@lmbpn.com. Thank you for your support of the author's rights.

LMBPN Publishing
PMB 196, 2540 South Maryland Pkwy
Las Vegas, NV 89109

First US Edition, January 2021
eBook ISBN: 978-1-64971-417-6
Print ISBN: 978-1-64971-418-3

THE THICKER THAN BLOOD TEAM

Thanks to our Beta Readers
Rachel Beckford, Larry Omans

Thanks to the JIT Readers

Dave Hicks
Jeff Goode
Daryl McDaniel
Veronica Stephan-Miller
Dorothy Lloyd
Wendy L Bonell
Deb Mader
Diane L. Smith
Paul Westman

If we've missed anyone, please let us know!

Editor
The Skyhunter Editing Team

CHAPTER ONE

The Lumos School seemed like a completely different place to Kylara Diamantine. It was wild how different it could feel after only a few months. When she'd left for winter break, she'd wondered if she would return. Now that she was there, though, she couldn't believe it had ever been in question.

It simply felt so good to be in a place surrounded by young, eager people trying to better themselves. Of course, it didn't hurt that she was something of a hero now.

"Oh, my God, will they ever stop staring at you?" Tanya whispered. They were in Magical Theory together and the mages who had kept to themselves before now giggled and levitated notes to Kylara. She already had a nice little stack of them. It seemed that some of the boys wanted to know if she had a boyfriend lined up for the Valentine's Day dance. Strangely enough, so did some of the girls.

"It's not so bad, is it? At least we're no longer outcasts."

"Speak for yourself." Karl Midnight snorted at the neighboring table. The class was supposed to work on sensing each other's inner magic, an activity that lent itself very well to gossiping instead of doing the prescribed work. "I helped to bury those skeletons too and no one sings my praises or sends me notes."

"How do you think I feel?" Tanya added. "If it weren't for my ability to make plants grow, Kylara wouldn't have acquired it and no one would have been able to stop those dragons."

"See, it's good," she said from her place between the others. "You two never agreed about anything before. My new popularity is bringing you together."

Professor Sharra dragged her focus away from grading and stood, brushed her hair back, and rubbed her hands over the shaved sides of her head. She needed a trim, Kylara thought when she realized she could hardly see the geometric tattoos etched on the side of the woman's head to help augment her magic power.

"All right, that's enough for today. Your homework is a thousand words of sensory details about another person's power. I will give extra credit if you're a mage writing about a dragon or a dragon writing about a mage."

A number of hands were raised.

Professor Sharra shook her head as she smiled. "No, I won't decide who gets to work with Kylara, but if I receive more than three reports about her, points will be deducted from your grades. Kylara, if anyone keeps bugging you, tell me and I'll deal with them."

"Part mage, part dragon, all snitch," Karl whispered and Tanya laughed. The entire class turned to see a red-faced Kylara.

With class dismissed, the three friends headed toward the cafeteria. Before they had stepped out of the building and into the snow-covered grass within the U, Kylara already had her first taker. It was Jasmine Patel, her former roommate and the only student mage besides her who had fought against the horde of dragon skeletons that had descended on the school grounds at the end of the previous semester.

"Kylara, I want to do the homework assignment with you. Cool?" Although Jasmine delivered all the words in a smooth, bossy monotone, Kylara was quite thankful for the 'cool,' at the end. Last semester, when the girl had discovered that she was not a dragon but a mage who could absorb dragon powers and take their form, she had been fairly open with her disgust. Fighting for their lives together had changed Jasmine, although her bossy, entitled veneer remained the same.

"That's cool. Is this afternoon all right?"

"Sure. I'll see you before dinner."

"Great, Jasmine, see you then."

The girl nodded and hurried to catch up with a group of mages. Despite the two of them having a way better relationship than they had ever had when they'd shared living quarters, they still weren't as close as Kylara and Tanya. But she was okay with that. You could only have one best friend, after all.

They entered the cafeteria and she grinned at the sheer splendor of the room. It never ceased to amaze her. Every time she entered the room, whether for breakfast, lunch, or dinner, she couldn't help but be impressed.

It wasn't only the marble floor done in the shape of a dragon in tiles of black and white. Nor was it the wooden pillars carved with intricate leaves and vines and covered in gold leaf. The frescos on the ceiling were wonderful, but Kylara thought that in a museum, she might find them less than impressive. It was the combination of all these elements that made the room beautiful, although even that didn't quite explain why she loved the dining hall so much.

The sound of the room had much to do with its appeal. No matter the time of day, there was always conversation going on. The sounds of students lost in study, debating the outcome of a sports game, or trying to flirt and failing reverberated faintly off the walls, which made the room feel fuller than furniture ever could.

There were also the aromas in the room. Today, if she wasn't mistaken, she could smell a stew of bison meat and dried red chilies—a taste of New Mexico. Kylara grinned. She was the only student who lived in the state. Most of the dragons and mages at the Lumos School came from the wealthiest corners of the world. The fact that it smelled like chili in there was a testimony to how good her year had been going. She had even made an impression on the mages who worked in the kitchen.

"Do you two want me to save you a seat or whatever?" Karl Midnight asked.

"How can you save us a seat when you still have to get your lunch?" Tanya asked.

Karl winked and a rope of dark, inky shadow launched from his feet. It slid away from him toward the buffet, where it split so it could take a bowl of chili, a plate of cornbread, and a cup of tea.

"That's disgusting," Tanya said. Kylara knew that it wasn't particularly gross to her roommate, but the two dragons couldn't help but scrap with each other. The only person who fought with Karl more was Samuel Lumos.

"Hey, guys!" Sam waved to catch their attention from where he was already seated alone at a table and smiled his brilliant smile. He was so radiantly handsome that Kylara sometimes wondered if he used his light powers to make his smile glow.

"Kylara?" Karl asked although he knew as well as she did that it was an unnecessary offer. His shadow powers had been one of the first dragon abilities she had absorbed. If she wanted to skip the line, she could do so as easily as he had.

"I can do it myself, thanks Karl," she said. "If you want to go save our seats with Sam, that would be great."

Midnight looked as if he'd rather let all the dragons in the cafeteria stab him with the points of their tails but he nodded and sulked with every step toward the table. She knew she shouldn't smile about it but it was amusing how he was able to wipe the perfect grin off of Samuel's face.

"I can't believe you did that, Ky!" Tanya looked scandalized as she put her hand on her shoulder. "We'd better hurry before those two tear each other apart."

The girls shuffled forward in the line for chili and cornbread and chatted amicably about nothing in particular while they waited. At one point, Tanya had to snap her fingers to bring Kylara's attention back to the conversation at hand. She had been distracted trying to return the waves from the other students. Now that she had saved all their lives, she was much more popular than she'd been when she had arrived with nothing but the clothes on her back.

They filled their bowls and Kylara thanked the mage serving them before they turned toward the table. She waved, nodded, and smiled at everyone she passed, but her real focus was on the two boys.

"I'm merely saying she wasn't alone out there," Karl said as they approached. Tendrils of his shadow power inched slowly across the table toward the golden dragon. Any time one got too close, Sam pointed a finger at it and vaporized the darkness with a tight beam of light. Kylara thought this antagonistic game they played was the only reason neither had murdered the other yet.

"I know she wasn't alone. I was there too," Sam responded. "But that doesn't change the fact that we'd all be toast if it wasn't for Kylara." He zapped a tendril of shadow that wasn't all that close to him as if to prove his point.

"Oh, not this again," Tanya said.

"Are you two still going on about how awesome I am?" Kylara asked. "Because if so, there's no reason to stop."

"I'm not saying you're not awesome," Karl said, his gaze on the table while he sent a thread of shadow around the edge to try to flank Sam. "I'm simply saying that we were all out there and you're the only one getting love letters. Not that I would ever go to that stupid dance."

"So you're jealous of 'love letters' you don't particularly want?" Tanya asked incredulously.

"I'm not jealous." Karl scoffed. "I'm disgusted. Everyone treated her like crap and now, they're all fawning over her. It's stupid."

"You used to treat me like crap," Tanya pointed out.

"Yeah, that's true, I guess," he admitted. Kylara had to give it to the boy with shadow powers and the long greasy black hair to match. He wasn't one to shy away from admitting to his poor behavior. "I thought Kylara was a lame country bumpkin who didn't even know how to fix her acne scars until she got more powers."

She gritted her teeth. While she liked Karl and respected him and the font of bravery he possessed despite no one liking him, he still sometimes said crappy things like pointing out the blemishes on her face. She ran a hand through her dark hair and dislodged some from behind her ears to fall over her face and cover the marks.

"Kylara, you're beautiful. There's no need to hide because Karl put his foot in his mouth. If you did that, you'd never come out ever again." Sam blasted the shadow creeping around the edge of the table. "Nice try, by the way. If I was like six years old and blind."

Karl chuckled at that. He also had a knack for laughing at himself that was appealing.

"Maybe people would pay more attention to the rest of us if we all did as well in school as Kylara," Tanya pointed out.

The dragon mage grinned. "It's not my fault I have special powers."

All three of her friends threw their hands up in protest.

"And your powers mean you're doing good in Dragon and Human History?" Sam got in first.

"Or Geography of Dragons?" Tanya asked.

"Fancy dress has a point," Karl added. "That is seriously the dullest class on the face of the earth."

She shrugged. "Maybe to all of you, but I...well, I like my classes."

"All of them?" Tanya asked a little skeptically.

"Sure. Remember that you guys grew up immersed in all this. My mom was a dragon but what she taught me...let's say if it wouldn't help me to catch a deer or clean a pump, we didn't do a deep delve."

"Oh, hey. Speak of the devil," Karl said and some of the dark tendrils on the table popped up to gesture behind Kylara.

Hester Diamantine strode through the cafeteria. Even though she'd been free for months now, it still filled Kylara with calming relief every time she saw her mom look at her with her perpetually grim expression. She waved with her scarred hand—a feature that had always endeared her to her daughter and made her seem superhuman for suffering a wound so powerful it had overwhelmed her dragon healing power.

"Hello, Lady Diamantine," Sam said as he stood and bowed deeply to the former member of Dragon SWAT.

"Hello, Sam," Hester said. A twinkle in her eyes that never reached her mouth told Kylara that she found the boy amusing. The girl knew that all her friends saw nothing but the dragon's hard, icy expression.

"Do you all mind if I steal Kylara for a few minutes?" Hester asked cordially. She mimicked Sam's overly formal style and in doing so made tea shoot out of Karl's nose when he tried to stifle his laughter.

"But of course, my lady," Sam said quickly, out of his element now that he'd tried to be too formal.

"What is it?" Kylara asked.

"I think it would be better if we talk outside. It's about our home or what's left of it after the fire."

She stood and followed the dragon out of the room, concerned that she hadn't been any better at reading Hester's expression than her friends had.

CHAPTER TWO

Kylara followed her mom out into the brisk winter air. Though it wasn't currently snowing, she could still feel the chill reach her bones. Hester didn't seem bothered by it but she never looked bothered by anything. It was what was simultaneously great and frustrating about her. The young mage wondered more than once what it must have been like for her Aunt Cassandra to hold Hester Diamantine a prisoner. Had there ever been any chance of her mage aunt breaking the dragon? She doubted it.

"Are you all right?" Hester asked. Although the words were said woodenly, they still meant a lot to Kylara. Her mom—despite her sometimes hard exterior—had always cared for her daughter.

"Yeah, it's only the cold but I can take care of that." She flexed one of the lesser powers she had acquired. Ruby Firedrake had inadvertently burned her with her ability to heat her body to scalding temperatures and since then, she had been able to do the same as Ruby. She warmed her body while the snow around her and Hester melted and finally evaporated.

Her mother smiled and shook her head in gentle amazement.

"What?" she asked. "It's not as impressive as turning your scales to diamonds."

"The fact that you can do both as well as your other abilities and control them all is what impresses me," Hester said and focused on the ring of grubby soil and grass around them revealed by the melted snow.

"Using all the different powers is the fun part," Kylara said and made wildflowers burst from the warmed earth to bloom around their ankles.

"That's good to hear, Kylara. It truly is. And to think I kept you trapped on that parched piece of land near the mountains because I was afraid of you gaining more powers like this."

"For your information, I miss that parched piece of land," she replied.

"Well then, that's why I wanted to talk to you." Diamantine had never been one to change a subject subtly. "I'm going to go back and rebuild."

"What? When?" Kylara demanded, surprised.

"Today. I wanted to tell you sooner but…" Hester shrugged a little uncomfortably. She had never been one to communicate anything but what was essential. There had been times when Kylara was growing up that the dragon had vanished for days, only to return and seem confused by her daughter's frustration with her. In her mind, the fridge had been full so what was the problem?

"Fine." Kylara had long since learned to take these abrupt changes in stride. "Will we fly there? I can be ready in five minutes."

Hester smiled more gently than she had since their conversation began. "Not we, Kylara. Only me. You need to stay at the Lumos School."

"What? That's crazy. It was our home that was burned, not yours. I lived there as long as you did. If I let you rebuild it alone, you'll mess my room up." She knew the dragon wouldn't laugh—Hester never laughed—but she hoped the humor would at least soften her resolve.

"It was our home, but I built it. I can do so again. You must stay here and build your life, Kylara. That's far more important than a house."

"But you only just got back. I thought the headmaster was more than happy to let you stay."

"It's not her decision. It's mine," her mother said firmly—like that explained anything.

"So change it."

"Kylara, be serious. You're no longer the little baby girl I found in a canoe. You're a powerful young dragon."

"Mage," she interjected.

"Whatever you are, you're far more powerful and inspiring than I had ever imagined you could become. You've already made me so proud, but you have to spread your wings a little."

"I spread my wings considerably when you were kidnapped," Kylara protested. "When the house was burned, I adapted. I did what was necessary to survive and I did what I had to do to rescue you! How can you leave me now?"

"Oh, hush now, Kylara. Can you even hear yourself? We watched numerous human films while you were growing up. How many of the college students had their mother living a building over from them? What will your friends and the rest of the students think if I'm always hanging over your shoulder?"

She didn't quite know what to say to that. Her mom was right and she knew that, except that she had not had a normal life, not by anyone's definition. The idea of doing something simply because it was the way regular old humans did it was not a great argument for a mage raised by dragons, but the sentiment was right all the same.

Hester studied her. "You grew up in my house and we spent every day of our lives together."

"Not every day."

"Most of them, though. I am so thankful that you grew up to

be as strong as you are. You're strong enough to be on your own now or at least alone here with your friends, teachers, and the guard mages," Hester's eyes twinkled, the closest she ever came to grinning. "It's not like I'll be that far away. Our land is in the same state, something that isn't true for anyone else here. If you need me, I'll get here as fast as I can fly."

"If I need you, I'll open a portal and come get you, Mom."

Her mother sucked a breath in through her nose as her eyes welled with tears. "You still want to call me that?" She exhaled slowly and fought valiantly to keep the tears from spilling out of her pale eyes that were so different from Kylara's dark ones.

"Of course I do!" She threw her arms around her mom. "You raised me. You taught me how to cook chili and how to clean a jammed pump. You'll always be my mom. You've always been there for me. Well, until you were kidnapped, but you still came when I needed you. I love you, Mom."

Hester squeezed her in response, and Kylara felt hot teardrops on her shoulder. "Your biological mother would be very proud of you, I'm sure."

"Only because you taught me to be caring and thoughtful and to treat mages and dragons like people," Kylara said, which earned another choked sob from her mom.

"You're so strong, Kylara," Hester said and although she pulled away from her daughter, she kept her hands on her shoulders as she stared into her eyes. "I can't wait to see what else you accomplish."

"You're about to accomplish detention," Karl shouted from across the courtyard as he headed to their next class.

"I love you, mom."

"I love you too, Kylara. But I should go now, as should you. I've worked with Kor, you know. He was a real pain in the ass if I was late. I can only imagine how it must be now that he's your professor."

"I'll survive," she said.

"I know you will," the dragon replied. Then, after one last parting hug, Diamantine took her dragon form and flew to the west in the chilly winter air.

CHAPTER THREE

When Lord Boneclaw first heard the mewling whine of the mage's voice calling him to the material plane, he had ignored her. She had warded herself against possession, but even if she hadn't, the lord who had ruled the dragon political sphere from the shadows for millennia wasn't particularly interested in coming back as an aging mage who derived most of her power from making spirits obey her.

He had considered simply rushing her body, overwhelming it with his malevolent energy, and bursting her like an overripe peach. He certainly knew enough of human anatomy to make this happen, but there would have been consequences. He almost certainly could have left the skull untouched while he obliterated the rest of her body, but that could lead to dangerous questions if it were discovered by the wrong people.

There had simply been nothing to lure him to the land of the living, not until the mage enlisted the help of a dragon with quite unusual powers.

The mage had called him to the material plane to inhabit his own body and that had changed things. Being dead hadn't been that bad. Boneclaw—more than willing to admit to himself that he was obsessed with power—had found ways to tether himself to the material realm. It meant that when he died, he didn't fall into the oblivion that most did. Instead, he went to what could be called in-between, a place of peace and rest that he had carved out for himself from the souls of the dead before he had died. There had been no reason to leave it until he sensed his bones walking upon the earth he had sought to rule for so long.

So when the time came, he had answered the mage's summons. When Cassandra had called his spirit, he came forth from his waiting place and flowed into his bones. Since then, he had been coming to terms with exactly what he was still capable of.

They were in one of his old lairs now, a castle in the south of France that the locals thought was haunted. This was largely because any time anyone tried to buy it, clean it up, or move in over the centuries, Lord Boneclaw had eviscerated them and stolen their skulls. Those kinds of rumors tended to persist, even though he hadn't been around for the last year to keep up appearances.

"Lord Boneclaw, I call on thee. Show thyself. I command it!" Cassandra shouted from the main hall on the first floor of the castle.

He could always hear her. No matter where he was in relation to her—even if they were on different continents—he could hear her. The thing was, however, that he didn't have to obey. The body Galen had restored to him gave him many things, one of which was a barrier between himself and the commands of the mage. But it wouldn't do for her to know that yet so when she called, he answered, despite the inconvenience and irritation.

Resigned to his current pretense, he changed into his shadow form—an ability he had learned from the pixies so long before and which could not be taken from him, even in death—and flowed through cracks in the stones of the castle. He poured out into the biggest hall. Billowing clouds of shadow filled the darkest corners of the room before his bones began to take shape. His front legs manifested first, then his shoulders and spine followed by his back legs, and finally, his head and tail.

He roared in displeasure at being summoned—a farce that both terrified Cassandra and kept her convinced that she was indeed the person still in charge of their relationship—then bowed to her.

Even this gesture of subservience filled the mage with terror. Or so he thought. Boneclaw was a master of reading auras and controlling his own, yet the emotional state of the mage remained frustratingly obfuscated. It was like what she felt was always hidden behind a fog, and the more he tried to shine a light to pierce it, the more it reflected at him.

Still, he knew his form scared young Galen to his very core, and Cassandra didn't seem very comfortable when he coalesced out of the shadows, either.

He knew it was because of his appearance. Plainly put, he was little more than a skeleton, a massive dragon skeleton with spikes of bone at his elbows, running down his spine, and jutting from his skull. It was the little more that made all the difference, however. His dragon form was held together with magic and the creeping, veiny webbing of his spirit tying the bones together. Instead of a skeleton of pure white bone like the rest of Galen's revenants were, Boneclaw was tainted with blackness. Cassandra thought it meant she could control the dead dragon, while Galen knew it meant he could not.

"I have shown myself to thee, as you commanded," the ancient dragon intoned formally. "Why do you interrupt my study?"

"For the very same reason I summoned you in the first place, Lord Boneclaw," she said and bowed respectfully, although not as deeply as she should have. When he was finally done with this farce, he would demand that the mage kneel before him and kiss the very earth he had trod upon. If she refused? Well, he very much liked the shape of this one's skull.

"I have told you I cannot make you a dragon. Perhaps when I still had all the powers I possessed in life, I could have but alas, not anymore." That was a lie. He had the ability to turn to shadow, was particularly proficient with his aura, and knew how to use bone spurs to lethal effect, but that was the limit of his capabilities. He had no power to turn a mage or anyone else into a dragon. No one in this realm did.

"Some of your abilities still elude you, then? Even with the months of practice we have granted you?" Cassandra asked.

Lord Boneclaw wanted to point out that he had given them months. They were in his castle, after all, purchasing supplies with treasure he had stashed away centuries earlier. But if the charade was to continue, he had to answer direct questions. The mage had done him the favor of explaining how she had expected her magic to bind his spirit.

"My powers over darkness are as formidable as ever, but I still cannot take my human form," he admitted. "Which means there is no chance I can help you achieve dragonhood. If I cannot shift between the two states, I cannot teach you to do so either."

The mage nodded and tried to hold the faux confidence in place, but he saw it slip or thought he did. He hated not being able to read this woman's aura. "If there is still nothing you can do for us, why stay in this realm at all?"

It was a challenge and an insult, but he ignored it for now. This petty mage's time would come. That was a promise he made to himself every time she overstepped her place as a mage, which was often. Besides, there were still things he wanted from his two summoners. "Perhaps if young Lord Stormwing could use his power on the skeleton of a mage, I could have a human form as well. Then I would be able to help you both, I'm sure of it."

"No," Galen said and looked up from where he was slumped in dragon form against a wall of the castle. "I won't bring a living person here so you can kill them and experiment on their bones. It simply will not happen."

It was the only position the boy had any opinion on at all. For everything else, he deferred to the mage—for meals, for what he did with his time, for everything. He was like a lost little lamb who only knew one thing—fear the wolf.

The ancient dragon could read the boy's aura as plain as day. He was scared of Boneclaw and himself. While he said he wouldn't attempt to take control of the skeleton of a still-living person, he could feel in Galen's aura that the boy wrestled with the idea of raising dead ones as well.

It was an unfortunate turn of events but he saw no way around it, not without breaking the boy's mind with his aura, which might render his power useless. It had never been a good choice in his opinion. He much preferred patience and subtlety to simply destroying his toys.

"We've been over this before, Lord Boneclaw. Mages are off-limits," Cassandra said sternly like he was one of her lowly elemental spirits instead of something so much more.

"Then there is nothing I can do to help you achieve your dream," he said and started to fade into shadow to return to his training.

"Stop!" Cassandra ordered in her bossiest tone. Boneclaw complied and made a mental note to add an extra second to her moment of death—whenever it came—at his hands.

"Was there something else you wished to know?" he all but growled, making it clear—even to this obtuse mage with her impossible to perceive aura—that he was not comfortable with being ordered about.

"What if there's a way that doesn't involve a mage body?" Cassandra asked as she had so many times before. "Both the Steel Dragon and Amythist and even young Galen received their additional powers in the pixie realm. That's where you earned the power over shadow as well, isn't it?"

He drew the shadow away from himself and took a step toward her. He had assumed that she must have guessed this secret of his, but she hadn't brought it up before. Was there some reason for this new flavor of impertinence?

"Yes, I gained my powers in the pixie realm. They helped me but I very much doubt that they would agree to such an arrangement again."

"But you know how you got powers. If we could go there together, perhaps I could learn a dragon power in the same way you did."

Lord Boneclaw clacked his skeletal claws on the floor of his castle as he appraised this mage. Something had indeed changed about her. She knew something.

"That would be very likely if it were possible to go to the pixie realm but we can't. Not without a pixie."

"But—"

"I know all about Constance Vigil and her ability to teleport. I fought against it and tricked her into using it while I was still alive, remember? It won't work."

Cassandra bowed slightly, the way Boneclaw himself would have bowed to a maid after asking her to pick up a particularly gruesome corpse. It was a respectful gesture done as disrespectfully as possible. "And if there was another way—a different way?"

Lord Boneclaw paused. Had the clever little mage learned something that was genuinely interesting?

"What are you talking about?" he demanded and used frustration to hide his real curiosity.

"My niece, Kylara Diamantine, has learned to gate like the pixies. She can transit across the planes exactly as they do. My air spirit watching the campus has seen her do it more than once."

For the first time since he had been resurrected, he was speechless. How was this possible? He had pursued numerous roads into the pixie realm for centuries and every path led to a dead end. Now, this welp of a mage with dragon powers she didn't deserve could do it at will? Curious. How terribly curious.

And then there was the implication of Cassandra's certainty. She had said that her spirits had witnessed such a feat more than once. This meant she had been withholding information from him and he decided she would suffer for that. But first, he needed to see how he could make use of this windfall.

"How did she come to have these powers?"

"I'm not exactly sure," the mage said. "She has an unusual collection of abilities, but all the others have parallels in the dragon world. This one—"

"She probably had a pixie do it on her and absorbed it," Galen piped up from his position near the wall.

Cassandra shushed the despondent boy irritably.

Lord Boneclaw would have raised an eyebrow if he had one. "She absorbed it? But how, pray tell, is that possible? You told me, Lady Cassandra, that the girl's powers have been manifesting as she grew. That is rather different than her absorbing them."

"What? That's not how it works," Galen said while the mage cast daggers at him with her eyes. "Kylara can use any power that's been used on her. I think. She might have to be hurt or something or maybe there's a limit? All I know is that she got plant powers from Tanya, light powers from Sam, and dark powers from Karl Midnight."

"How very interesting," Lord Boneclaw all but purred. "And to think that Lady Cassandra has been giving me a completely different perspective."

"Oh," the boy said. The look he gave Cassandra was one of apology and concern. The ancient dragon smiled all the more broadly at that.

"So, the mage doesn't merely acquire powers from dragons, she takes them from whomever she wishes," Lord Boneclaw hypothesized. This was interesting, very interesting. He would very much like power like that. If there was a way he could meet the girl in the pixie realm, perhaps he could learn the power as well.

Cassandra blathered on, oblivious to what he now understood was possible. No, not merely possible—his destiny. "So if I could convince my niece to go there, maybe I could acquire a power, right? You know places where it can be done and will show me."

"Yes," Boneclaw answered and let the shadow consume him and melt his bones into insubstantial blackness. "Yes, there may be a way, but I must study the boundary between the two realms further. If the girl is able to open a path at will, it may be that there are other channels I had not found before."

"I won't let you vanish into the bowels of this castle for another month," she whined. He still couldn't sense her aura but he could hear her desperation in her voice. She wanted to be a dragon—longed for it. He smiled, pleased by the knowledge that he could use that.

"In three days, I will tell you what I have learned and together, we will help break down the barriers between mage and dragon kind."

Cassandra nodded and released him with a gesture. It meant nothing in reality, but Boneclaw tried to pay attention when she did it to keep the charade of her control over him intact.

His darkness flowed through the castle, seeping from crack to crack like water flowing deep beneath the earth. He continued his steady descent until he reached the dungeon. Originally, the subterranean room had been a cellar for wine, cheese, and root vegetables, but he thought the cages and manacles attached to the wall were a pleasing and practical touch.

He flowed through the space while he probed for ways into the pixie realm and his ethereal, shadowy form eased between iron bars and the links of chains as effortlessly as mist. The cellar was too small for him to take his dragon form so he was stuck in his shadowy body, but that didn't bother him at all. Nor would it interfere with his research.

Lord Boneclaw reached out for the pixie realm and tried to

sense it as he had so many times. Long before—millennia, he was sure—he had been able to sense the pixie realm in the very darkest of shadows. It had seemed like he could sense the dimension that had given him his powers but over time, that had faded.

Now, though, another factor had come into play. There was a magic in his resurrected bones that he had never tasted before. Lord Boneclaw was sure most dragons would find it unpleasant as it was rank with death, but he didn't make such childish distinctions between light and dark or life and death. Power was power and this one tasted new.

Lord Boneclaw made one bone—the foremost bone from his pointer claw—become substantial and appear on a table in the dungeon. He used this as a kind of inter-dimensional anchor. He could feel that the magic inside it was pixie magic. Was that because Galen had learned the resurrection power in the pixie realm? Did that mean any powers learned there would leave some kind of connection? All these were questions to explore later.

Right now, he focused and pushed harder on this connection. When he did so, he was rewarded with the sense of a place he had never been to before. It was a place of life and death where tall trees sank their roots deep into soil made of the decayed bodies of thousands. Although not all things were decayed and dank. There were beings—well, perhaps that was too kind—undead beings there. He could feel them calling to his bones, asking for direction or if he needed help.

Boneclaw answered in the affirmative.

The skeletons responded and chittered in excitement at meeting this source of magic so much stronger than themselves.

Oh, this was interesting. This was beyond interesting. This was something he had longed for over the millennia and now, through what almost felt like dumb luck, it was his. He had a secret entrance to the pixie realm and even better, it wasn't a place the pixies would easily stumble upon.

The ancient shadow dragon knew they didn't like the creatures of their realm any more than dragons did. These skeletons had responded to him but they would almost certainly defend the area viciously against all attackers. It was a wonder that Galen had managed to master them with his power, a wonder and—to Boneclaw anyway—a blessing.

As he eased himself into this swamp of death, a plan began to form in his head. This was interesting, exceedingly so, but the last thing he wanted was to raise more dragons and risk Cassandra bringing back their spirits as she had with him. If that happened, she might realize how little she controlled him. That simply wouldn't do.

The key to all of this was still Kylara Diamantine. If he could take her power, he would be truly all-powerful. And now that he had a path into the pixie realm, it might very well be possible.

But for all this to work, he'd need the girl to dance on his web. Which meant it was time to pay her a visit and see exactly what threads could be used to pull her where he wanted her to go.

CHAPTER FOUR

Practical Dragon Powers was easily Kylara's favorite class. During the previous semester, every duel had been conducted at the top of massive pillars which the dragons could not leave. This semester, duels were conducted either on the ground or in the air and were fought to first blood or forfeit. That made it much more fun in her opinion.

Better yet, since she had saved the entire school from Galen's out of control skeletons, she was no longer seen as a vacuum of magical powers. Now, dragons wanted her to have their powers, or some of them did, at least. It meant that when it was her turn to duel, she had numerous choices to choose from.

Today, she faced a dragon she didn't know very well but had wanted to fight for a while. Her name was Leslie Calciatus, but everyone called her Shelly on account of her special power. She could grow ridges of calcium from her spine, forearms, and tail. All of them had the pearlescent quality and fractal patterns of a snail or clamshell, hence the name.

Shelly wasn't an aquatic dragon, though. She had no gills and she used the unusual calcium growths as weapons more than anything else. Her specialty was launching the discs and spiraled spikes as projectiles, a skill she had greatly improved under the Silver Bullet's tutelage.

"Ground or air?" Kor asked Kylara as she was the challenger.

"Ground," she said, knowing that Shelly was not the best flyer. She wanted to enjoy the best fight possible.

"Excellent. To blood or forfeit. Shelly, rip her to pieces."

The dragon wasted no time. She leapt from her starting place toward her opponent, who braced herself to catch her bulk. Shelly tucked into a front flip and launched a spinning clamshell-shaped projectile from her tail.

Kylara raised her diamond scale-encrusted arm barely in time and the projectile ricocheted away.

Her adversary landed squarely on her feet, then reared on her hind legs so she could slash with her front limbs. To call them claws would be an understatement. She had turned every available inch of scale into long, razor-sharp discs and swung these at Kylara, who tried to defend herself as best as she could.

"How hard is that, diamond?" the dragon demanded as she pressed her attack.

"Hard enough," Kylara said and barely managed to dodge the girl's attacks. Shelly fought differently than most dragons, simply because she could attack with far more than only her claws and teeth. Every inch of her was deadly sharp and she knew it. She continually threw herself at her adversary and kept her on the defensive.

But Kylara's diamond scales weren't the only trick she had and she reached out with tendrils of shadow energy. They crept across the ground to bind Shelly's feet, but the girl had done her homework. She understood that if the shadow restraints were severed, everything beyond that point would puff away into nothing.

Without hesitation, she used this knowledge to effectively stop the shadow powers. It didn't matter as Kylara had other tricks up her sleeve. She called on the power she received from Sam and let it grow in her belly to burst out as a brilliant blast.

"Watch for her light!" Kor shouted a warning to Shelly.

The young dragon mage ground her teeth at her teacher but she understood why he was taking sides. Most dragons were lucky to have one power. She had at least five that were directly useful in combat and perhaps more depending on the terrain and how clever she felt.

She opened her jaw and unleashed a blast of light, but Shelly —again—was ready. The dragon grew a massive round shield that was reminiscent in shape and texture of a clamshell and used it to deflect the attack.

Fortunately, that wasn't all Kylara could do. The earth beneath their feet wasn't exactly thick with plant growth but there was still more than enough for her to work with. All they needed was a little water.

She looked at the winter sky and called the clouds to her. They billowed together and coalesced into a large gray rain cloud directly above the class. Before she made the clouds open to soak the plants and give them water to grow—and inadvertently soak her classmates, something that not even dragons liked in the cold of a New Mexico winter—she called down a bolt of lightning to strike her opponent.

But Shelly had seriously done her homework. While Kylara had called the storm, she had been working as well. She had constructed a profoundly tall spiral seashell. It was so tall it looked more like a narwhal horn than a shell. The top was a good ten feet taller than the crouching dragon, and the base was planted deep into the ground.

The lighting called from the sky struck this lightning rod and spared the dragon.

"Now mind the plants!" Kor coached.

Kylara leaned back and called for the cloud to burst upon the class. This earned her a collection of groans but it wasn't like anyone ran to the warmth of their dorms. Kor had made it quite clear that dragons didn't have the luxury of always being warm and dry.

As soon as the moisture touched the soil, the plants drank it with their roots and tried to bind Shelly to the earth.

The young dragon resisted, however. She ran circles around her opponent and bounded in such high leaps that she looked more like a rabbit than a dragon.

"That's like I showed you, good!" Kor shouted.

Shelly was grinning now and clearly relished lasting this long against the most popular girl in school and an undefeated duelist. As she ran, she hurled more of her shells at her adversary but her aim was off. Instead of puncturing the dragon mage's tail, three clamshells were impaled in the ground right next to it. Kylara ignored them and focused on binding the other dragon with plants.

The girl continued to run until she was on the other side, then threw three more of the clams. These two didn't strike home but Kylara finally understood that a direct blow wasn't the real plan. The shells were so tightly placed on either side of her tail that she couldn't move. Shelly had effectively anchored her in place.

"Do you like that, Diamantine?" Shelly called and tossed more shells to pin Kylara's hands to the dirt.

"Bring it on!" she shouted and poured all her strength into her plants. She found the seed of a mesquite tree and made it explode into life. It caught hold of one of Shelly's legs and held her fast. She didn't try to break free, though, and continued to use her shells against Kylara instead.

Soon, the two opponents were both pinned and laughed unrestrainedly while Kor shouted at the two of them.

"This is the most embarrassing show of dragon powers I've ever seen. You pathetic little cretins! Stop laughing! There's nothing funny about a draw."

"It's not a draw," Kylara said and tried to gain control of her laughter. "I forfeit. Shelly, that was great."

"I'll take the win!" The young dragon beamed. "But honestly, if you had pushed it any further, I wouldn't have been able to produce any more shells."

"Are you serious?" She tried to pull her hands free from the shells as she made the new mesquite tree binding the girl retract its roots below the surface.

"Yeah, if I can't move, I can't do much."

Kylara shook her head. It seemed she was the one who needed to apply herself a little better when it came to doing her homework.

"Both of you should be ashamed of yourselves," Kor snapped before he incinerated the tree that had grown in the middle of his combat field. "Fighting to a draw and arguing about who should have forfeit first. It's pathetic. Disgusting. Consider your grade for this duel an F. Next!"

Two dragons stepped forward as Kylara and Shelly took their human forms and went to rejoin the other students.

"That was badass," Karl Midnight told Kylara as she approached. "I'm impressed that she learned how to stop my shadow power."

"It's not your shadow power," Sam cut in before she could thank Karl for the compliment. "It's hers now."

"Oh, don't be all prissy because your light power was stopped by a shell." Karl had been far friendlier to her as of late—and to Tanya as well after a fashion—but he and Sam seemed incapable of agreement on anything.

"Your shadow power was stopped by a shell too," the golden dragon pointed out.

"I thought you said that was Kylara's." Midnight grinned mischievously, knowing full well that breaking the logic of his argument would bother Sam far more than it would bother him.

"Guys, it's cool. It was a good fight."

"You should have won, though," Karl pointed out.

"We can agree on that, at least," Sam grouched. He never liked it when Karl beat him to what he had wanted to say.

Kylara looked from one boy to the other, not at all sure how to respond. Tanya usually helped to deflate the tensions in these situations, but she wasn't in this class. Her anxiety began to increase a little, so it was a huge relief when Amy Williams soared toward them on her skateboard in the sky.

She dropped from above into a massive triple backflip melon grab, then landed smoothly and balanced on the rear truck of her skateboard with the help of her insanely powerful telekinesis.

"How's the world's weirdest mage doing?" Amy asked with a lopsided grin.

"Fine. I'm still trying to learn new powers. Shelly and I just fought so I have to wonder if I'll start to grow shells."

"That would be dope," the mage agreed. "Have you had any luck yet?"

"Naw." She shook her head. "I don't feel any different. I think I maybe need to be hurt or something."

"Right on. Keep getting stabbed then, I guess."

"Or not," Karl added. Kylara respected that he was one of the few people she knew who openly disagreed with the world's most powerful mage.

Amy chuckled, which in turn made Sam furrow his brows in anger. "I guess you do have a good range of powers already." The mage smirked. "Shells, though? They might be cool."

"Is there a reason you are distracting my students from the current duel?" Kor raged, his gimlet stare fixed on the intruder. Karl wasn't the only dragon willing to stand up to the being of power dressed as a skater punk.

"Yeah, Kor, I am about to leave. This is me saying goodbye to my friends and all, not something you would know much about!" Amy shouted, which earned a ripple of laughter from the class.

"Ha! Friends are for the weak!" Kor boomed. "You have two

minutes to do your little huggy-poos and kissy-wissies." Kylara had never heard the words "huggy-poos" or "kissy-wissies" said with such vitriol before. It was more than a little disconcerting, especially given the bombshell that the mage had dropped in her lap.

"Wait, you're leaving? As in the school?" she asked, hoping she had misunderstood.

"It's a big world out there and believe it or not, many are still not ready for dragons, mages, humans, pixies, and dwarves to all follow the same set of laws. Cassandra hasn't appeared since she vanished during the fight. We're aware that she might come back, but that doesn't change the reality that I'm needed elsewhere. It seems someone's been messing with some of the monuments in Detroit of the Steel Dragon's battles and the whole area reeks of magic. I've been recruited for the job."

"I guess that makes sense," Kylara said. She certainly didn't want to look like a little kid in front of one of her literal heroes who had referred to her as a friend.

"It's not like we're all that far away." Amy smiled before she frowned and put a finger to her chin. "Well, I guess we will be over a thousand miles away but I can open portals and you can open portals. What I'm trying to say is that even though this feels like goodbye, we'll always have the portals, yeah?"

"Yeah, the portals," she agreed and smiled at the fact that she and the world's most powerful mage were both joking about a power that not many besides the two of them could do unassisted.

"And keep working on your studies, you hear me?" the mage said, hopped onto her skateboard, and did tricks in place that seemed to break the rules of physics. The board was completing far too many twists and flips for nothing but her feet to be controlling it.

"Exactly like Kristen Hall," Amy continued, "you really could grow to be an important bridge between the two cultures. I know it's a large and daunting prospect but hey, this shit kind of happens to us sometimes and we have to be ready for it. Oh, dang, sorry about the language." She smiled and made it clear that she didn't particularly care.

"Right. A bridge." Kylara tried to not feel overwhelmed at the concept of the future of world peace resting on her shoulders. She tried even harder to not let Amy know that she didn't feel up to the challenge.

The famous mage flashed a last smile before she became fully airborne and streaked away on her skateboard.

Kylara waved goodbye until she was a barely distinguishable dot on the horizon.

CHAPTER FIVE

Amy was right about nothing weird happening on campus, but like most situations, change waited to confront them all.

After a few weeks and a few dozen invitations to the Valentine's Dance that Kylara ignored, the peace that had settled over her second semester at the Lumos school came to an abrupt end.

It happened when they were in Practical Dragon Powers and during a test in which pairs of partnered dragons and mages were instructed to team up and duel against other dragons and mages.

Kylara had waited her turn patiently, listening to Jasmine go on about the dance she'd missed. "I still don't see why you had to miss it. You had, like, a thousand invitations."

"Yeah, well, not from anyone I liked." As she said this, her gaze drifted from Sam to Karl. They were arguing over a mage who looked terrified about having to partner with one and fight against the other. It would take at least a week for all the mage and dragon duels to take place. Kylara and Jasmine were among the first since they didn't have to go through the effort of breaking through the dragon-mage barrier. Kylara had wondered if Kor would pair her with a dragon since she was technically a mage, but he'd never mentioned it.

"Oh? And who did you want an invite from?" Jasmine asked rhetorically as she hadn't failed to notice where Kylara was looking.

"I...no one. I don't know."

It was at that precise moment that a portal opened and interrupted the class. When monsters began to pour out of the rip in space-time, Kylara was probably the only person on the entire campus who was relieved at the arrival of a horde of dragon skeletons.

"It looks like Galen's back!" Sam shouted as he took his dragon form and flew toward the intruders. These weren't the full-size ones that had attacked last semester but small ones the size of cats and dogs.

"It's about time he showed up," Karl yelled and whipped tendrils of black shadow magic out to ensnare the dragon Sam knocked from the sky. Despite the constant arguing between the two, they had certainly learned to work together in a fight.

"Students, stand clear. The Silver Bullet has this one!" Kor boomed and launched volleys of silver spikes from his tail. Each of them found its mark and in mere moments, three skeletons were destroyed. No wonder they called him the Silver Bullet.

Most of the students began to run to the dorms but Kylara didn't budge. She called on her plant powers to reach out and entangle the creature Karl held with his powers. The plant roots, hungry to return this aberration to its resting place beneath the soil, dragged the tiny dragon skeleton into the earth where it ceased to struggle.

"I'll work with Tanya!" Jasmine shouted and a gust of wind followed as she launched herself upward by grabbing her robes with her telekinesis.

Kor roared as he sank his mind into battle mode. He was

formidable and lashed out with silver claws while he launched a continuous assault of spikes into the skeletons from his tail.

Kylara and her team worked well together and the results were impressive, given that they were all students. Sam knocked down any skeleton that took to the air and Karl bound and held them until Kylara was ready to sink them into the dirt using plant roots.

"I don't think Galen is doing this," Tanya shouted to her friends as she flew closer to join the battle with Jasmine on her back. She landed and added her plant powers to Kylara's to draw another group of the invaders underground. The friends had lost count of numbers and the skeletons continued to pour out of the portal.

"He's the only dude we know who controls skeletons," Karl pointed out and his words dripped with sarcasm.

"I think Tanya's right!" Kylara shouted, left the plants to her friend's expertise, and joined the melee with Sam where her diamond scales would be put to better use.

"Explain!" the golden dragon said before he snatched a tiny monster in his jaws and tossed it toward the others.

"Aunt Cassandra probably took Galen but she doesn't know anything about portals! She can't open them like I can."

The words weren't even cold when the portal closed without even a flicker of warning.

The few creatures left on this side of it struggled for their survival but they were too small to accomplish much. Kylara and her friends, together with Kor's battle mastery, dispatched them easily.

"You kids didn't do that badly," the instructor bellowed. "You almost got as many working together as I did on my own. Consider your midterms passed. Now, get back to your rooms. Campus is locked down. You have five minutes before you all have detention."

High-fives echoed off the snow-covered buildings as Kylara

and her friends hurried to their respective dorms. They talked while they walked, although their professors would perhaps have called it conspiring.

"I can't believe the Silver Bullet passed us based on that." Sam grinned broadly.

"Lucky for you. I got in trouble for rushing out of class." Tanya pouted. "My professor said that Kylara could handle it."

Everyone groaned at that.

"Come on you guys, you know I need your help," Kylara said.

"Yeah, we know," Karl agreed. "But that doesn't mean we won't give you crap for taking all the credit."

"I agree with Karl for once," Tanya said.

"Twice. I agree that wasn't Galen," Karl said and the conversation sobered immediately.

"How come?" Sam asked.

"Because it wasn't a portal to anywhere on earth," Tanya stated. "Those skeletons came from the same weird pixie swamp where I got my plant powers and Galen learned to control them."

"Cassandra can't do that either," Kylara said. "If she could, we'd know about it."

"Do you still think they're together?" Tanya asked.

Kylara nodded. "I do. I saw her talking to him before she vanished and I honestly don't know how else he could have gotten away."

"Maybe he can open portals to the pixie world," Jasmine suggested.

"I don't think anyone can do that," Sam said, "except Kylara."

"Well, it wasn't me," Kylara said.

No one said anything to that. There was merely a moment of awkward silence before they all went their separate ways.

"Thanks for getting detention for me," Kylara told Tanya as they trudged to their room.

"Psh. I was only hoping everyone would start to think I'm the crazy, reckless, popular one."

"Do people truly think I'm all three of those?" she asked.

"I know I do." The young dragon smiled, unaware that she was making her roommate uncomfortable. This was likely because she was a dragon used to sensing auras and Kylara wore an aural dampening pendant around her neck. "None of us even have a bead on your powers. You know?"

"Yeah…I guess I do…"

CHAPTER SIX

"Lord Boneclaw, please forgive me, but I still don't understand."

At least the mage's tone had grown more respectful, even if her incessant questions never slowed. "Why would you send those revenants onto campus to attack Kylara if you believe her power is the key to your master's dreams?"

He might have blasted her with fire in that moment if he couldn't already see the threads of his web dancing under his new plan. She still needed to think she was his master, as annoying as it was.

"I had to be certain of her powers," he explained soothingly. "The ability to learn new powers is a mighty one, and your niece had done well in using these powers to benefit herself. That is why I opened the breach your air elemental observed."

The mage nodded, although she chewed her lip. Boneclaw still had to rely on facial expressions to understand what she was feeling and he was quite sick of it. "You should have told me what you were planning. If I had seen those revenants attack in person, I would have intervened. My elementals know that they cannot allow Kylara to die and might have tried to help."

"Which might have ruined everything," he told her. "It will

take careful planning and a deft touch to separate your niece from the others—defter still to make sure she does not suspect that you are working with me."

"I don't see why that must be kept a secret," the mage argued. "She knows I can summon spirits and has seen the evidence of that herself. What does it matter if I summoned you?"

"Not everyone will believe in your power over me," Boneclaw said, aware of how ironic it was for him to tell Cassandra that her power would not be believed when the only person who believed it worked was her. "If the Steel Dragon finds out that I am back, I can assure you that she will interfere with our plans. That is what she does—always the wrench, never the engine."

"Then perhaps if I contact Kylara personally—"

"No, no, that will not do." He managed to keep his tone placid despite the rage he felt at Cassandra's impetuous urge to constantly undermine his plans. "If you contact her now, she will simply tell some of her professors. What happened when she failed to do exactly that is most likely still too fresh in her mind. If you reach out to her, she will tell them, and any hopes we have of you realizing the ability to become a dragon will be dashed. Please, master, let me continue with my plan." It did not feel good to beg but it would be worth it to get Kylara's power. "If I am correct, she will come to us in time."

"And you swear you won't hurt her."

"I would never hurt her while she holds the key to the power you crave." That, at least, was true. He wouldn't hurt the girl before she had shared her ability with another. The omission was that Cassandra thought that person was her but in reality, it was Boneclaw.

The mage looked conflicted but she eventually agreed. "Very well. Many of your arguments make sense. You may proceed."

The ancient dragon bowed to this self-important, delusional mage and vanished into shadow.

His time would be much better spent if he didn't have to keep explaining to the mage or hiding his actions from her, but her usefulness was such that he couldn't do away with her yet. At least she respected the time he spent studying in isolation.

He paused as the final word triggered a thought.

That was what he knew must happen to the young mage with the powers he craved. She was extremely powerful, especially for her age, but nowhere near the apex of where she might eventually be. Lord Boneclaw liked that. Her power would grow, which meant that if he could take it now, it would grow with him. He knew he could take it from her if it weren't for her pesky allies.

That was why he needed her to become even more isolated than he was.

As long as she was at the Lumos school and surrounded by her friends and worse, true meddlers like Kor and Amythist, she would not act without thinking. She would be tempered by those who sought to twist the world into their own sick images.

The ancient dragon knew that if he attacked Kylara while she was at the school and did manage to defeat her—something he thought he was very much capable of, even in his current state—his victory wouldn't be the end of the fight. Amythist and Kor were both powerful, obnoxiously clever enemies. He thought he could beat either of them in one-on-one combat if he was able to choose the terrain, but he had no illusions of victory if he faced them both together on the campus grounds, which they knew better than he ever could.

And then there was what would happen if he did manage to defeat them both. If Amythist was slaughtered—which she deserved—at the hands of a raised dragon skeleton with shadow powers, even the dense brain of the Steel Dragon would realize that he had returned. He wanted that fight—desperately and with every bone in his body—but not yet. There were advantages to be gained with the waiting and no advantage to rushing in early.

No, the path forward was to focus on taking Kylara's powers.

If he could cut her off from her friends and get her isolated and off campus, she would be his.

And after watching her fight against the revenant skeletons, Boneclaw knew precisely how to accomplish that.

CHAPTER SEVEN

A week passed and no more portals to the pixie realm opened on campus. That put much of the school at ease, and most of the student body and staff fell into the familiar flow of the semester again.

Kylara, however, jumped constantly at shadows. Whenever she saw a bright light that seemed out of place, she assumed a portal would open to let skeletons stream through. She felt like she was living every moment on edge, waiting for the next attack or the next attempt to destroy or disrupt her life.

"You don't have to worry so much about it," Karl said to her at the start of their Dragon Powers class.

"You say that but it's not you they're after," she replied.

"You say that," he responded, mimicking her, "but it's not like we won't help you fight more of those monsters. I got some of the attention that I've deserved for so long, so you better believe I won't leave you high and dry when this 'doing good things' stuff might help my reputation."

"You're incorrigible."

"And you're stressed." Karl sent two tentacles of dark energy that began to knead her shoulders. "Do you mind?"

"No...no, not at all. That feels weirdly amazing," she told him. It felt like all her stress was in her shoulders and his powers seemed to be able to get under her skin and work it out.

"It's because I can put some of my finest tendrils under your skin and pull on your muscles directly."

"Karl, are you serious right now?"

She turned to where Sam stood with his hands on his hips and a look of disapproval on his face that would have rivaled even Hester Diamantine's.

"Hey, Lumos. That's so weird. Kylara, you just got even more tense," Midnight said.

"Maybe that's because you're literally under her skin," Sam snapped pointedly. "Get your freaky magic off her."

"Oh, come on, you perv," Karl countered. "You've put your power inside other people. How is this different?"

"Seriously, Sam, it's not a big deal. Karl was about to stop."

"You don't have to tell me to stop because of him," the dark-eyed dragon said. His tendrils of shadow did not budge from their place on her shoulders.

"No, Karl, it's fine. I said stop."

"You heard her," Sam sneered. "Now get off her."

"Sam Lumos and Karl Midnight! You're up!" Kor bellowed from the center of the dueling field.

"No problem, Ky. No problem at all." Karl reabsorbed his powers.

"Oh, there is most certainly a problem," Sam said.

"Well then, it's a good thing it's time for us to duel. Did you ever find a mage willing to work with you?" Karl asked jeeringly.

"I did. It's not that difficult when you treat people with respect. What about you?"

"Yeah. I have one. Let's do this."

"Boys! Now!" Kor boomed as the two students took their dragon shapes and strode to the middle of the courtyard.

"Mages?" the Silver Bullet asked. His expression suggested

that he sensed the tension between the two young men and relished it. "Or will this be merely a dragon on dragon duel?"

"I thought it had to be with mages," Sam said.

"That was the plan but…" The instructor glanced from one to the other and shrugged. "You two look like you'll both be trying for an A. I don't need mages to get hurt over a couple of grade grubbers."

"No mages would be fine with me," Karl grumbled.

"Me too."

"Excellent." Kor beamed. "Ground or air?"

"Air," Sam said.

"I don't have a problem as long as I can slam the pretty boy into the mud."

The instructor didn't even pretend to care about the open hostility. If anything, he seemed eager for a duel fought with a motivation beyond good grades. "You'll both start airborne but being grounded doesn't disqualify. We'll play to blood or forfeit, as always."

"Excellent," Sam said.

Karl said nothing and simply vaulted upward and flapped his wings to gain height. Tendrils of dark began to stretch from his wings like streamers from the world's darkest kite.

Sam took to the air and gave chase.

The duel started with the two dragons circling, each trying to outmaneuver the other so they could land a blow in a vulnerable area with their powers.

This didn't accomplish much and the temper of the combatants didn't allow the tentative skirmish to last long.

"Do you feel stressed?" Karl goaded as he lashed out with a bevy of dark tendrils.

Sam blasted the approaching web of darkness with light energy and dissolved them into nothing. "Is this how you came on to her?"

Came on to her? Kylara gasped quietly. They weren't being so petty...were they?

"At least I made a move, loser!" Karl replied as he used his shadow powers to increase the size of his wings twofold. With the larger surface area, he gained speed and powered into Sam.

The young golden dragon was tougher than his opponent when it came to hand-to-hand combat. When Karl made impact, his claws were ready and tore bloody gashes across the shadow dragon's belly. Karl, however, hadn't chosen a conventional attack. The shadow wings transformed into a thousand ropes to bind Samuel and make the two plummet like stones.

"Match to Lumos." Kor boomed.

They landed heavily but neither tried to separate. Instead of drawing apart at the first sign of blood—as was required—they continued to brawl. It was a messy, uncoordinated, and inelegant affair. Claw and tooth of both dragons focused on small sections of the other. They both understood how healing powers worked, so each combatant tried to batter one spot repeatedly to make the other dragon truly feel it.

"Boys, *boys!*" Kor bellowed. "For the love of your mothers, stop this nonsense!"

"Tell him to stop hanging out with people he doesn't deserve!" Sam shouted before Karl shot a tendril down the golden dragon's throat.

Despite Sam drawing first blood, he seemed to be in a weaker position now. Even before he had been denied his ability to breathe, he hadn't been able to stay in control of all of Karl's tendrils of darkness. They lashed out, caught hold of him, and bound his limbs tighter and tighter. Some, however, fell victim to his light powers. He was simply too good a fighter. Every time it seemed like Karl was about to overwhelm him, he would break free and resume a battered assault on his opponent.

Both were bruised and bleeding in multiple places. The problem, Kylara knew, was that they had trained together so many times that they both understood the other's limitations. It surprised her that they were fine with exploiting the other's weaknesses for her sake. That was a problem.

"If this is because of me, you both have to stop—now!" she roared at them.

"It's not because of you," Karl responded, his tone rough. Sam had broken the tendril that wedged in his throat and currently had his teeth sunk into Karl's neck. His teeth were red with the other dragon's blood. "It's because this jerk won't let me even talk to you without getting all uptight."

"Talking is fine. It's you putting your creepy tentacles under her skin that I have a problem with." Sam's words were barely audible with the other dragon's neck in his mouth.

"I am not a prize to be won," Kylara yelled furiously and inadvertently called up a storm cloud in her agitation. "And if either of you ever wishes to speak to me again, you will stop this *now*."

Thunder boomed overhead and a bolt of lightning ripped out of the sky and sizzled into the earth scant feet away from Sam and Karl. The shockwave was enough to knock them both away from each other. They tumbled for a few feet and lay still to let their healing powers mend their multitude of wounds.

Kylara felt exhausted. Forcing the lightning to strike the ground instead of what she had truly wanted it to hit—the two numbskulls fighting over her like she was the last slice of a cake —had cost her considerable energy and concentration.

With a pounding headache, Kylara scowled when she witnessed three new portals open in their vicinity.

"Behind me, students!" Kor bellowed as skeletal creatures poured through. It wasn't only dragons this time. All kinds of bizarre remains came through, as well as some that were more terrible simply because they were so familiar. Wolves, bears, lizards, snakes, and bats were easily recognizable despite the lack of flesh, scales, and fur, as were the animated bones of humans, dogs, and cats.

Kylara had no idea where to begin. There were so many and some of them were so small that she couldn't see how she would bind them with plant roots.

"Jasmine—" She broke off when she remembered that the girl wasn't there. Neither was Tanya and Karl and Sam were both still bloody and on the verge of unconsciousness from their pointless brawl.

"The dorms, dammit. Make for the dorms!" the Silver Bullet shouted as he launched his silver tail spikes through skeleton after skeleton. Kylara tried to focus through her headache. She couldn't let anyone get hurt. That was the priority. She looked for the invaders that were closest to other students and attacked those first, caught them with her shadow powers, and hurled them to the dirt.

There were so many students but even more—easily ten times more— skeletons. She struggled to stop them, but how? She needed her friends and couldn't do this alone. And yet she had to.

A low roar made her turn to see a true abomination emerge from one of the portals. If she had to guess what it had been before its flesh had been stripped away from its carcass, she would have said mammoth and hoped to get partial credit. Because mammoths didn't have massive, whiplike tails with a biting alligator skull at the end. Nor did they have four legs and two arms in front of them that might have belonged to a massive, truck-sized sloth from prehistory. Worse, mammoth faces centered around a boneless trunk had become a dozen grasping hands ringed around a hole where its mouth would be.

Kylara lashed at the creature with dark energy but it was too large and too determined. It powered into her with its massive tusks, struck her in the temple, and hurled her back into a tumble.

The young dragon mage wasn't quite knocked out but she would have been if she hadn't been in dragon form. She knew her brain suffered an injury, though, as she witnessed what happened next through the fugue-like state of the brain trying to hold on.

As soon as she was struck by the great mass of bone, the portals vanished. Stranger still, the skeletons stopped fighting. They simply crumbled and lay inert as if some horrible decorator had thrown a Halloween party but never quite managed to clean everything up.

Kylara closed her eyes in an effort to clear them and opened them again to find everyone standing around her. Okay, so maybe she did black out for a moment there.

"Is everyone all right?" she asked.

"We are now," Tempest—one of Karl's old friends—said. "Since you closed those portals from the pixie realm."

CHAPTER EIGHT

Classes were canceled and the campus was locked down after what happened in Practical Dragon Powers. Kids still had to eat, however, so Kylara and her friends were clustered together around a table in a corner of the dining hall. Even the out of the way spaces in the room were gorgeous, she thought, a little cheered by the beauty of the space.

"Wait...so we're clear here, you were super-pissed at these two morons for both having a crush on you and maybe lost control and opened a couple of portals?" Tanya asked.

Sam and Karl battled for dominance and protested vociferously that neither of them had a crush on Kylara and they were merely worried about her. Tanya silenced them with a disbelieving expression and they both turned looks of concern to Kylara.

"I...I'm not sure. I know I accidentally summoned a storm, but I've done that in the past. I've never opened a portal like that before." She tried to explain but it sounded like excuses somehow. It was hard to think clearly about the event. She had been so mad at Sam and Karl, and in the next moment, the gates had opened and the skeletons had streamed through. How connected were those events? Had she become angrier and her fury had caused the problem? She didn't think so but also knew she had to consider it.

"Well, can you?" Jasmine asked. She had joined them, which was probably for the best as it stopped Tanya from prying too much into the boys' feelings—something she was prone to do because Kylara thought she liked Sam.

"I don't know," she had to admit. "Opening portals feels completely different than summoning a storm. I don't think I'd confuse the two if that makes sense."

"Not at all." "Nope." "Maybe?" The three dragons replied.

Jasmine was the only one who nodded. She was the mage, after all. "Types of magic are distinctive, but not completely distinct," she explained, her tone as ice-cold as always. "It is possible that you could have 'leaked' energy into that part of your power profile and done it without meaning to?"

"But why would I do that? I could have put every single person there in danger," Kylara asked as if her subconscious was somehow controlled by the rules of her rational mind. She hated to sound arrogant but she thought it did. She had trained for years under Diamantine with an almost obsessive focus on her dragon powers and not letting them get away from her. She knew how to prioritize healing smaller wounds over big ones. She knew how to transform into her human form before landing, even though doing so screamed against every dragon instinct she had.

"You did say you summoned the storm without meaning to," Tanya pointed out. "Maybe you were so angry at these two testosterone-fueled goons that you tried to banish them or something. Seriously, you were as mad as a hornet." To emphasize her point, Tanya glared at the two boys, who wilted under her gaze.

"I guess it's possible, but I honestly don't think so. I've been in combat with these creatures before. I've been hurt by them too, but nothing like this has ever happened before. I don't see why this would suddenly be different." She hoped she sounded more confident than she felt. It was a small blessing that the pendant around her neck protected her emotions from the inquisitive auras of dragons.

"But Kylara, everything about you is always changing," Jasmine pointed out. "First, you were a dragon with diamond powers, then a dragon who could absorb other dragon powers, then a mage who could do that. Only now, you can also use pixie powers. You have been the greatest source of chaos on campus. This fits with that pattern."

She slumped. It was demoralizing to hear a mage—a group of people so obsessed with patterns that they regularly had them tattooed on their skin—talking about her fitting into one.

"I...uh, no offense," Jasmine added lamely. "I think it's quite interesting, to be honest." Like being interesting to a mage was supposed to make it better.

"The thing is, Ky, you're the only dragon who can do this, right?"

Before she could nod, Jasmine spoke. "Or mage. Traveling to the pixie realm is not something that is easily done. Mages don't possess that secret. The only beings who do are pixies—and you, of course."

"Which means that either you're doing it—"

"I'm not!" Kylara protested to Tanya.

"Or we have like a rogue pixie on the loose." Her roommate shrugged. "Honestly? To me? That sounds way worse. Who knows what pixies are capable of? If we can get powers in their realm, what kind of powers do they have?"

But before she could answer, Ruby Firedrake, the dragon in charge of her dorm, waved to her from across the dining hall.

"Kylara! I checked your room and couldn't find you. I'm glad you're here and not out breaking curfew." She said it in a friendly enough way but the threat was clear. *Break the rules and I won't cover for you.*

"What's up, Ruby?" she asked, concerned that she knew exactly what was up.

"The headmaster wants you in her office. Now."

"But I was eating—"

"I'll fix you a to-go plate and leave it in your room," Ruby smiled cordially.

"But no food is allowed in our rooms," Kylara pointed out weakly.

"There's also no saying no to the headmaster. Now move it or I might become a rules stickler and you'll have to go to bed with nothing but the three bites of sandwich you already ate."

Kylara looked at her sandwich, took a farewell bite, and followed Ruby to the headmaster's office.

CHAPTER NINE

"See you later, Ky, and good luck!" Ruby said after she'd opened the door to the office and gestured for the young dragon mage to enter.

If it had been only Amythist in her office, it might not have been so bad. Kylara liked going to the headmaster's domain. She had been there more than once—not much of a surprise given that she had come to the school basically as an orphan, albeit an orphan with extremely unusual powers.

The space was the antithesis of intimidating. It was positively filled with an assortment of fascinating items. Bunches of herbs, tied with string and hanging from the ceiling, dried slowly as they filled the room with a wonderfully diverse palette of aromas. Potted plants were everywhere, some of them thriving, some of them long dead. There was a tea kettle too, usually in mid-use, sheaves of paperwork, and a computer that looked dustier than most of the dead plants.

It was a calming place, a room she liked to explore with her eyes while talking to the pleasantly tempered headmaster. But alas, a one-on-one meeting was simply not meant to be.

Inside, Headmaster Amythist was seated behind a steaming

cup of tea. This was not unusual. The problem was that Professor Sharra was also there, as was the Silver Bullet, flanking the headmaster on either side.

Kylara understood that she was in fact in deep trouble when she noticed that the headmaster and the professors were already sipping tea and that the ancient dragon had not offered her any.

"I'm sure you know why you're here," the headmaster began.

"Because you think I did something I didn't do," she said. It emerged perhaps a little too combative, but she had already been attacked once.

"We merely want to know a little more about your powers," Professor Sharra said amicably.

"That way, we can find out if you opened those gates between our world and that slimier one," Kor said.

"I'm telling you, I didn't do it," she stated, her tone flat but not disrespectful.

"Please, Kylara. Your powers are a strange and unusual gift. Let us ask a few questions and draw our own conclusions," Amythist said. "In truth, we should have done this far sooner. Do not see this as a punishment but more as a kind of examination. Now, please take a seat and tell us when your power first manifested."

What followed felt more like an interrogation than the promised examination. Between the three of them, they had a good understanding of what she could do. But given the dangers the portals represented, that was no longer good enough.

Even the tiny discrepancies in their understanding of her abilities were discussed until they felt they had uncovered every detail. By the end of it, she felt more like a wild animal that had been captured and forced to give blood samples than a student who had willingly agreed to answer a few questions.

And always, there was the implicit assumption that Kylara had opened the portals.

"So, to be clear, which of your powers have triggered without you intending them to?" Professor Sharra asked what felt like her thousandth question.

"Storm powers. That's it," Kylara said.

"You're sure?"

"I don't know! Well...I guess I've healed with light powers without exactly meaning to."

"You see? That proves it," Professor Sharra said to the other two adults and acted as if the young dragon mage wasn't there at all.

"I agree with the mage," Kor said. "If one power can be triggered accidentally, it's certainly possible that all can."

"For the last time, it wasn't me!" Kylara shouted and immediately regretted it.

The three faculty members all looked down the noses of their human bodies at her. She swore she could see two sets of eyes flicker to dragon for a moment, though.

"It's nothing to be ashamed of," Professor Sharra said. "You're an exceptional case so it's to be expected that we might need to take exceptional steps to assist you in controlling your powers. But we have to understand what's happening to you."

"It's normal for these things to happen at your age," Kor said as possibly the most awkward preamble she had ever heard. "Why, when I was your age, you'd be shocked at the places where I started sprouting silver spikes."

"Can we not?" she mumbled, terrified of where this was going.

"It went away!" Kor laughed at her discomfort. The spikes had probably appeared on his nose or something and he had phrased it that way merely to make her uncomfortable. It was immensely annoying that it had worked. "But it took practice and help from my elders. Do you understand?"

"Look, I don't want this to happen any more than any of you do. I'm one of the only students who can fight these monsters, right? How does it make sense that I would open the gates to the skeleton swamp? I've never even been there."

"But your friend Tanya has, correct?" Amythist asked.

Kylara nodded.

"Well, perhaps, in a moment of stress, you simply wished those two boys would simply go away. I've certainly felt that way before."

"Okay, I'd much prefer to go back to Kor's weird teenage body details than wherever this is going," she pleaded. "But I'm telling you that I didn't do this. I've used portals in combat before. If I wanted to get rid of them, I would have sent them somewhere in the desert. Plus, I don't have the ability to raise skeletons, Galen does. Maybe he teamed up with a pixie or something."

"How sure are you that you cannot raise skeletons?" Kor asked.

"Kor, that's enough," Amythist said.

"Headmaster, he might have a point," Professor Sharra said.

The ancient dragon inclined her head at Kor for him to continue. Kylara wondered if the headmaster had a gesture to make everything stop.

"Well, you've fought the skeletons and they've swiped at you and whatnot, correct?" Kor asked.

"Yeah. That's true."

"So maybe you do have skeleton powers."

"I honestly don't think so," Kylara said. "I haven't acquired any new abilities lately. I think maybe I'm...I don't know...full or something."

Professor Sharra and Kor shared a look while Amythist sighed slowly. "If this is how you feel, young Lady Diamantine—full, overwhelmed, brimming with power—then it is with my greatest apologies that I must ask this next request of you."

It was incredible how quickly one's motivations could change. Only a week before, Kylara had longed to go home. Now, however, the thought of being expelled made her want to hurl.

"Please, Headmaster, I'll do anything. Don't expel me. I've learned so much already and I'm sure I can control whatever this is."

"I'm sure you can too, my dear. You merely need a little practice without so much pressure on you."

"Yes! Practice sounds great." She was overwhelmed with relief when she realized that she would be able to stay.

"Excellent. Then I hope you won't mind wearing this." Amythist withdrew a thin, almost dainty silver bracelet from her desk.

Kylara recoiled immediately. She had heard about these before. Two of them had bound her mom when Cassandra had captured her. Mages were forced to wear them and Kristen Hall, the Steel Dragon herself, had been forced to wear one in prison.

"I'm confused. You're…you're locking me up?" she asked.

The headmaster smirked into her tea. "If Kor had his way, we might have, but no, child. This is not the kind of bracelet that is used to imprison dragons."

"Oh," Kylara shook her head, relieved. "I saw it and thought you were going to take my powers or something."

Amythist chewed her lip for a moment before she smiled even more broadly than before. "It will take your powers away, dear, but not all of them. This is the kind of cuff mages wore before the rebellion. It's designed to dampen but not snuff out magical abilities."

"But I was fighting against the skeletons. If you dampen my powers or whatever, what am I supposed to do if they appear?"

"Our hope is that with this bracelet, no more of them will show up," Professor Sharra pointed out.

"And what if they do? What then?" Kylara demanded.

Kor laughed out loud. "Then we're wrong." He grinned. "If these breaches keep forming even when you're cuffed, we'll know it's not you. If that happens, we pop the bracelet off and we're back to square one."

"I don't know…" The voice within remained hesitant.

"I know it's a sacrifice, my dear, but it is a good way to know for sure."

"Isn't there any other way?" she asked, liking this plan less with each moment.

"Not unless we jeopardize your education," Professor Sharra said. "Which we all agree is not an option. We want to help you master this power, Kylara. We truly do. The bracelet is less than ideal but you'll get used to it. And you won't have to wear it for decades like I did."

"Decades? Honestly?"

Professor Sharra nodded. "And you're far tougher than me. Come on, let's get it sized."

Without warning, a portal exploded into being inside Amythist's office. Everyone stood, Ky included, and readied themselves for an attack. As soon as the girl saw the skateboard sailing through the gateway, she relaxed.

Amy glided into the room, saw the bracelet in Sharra's hand, and snarled at it. "It looks like I am just in time. What the hell do you people think you're doing?"

The ancient dragon frowned at the newcomer but returned to her seat as if people opened magical gates into her office all the time. "You could have knocked, dear."

Amy snatched the bracelet out of Professor Sharra's hand with her telekinesis and floated it across the room. She reached out gingerly to touch it like it might burn her, then left it hovering in the air instead of taking hold of it. "After everything we went through to end the slavery of mages, how could you even consider doing this?"

"We are trying to help the girl." Professor Sharra walked toward the mage, her hand extended to take the bracelet, but waves of power prevented her from coming close enough to seize it. Beads of sweat broke out on the professor's brow as she tried to crack Amy's shielding, but there was never any question which of the two mages was stronger. The visitor ignored her entirely and focused on Amythist instead.

"Help her? By putting one of those damned things on her?" she snapped. "I almost had to wear one of those. Kristen Hall stopped that practice. Amythist, of all the dragons out there, I'd never have guessed you would stoop to this."

The ancient dragon rose with a sudden movement that startled everyone. Her eyes seemed to glow with a purple light and her brows drew together. "You are always welcome in my home, Amy, but rudeness does not become you."

"Resorting to the trappings of slavery does not become this school," the mage replied. "Lumos would roll over in his grave if this were allowed to happen. Come on, Kylara. You can come with me. We'll find a way to train you in your powers without this...pile of crap they're trying to lay on you."

Ky's heart jumped at the idea. She took a step toward Amy without even thinking about it. The mage had been one of her heroes for as long as she had known about her. Getting to study magic under her would be a dream.

She halted after a single step, though. Going with Amy would also mean leaving her friends, who had come to mean a great deal to her. It would mean not getting to prove to these stuffed shirts how wrong they were—and oh, how she wanted to rub their noses in it when this was all done. She knew it wasn't her power opening those portals. All she needed was a way to prove it.

The bracelet represented a way. Perhaps not the most pleasant way in the world and she certainly didn't like Kor's attitude. Or Sharra's, for that matter, now that she thought about it. But she understood why Amythist was willing to accede to the idea. She also wanted Kylara to have a chance to prove that it wasn't her magic making these events happen.

"I think I have to stay," she told Amy.

The shocked and hurt look on the mage's face felt like a stab in Kylara's gut. "I see. You've never worn a cuff, Kylara. It's not pleasant. Are you sure this is the path you want to take?"

Now that she'd said it, Ky wasn't anywhere near as sure as she'd been a few moments before. But she'd declared her decision and had to stick with it. "Yeah. This seems like the best way to prove it wasn't me doing those things."

"As you wish," Amy said. Her voice sounded hollow and sad. "I'm still appalled. This…isn't all right, and I'll address it with Kristen. But if Kylara will do it willingly…well, she's an adult and able to make her own decisions."

With that, Amy hopped onto her skateboard and streaked through the window. After she'd departed, the bracelet fell, no longer suspended by her magic. Professor Sharra scooped it up and went to Kylara's side.

"That was very brave of you," Sharra told her. "I believe you made the right decision."

She hoped so but she was already feeling regrets and the bracelet wasn't even on her wrist yet.

It was both amazing and horrible that something so small and delicate could make a person feel so different.

Before putting the dampening bracelet on, Kylara had known of them, of course. Her mother had explained them to her and how they had used the devices to capture rogue mages and render them safe enough to transport. The young dragon mage had known—academically, at least—that this meant the bracelets were powerful. And yet, in her gut, she had always vaguely harbored the idea that the mages simply weren't that strong. If they were, how could such a thin band of silver do anything to stop them?

Amy Williams had done much to change the internal bias that

Kylara possessed, but seeing a fettered mage in combat was not the same as feeling one's power taken away.

Because that was what it felt like—like something had been taken from her. She still had magic but it lacked much of its strength. As she walked to her dorm, she tried to flex some of her powers.

The lights she could make burned only half as brightly.

Her shadow powers didn't stretch nearly as far as they did before.

She could still feel the wind and moisture, but not as acutely. The plants didn't call as loudly to her, either. It felt like someone had wrapped her hands in thick gloves, put weights on her back, and fettered her ankles with chains.

It was horrible.

And the only way she would get out of it in the immediate future was if there was another attack on campus.

CHAPTER TEN

Boneclaw was thrilled with the result of implementing his plan to catch Kylara in his webs. Best of all, it had been so easy.

The skeletal creatures from the pixie realm didn't obey him the same way they did Galen. They didn't see him as an other but as one of them, which made sense, what with him being a skeleton like them and everything.

While they obeyed Galen blindly, they looked at Boneclaw more like a part of their pack, which suited him perfectly. For years, he had manipulated others into thinking they were doing what they wanted to do when in reality, they were doing what he wanted. The fact that these magical bone beasts didn't have a brain didn't make them any less easy to control.

Boneclaw had opened a gate using the connection he had to the swamp simply by dint of the power Galen had found there—the same power that now coursed through and animated Boneclaw—and the bone beasts had been more than willing to allow their big, strong ally to order them to do what they wanted to do anyway—feed.

The ancient shadow dragon had watched the entire encounter from a clump of shadows in the nearby woods. It had been a little tricky to circumvent the charms and wards the mages had put on the campus but eventually, he had worked his way in. It wasn't the mages' fault that he had made it through their defenses. He was, after all, an entity that had never existed on earth before—a revenant made into a dracolich with his own spirit. Add to that potent combination his ability to move through shadow, and Boneclaw was unstoppable.

Well, almost. His patience would give him invulnerability and immortality in the end but in the meantime, he could wait and watch the players dance on strings they didn't even realize were attached to them.

Kylara's classmates had played their part in his grand charade masterfully. They saw her struck on the head. They saw the three breaches between this world and the realm of the pixies close immediately. It didn't take a master of deduction to draw the conclusion that perhaps the girl who could open portals to the pixie realm might have had something to do with the fact that three of them had opened unexpectedly on campus.

But that disgusting pixie-loving Amythist had gone so far as to cuff the girl. How beautiful, how perfect, and how understandably rash that decision had been. Boneclaw wanted to foster distrust between Kylara and the school officials. That was the central tenet of his plan—to make her feel so isolated at school that she felt the only decision she had left was to leave. By blaming her for Boneclaw's breach and shackling her as a consequence, Amythist was only fueling his plans.

He understood, of course, that Kylara wasn't a complete outcast yet. That would take time. Everything took time, and time was the most precious of resources. It was the one thing that worked the same for everyone. No matter if they were human, dragon, or mage, time ticked onward.

Dragons had more of it, true, but it didn't mean they could burn through a year of work to make something come to fruition any faster than a human could. That meant Amythist's actions were a true gift to Lord Boneclaw. By taking the girl's powers and burdening her with guilt, she would become isolated all the more quickly.

There was more work to be done, however. He didn't want to risk a direct foray onto the Lumos School grounds. While he had snuck in and spied, that was quite different from taking his skeletal form and snatching Kylara up to whisk her away.

What he wanted—what he needed for his goal to be achieved—was for the girl to leave the campus so she'd be on her own and away from anyone who might assist her. His plan had been to foster her emotional isolation and then scoop her up in a moment of weakness.

And now, with one foolish decision, the headmaster of the school had unwittingly made her feel more isolated and also taken her power away. Boneclaw wasn't one to rely on brute force, but with Kylara operating in a reduced capacity, he would be able to strike without fear of her fighting back.

But there was still much to be done. Isolating the girl would be worthless if he couldn't take her power for himself, so he had spent his time working on cracking that particular nut. The shadow dragon knew from experience that a body from this realm could absorb new powers in the pixie realm. He had done it to get his shadow powers, as had Kristen Hall to get the light powers she'd needed to stand against him. He had to be certain that once he took Kylara there, he would be able to either duplicate her ability or siphon it away and give it to himself.

This meant that much of his time was spent investigating the swamp that was so intimately tied to his bones. There was something about it that made the skeletal magic possible. A give and flow infused the energies and there was something special about the interplay between life and death. It wasn't a sure thing, not at all, but he hoped that with time, he would be able to unravel the swamp's secrets, the power that made the impossible possible.

It meant that his mission to cut Kylara off further from those she loved couldn't be done by him alone. He needed to train, to study, and to be ready to take her power—ideally without the dragon world at large learning about him. The problem was their infernal teamwork. Kristen Hall had never shied away from asking for help.

Lord Boneclaw knew that if he attacked before the moment was right, they'd all simply band together and work against him. It was an infuriatingly frustrating strategy when the weak banded together to stand against the strong.

The ancient dragon decided that he would have none of it. He would take Kylara's powers one by one, then take the powers of other dragons until he was strong enough to stand against any who dared to resist him.

For all that to happen, he would need time to study the pixie realm, however. It was time for him to call on one of his allies, as paltry the selection was.

"Lord Galen," Boneclaw said robustly after he'd traveled through shadow from the campus to his lair in the castle.

"What do you want?" Galen asked petulantly. "I told you before. I won't kill anyone."

"No, Lord Galen, of course not. You have made yourself clear. I will not harm a mage for you to test your powers on." *You damn fool,* Lord Boneclaw thought but did not voice it. "What I need is to know more about Cassandra's holdings. Tell me...are there any of them you would wish for me to take you to?"

"Well...uh, yeah, this castle is fine and all, but I miss the States."

"I, too, long for the New World," he said but didn't tell the boy that he had already traveled there at night by flying over the Atlantic Ocean at the speed of shadow.

"Can we go there? Will Cassandra be okay with that?"

"It was she who wished me to explore her domains," he said, his tone almost a purr, and the young dragon—as foolish as he was—believed him.

CHAPTER ELEVEN

Despite feeling completely drained, Kylara needed to understand exactly what she was still capable of. That was why she had dragged Tanya out of their nice warm dorm room and into the frigid twilight air of early March in the New Mexico mountains.

"Once more," she insisted. Her breathing was already heavy and more ragged than it should have been after twenty minutes of dueling.

"What are you trying to prove?" her roommate asked as she flapped her wings and flew toward her. Her movements were graceful and effortless—the movements of a fresh dragon with full access to their strength and speed.

"That even under stress, I'm not opening these damn gates."

Tanya exhaled a blast of flame that fell on Kylara's diamond scales. Those, at least, were unchanged by the dampening bracelet. They deflected the fire as well as they had before but only for about three seconds. In the next second, she felt the flesh beneath her scales begin to burn.

Tanya flew past and circled slowly above while Kylara dumped her healing abilities into the burns. "I feel like my healing power is half-strength," she complained.

"Then maybe we should go inside," her roommate suggested, the sarcasm in her tone almost aggressive.

"Only a little longer," Kylara said. "I'll try the dark power, all right?"

"Ky, you know I hate that one. What Karl did to me was too much."

"Then dodge me, okay? I'm not Karl." Kylara knew it was a crappy thing to say as she said it, but she didn't know what else to do. She had to know her limits for when the portals opened again. She had to. And it wasn't like she intended to hurt Tanya. She merely wanted to see what she could do.

She lashed out with two tendrils of dark energy and cast them into the air like the feeding tentacles of the world's blackest jellyfish.

Tanya yelped when she collided with one she had failed to see in the twilight.

In the next moment, the earth beneath Kylara's feet erupted.

At first, she thought that perhaps the shadow power was somehow rebelling against her—a terrifying thought, to be sure. But she realized quickly that it wasn't her powers working against her wishes but rather her friend's magic.

"I said to dodge!" she protested.

"You wrapped in plants makes it easier for me to dodge your attacks," her roommate pointed out and forced the plants to grow even faster. They had more than enough water to use since the young dragon had blasted the snow around Kylara with fire. Roots and runners reached out to snare the dragon mage's tail, feet, and claws.

She continued to try to fight with her dark energy, but it was too weak. Tanya was able to blast it away with fire, something that usually only worked on the thinnest of black threads. She growled in frustration and tried to launch a beam of light at Tanya, but the dragon had been practicing with her plants.

As soon as the young dragon mage's throat began to glow

with luminous energy, Tanya made a plant directly in front of Kylara's dragon snout extend vertically. Huge leaves unfurled and absorbed the light energy. Before she could even voice her surprise, flowers fueled by her energy began to buffet her head while the roots of the plant entangled her claws even further.

Kylara struggled against the roots. She pushed, shoved, and tried to tear them, but simply didn't have what it took. She was exhausted—more tired than she could ever remember being. Calling on her powers only drained her further. She collapsed and the plants continued to grow around her, ignoring her weak-willed commands to stop and leave her alone.

"You know, I should leave you out here for being such a jerk," her friend said once she was bound tightly and completely.

Although she tried to apologize, her mouth was bound with hundreds of grass roots, so all she managed was, "Mmph."

Tanya was more than happy to let that serve as her roommate's half of the conversation. "What's that, Ky? You're sorry for attacking me with the exact power I asked you not to use? How kind of you to apologize."

"Mmph!"

"You didn't know I could use light powers to make my plants grow faster? That is so weird because I told you an hour ago when you were too busy moping about being so powerful that teachers thought you needed a break from your own strength."

"Mmph?"

"Yes, Kylara, of course I accept your blockheaded apology. What kind of a friend would I be otherwise? Now, I'll release you on the condition that we go to our room, maybe use your heat powers to make tea, and we don't do any more training with plant magic in the freezing cold and dark. If you agree, say nothing. If you say mmph, again, I'll take that to mean that you like being wrapped up like a piece of meat and that you'll be fine until morning."

Kylara—wisely—said nothing.

Tanya called on the plants binding her and they all slithered away to bury their roots in the soil and leave nothing above the surface except a particularly overgrown patch of grass that was roughly in the shape of a dragon.

When they reached their room, Kylara made them both tea—although after their training session, even that almost drained her of what strength she still had.

"I still don't see why they have to do this to me when I've been the one fighting." She sipped her tea and frowned. It seemed Amythist knew a thing or two more about brewing tea than she did. While the headmaster's tasted like bouquets of flowers, hers tasted of cut grass—vaguely pleasant in an odd way but not the same cup of tea.

"Well, yes, I think it sucks. None of us would argue that point, but…"

"But what?" she asked.

"But you've never had to feel what it's like to be helpless."

"Well, it sucks."

Tanya laughed. "I know. There's nothing worse. And it's so dumb that they're doing this to you. Assuming you didn't open the gates—"

"I didn't!"

"Right, Ky, I said assuming you didn't. There's no need to get all upset."

"Everyone is acting like it's possible when I'm telling you I didn't do it."

"Can you please let me finish my thought? I'm on your side, Ky. You should know that by now."

A pang of hurt seared through Kylara's memory when she recalled how Tanya and Sam had turned their backs on her after she'd saved them and revealed herself to be something other than the dragon they knew. She pushed it hastily from her mind. That was behind them now. "Right. I know, Tanya. I'm sorry. I'm stressed, is all."

"As well you should be. Assuming you didn't do this, dampening your powers right now is crazy. If it wasn't you, it has to be someone else, right?"

"Exactly."

"Which means the campus is under attack and they're taking away our best defender."

"Thank you."

"I was talking about Amy Williams but yeah, you're also kick-ass in a skeleton fight."

"Thank you?" Kylara sighed and wondered what Amy would think about this. She'd heard nothing from the mage after she'd refused her invitation to take her with her.

"It's so insane to think that we're under attack again, and we don't see any movement from the administration."

"Maybe they don't know anything," she suggested. "It seems crazy to blame this on a student, but maybe it makes sense if they have no other leads."

"What do you mean they have no other leads? We know there's a dragon who got their powers from that swamp. We know there's a dragon who can summon skeletons of all types of weird creatures."

"Yeah, but no one has seen Galen since his skeletons got out of control," Kylara pointed out.

"That doesn't mean he's not still a part of this," Tanya was quick to say. "He's likely been working on control of his powers. That's what he did last time when he vanished, right? It makes sense that he would have been doing it again. My question is why he would be messing with you now?"

Kylara paused and sipped her tea. The implications of that were…uncomfortable, to say the least. "But…if you think it's Galen and that he's messing with me…then all this is about me again?"

Tanya giggled her most condescending-yet-endearing giggle. "Kylara, this is obviously about you. Either you opened them—"

"I did not open those gates!"

"I was going to say or it was supposed to look like you did."

That made Kylara freeze. Her teacup was still in her hand, momentarily forgotten. "Why would you say that?"

"Well, the portals opened when you were angry. We've already established that."

"Yeah, but it's not like I was the only dragon who was angry. Kor was furious, and well...Sam and Karl were too."

"Right, but Ky, none of them can open gates to the pixie realm. The obvious assumption is that you did. Please, run with me here and accept that for the time being, pixie portals mean Kylara Diamantine to the students and teachers here."

"Fine, I'll accept that everyone is short-sighted and judgmental, no problem."

Her roommate smiled so sweetly that her dimples puckered. It was her equivalent of rolling her eyes, but Kylara appreciated the smile all the same.

"Okay, so it looked like you opened the portals because they closed when you were knocked out. The question is why? Why did that happen? Why did the portals vanish the minute Kylara Diamantine was knocked out?"

"That's not what happened," she said, her throat dry despite the tea.

"Maybe not, but it is most certainly what appeared to happen."

What did that mean? Before Kylara could pursue the train of thought too far, Tanya leaned forward conspiratorially and answered the question herself.

"It means someone was deliberately trying to frame you, Ky."

She stared at her friend for a long while, trying to think it through. "But how would that work? They would have had to be right there for this to make any sense."

"I bet they were. I bet they watched the entire battle and simply waited for you to get knocked out or otherwise incapacitated so they could close the portals and set you up to take the fall. It's the only thing that makes sense, assuming—"

"Assuming I didn't open the portals myself, yeah, yeah, yeah. But if I'm being framed, doesn't that mean me having my powers is all the more important?"

Tanya shrugged. "I...maybe? I can see why you think that but look at it from the headmaster's perspective. She knows that either you—the girl with weird powers and the ability to open gates—opened a gate to the pixie world accidentally, or someone made it look like you did. Either way, taking away your powers is a good thing."

"No, it's not. If I'm being framed—oh." Finally, Kylara understood. "If I'm being framed and whoever is doing this can open portals but is blaming it on me, taking my powers away renders the culprit's ability obsolete unless they want to blow their cover."

The other girl nodded enthusiastically. "Precisely. If this was a direct threat, Amythist would simply call Amy again, but it's not —or not yet, anyway. If there is something afoot, it won't do to simply shine the light on it. She has to lay a trap first."

"And I'm the bait?"

Tanya smiled. "Eh, I was the bait for Cassandra. It's not that bad."

"Not that bad if the predator never gets to the bait, you mean."

Her friend's eyes widened at that. She had never been a trapper and wouldn't have known that bait didn't usually survive being used to trap prey. "Still, Cassandra was stopped before. They can stop her again."

"Do you think it's my Aunt Cassandra?" she asked.

"Who else could it be?"

"I don't know, but this doesn't seem like something she would do. When we last spoke, she was so excited about my power. She wanted it for herself. I don't think she would have cared so much if she could simply go to the pixie realm and earn her own powers there. It's possible, I guess, but I don't think so."

"I guess she did arrive and help to save the day when Galen lost control," Tanya conceded.

"Exactly. I don't know why she would do this. I guess it could be Galen, but I don't see how he could be spying on me. His skeletons never spoke or anything like that. I got the impression that they weren't exactly capable of higher-level thought."

"Yeah, I agree with that. It's why I thought it was your aunt, honestly. She's more powerful than him for sure." Tanya paused for a moment to think. "Do you think she could have taught him something about those portals? Like maybe mages can't do it, only dragons?"

"I'm a mage, remember? I was born in a human body and from a woman, not an egg. Mages can obviously use this power."

Her friend nodded and absorbed everything in uncharacteristic silence.

"So what do we do?" Kylara asked finally.

"All I know is that you have to be very careful, Ky. It's almost better if you're wrong about your powers."

"I'm sorry, Tanya, but I truly don't think I am."

"Then you have a new enemy and whoever they are, they're close."

CHAPTER TWELVE

Kylara didn't exactly hope for another gate to open and more skeletons to attack, but when no attacks came, she had to come to terms with her disappointment all the same.

"I don't get it," she said to Karl and Tanya. "Why did the attacks stop now that I'm weaker?"

Her friends shared a look of eyebrow-raising agreement.

"What is that supposed to mean?" she asked a little too loudly, which drew the attention of Professor Sharra. The woman sashayed closer and her cloak flapped with her quick movements.

"We should be practicing," the professor of Magical Theory told the three students. "There is no need to discuss meaning or anything else at the current moment. Now, each of you should be able to lift our textbook at least two feet off the table by now. We'll go ahead and call this a pop quiz. Who wants to go first?"

Kylara, Tanya, and Karl all groaned at the surprise grade.

"But Professor, you haven't made anyone else do a pop quiz," Tanya protested and gestured around the magically enlarged room at the other students. Mages and dragons of unusual powers were all standing or seated in small groups.

Above almost every group was a floating textbook or two. It

looked almost impressive until one of the books collided with a shelf of vials and jars, which immediately shattered.

"We'll be ready when you're back, Professor, I promise," Kylara said and grimaced at the mess of broken glass.

"You'll do it now," Professor Sharra said and with a flick of her wrist, all the broken vials and jars repaired themselves and put themselves in their original places.

"But we don't have telekinesis like you do," Tanya protested.

"You have abilities that you must learn to use. Don't tell me you've been doing nothing, young lady. You're not being graded on your telekinesis or lack thereof. You're being graded on lifting that book two feet off the surface of the table and holding it there for ten seconds. And you're being graded right now."

"Fine," Tanya grumbled and slid her hand into her pocket. She pulled out a handful of seeds and scattered them on the table. Her expression deadpan, she upended her bottle of water on the seeds and plopped the book onto the wet surface.

"Those books aren't cheap, young lady," Professor Sharra grumbled.

"I know, professor. It won't be damaged." The young dragon extended her hand and held it flat so her palm was facing down. She made a fist, rolled her hand, and slowly opened her fingers so they pointed at the ceiling.

As she did this, the seeds popped from their hard casing, extended roots, and using her fingers as a guide, grew upward with the book on top of them. They reached a height of about a foot off the desk before they slowed. Tanya inhaled sharply and moved her hand in a twisting motion, which made the long-leafed grass grow intertwined instead of simply straight up. With this added stability, the book soared past the two-foot level.

Professor Sharra counted to ten and nodded her approval. "Very nice. I'll give you an A-minus."

"A-minus?" Tanya scoffed. "What did I do wrong?"

"You touched the book."

"To put it on top of the seeds."

"Right, which only bought you a millimeter or so, which is why you're still making an A. Next time, consider using the roots or leaves to reach under the book."

"Right...sure," the girl said, annoyed but also intrigued by the challenge. While Professor Sharra turned to the other two students, Tanya fidgeted with her grass and made it move the book in various directions.

"Who is next?" the professor asked.

"I'll do it," Karl said as if doing so would be only marginally more pleasurable than shoveling manure.

The instructor looked as if she intended to reprimand him for his attitude but before she could, black tendrils crept from Karl's fingertips, across the surface of the desk, and under the book. They pushed upward and intertwined like Tanya's grass had, or like the branches of coral. He lifted the book easily twice as high as Tanya had and held it there, looking down his nose at the professor while she counted.

"Well done. Full points," Professor Sharra said. "But you'll serve detention if you can't fix your attitude."

"Yes, ma'am," Karl said and his voice remained less than pleasant as his posture straightened.

"Kylara, are you ready?" The woman turned to her and ignored Karl, thus revoking what power a crappy attitude could have.

"Yeah, sure," Kylara said and reached out with her shadow powers.

Despite the power-dampening bracelet, she was able to extend the creeping tendrils of darkness across the tabletop with relative ease. She sent them beneath the book and pushed them upwards. They rose six inches...a foot...eighteen inches...then slowed.

"You're almost there," Professor Sharra encouraged.

"I'm...hold on..." She grunted and dug deep into her well of inner magic to fuel this power. Frustratingly, her well remained out of reach. She could still feel it, much like you could feel the pressure of the water behind the glass of an aquarium, but it was entirely different from simply getting wet.

"Dude...Ky, come on, I've seen you bind an entire skeleton dragon," Karl joked, although there was concern in his tone.

"I only need...a second..." Kylara dug deep and pushed the book up another inch, then another, and another. Finally, she managed to reach two feet. The professor began to count but only made it to six before the book clunked to the floor.

"Sorry, I don't know why that happened."

"It's all about making a matrix for structure," Karl said.

"Maybe you should try plant powers?" Tanya suggested.

"I can do this," Kylara said and launched her tendrils of darkness again. This time, she lifted the book to the two-foot mark much faster, but the professor only counted to three before it fell again with a thud.

"That will be enough for now, Kylara, thank you," Professor Sharra said politely.

"Please, give me one more attempt," Kylara demanded. She wiped the sweat from her face and her hand came away bloody.

"Ky!" Tanya blurted.

"Are you all right?" Karl asked her.

"It's completely normal for a mage to get a nosebleed if they push themselves too far," Sharra explained. "The body will try to provide energy for magic, even when that magic is not there. Blood is where it pulls it from, which often causes the fragile capillaries in the nose to burst."

Kylara couldn't stop staring at the blood in her hands—her blood. She had gotten a nosebleed before from overexerting herself, but the last time that had happened, she had summoned a forest of growth to inter dozens of skeletal dragons underground. That was considerably more than lifting a book off a table.

"It's not a big deal, Kylara," Professor Sharra said. "The cuffs are an incomplete science. They limit some powers far more than others. What's important is that you haven't opened any gates since it's been on."

"I never opened any gates!" she yelled loudly enough to cause a dozen of the books that the other mages were practicing with to tumble noisily. All the student's gazes settled on her now. Every mage and dragon in the class stared at the blood trickling from her nose because she was too weak to lift a stupid book off a stupid table.

"Jasmine," Professor Sharra said and broke the silence. "Can you please escort Kylara to the nurse's office?"

"I don't need to go to the nurse," Kylara mumbled, more embarrassed than anything else right now.

"Very well. Miss Patel, if you could take Kylara to the headmaster's office instead, that would be fine, thank you."

A chorus of rising, "oohhhhh," proved that kids in school were kids in school and that it didn't particularly matter if they were seven, seventeen, human or dragon.

The young dragon mage's brown skin flushed with embarrassment and she locked her gaze on the floor as Jasmine Patel led her from the room.

They marched across the cold campus. For once, Kylara could feel the wind cutting to her very bones. She was used to having her dragon healing power to warm her, plus Ruby Firedrake's heat ability had become more or less second nature. Now, perhaps because she had exerted herself so completely in class, neither power responded to her pleas for warmth. Meanwhile, Jasmine had summoned a whirling cyclone of either wind or telekinetic force no snow could penetrate and wrapped it around herself.

It was a very cold dragon mage and a rather comfortable Jasmine who entered the main campus building and went to the wonderfully warm and aromatic headmaster's office.

"Ah, Ladies Diamantine and Patel. And to what do I owe the honor?" Amythist said after she'd poured them each a cup of tea.

"I want this cuff off," Kylara demanded and pounded a fist on the table hard enough to rattle the teapot.

Jasmine spat out the tea Amythist had given them. "Kylara! Mages do not speak to dragons that way—ever!"

"Oh, hush now, dear, it's quite all right for mages to speak to dragons however they wish."

The young mage slumped and Kylara straightened until the headmaster continued.

"Of course, it is completely inappropriate for a student to talk to the headmaster of her school in such a way, and if it wasn't for that bracelet shackled about your wrist, you'd be in detention already."

Jasmine snorted so loudly Kylara could practically hear her say, "I told you so."

"But Headmaster—"

"Miss Diamantine, I know those are unpleasant. I truly do. Furthermore, I know some of the details of how they were used throughout history that would make your skin crawl. But that does not change the fact that it's working."

"But that's why I have to take it off. I was learning so much about my powers. I was pushing my limits every day."

"I know. I get updates on all my students, and all of your professors have been quite impressed with your semester thus far," the ancient dragon assured her.

"Then why do this to me?"

Amythist held up two fingers. "Two reasons. One, when we are excelling at a level beyond our peers, it means we have mastered what there is to know of that challenge. Your succeeding in school means you were not being properly challenged."

"Oh, come on!" she blurted, unable to control herself. "By that logic, you'd want all your students to get B's instead of A's."

"That is precisely what I want, believe it or not," the headmaster quipped, which made Jasmine's eyebrows rise even higher than Kylara's.

It was the mage's turn to stammer a protest. "But Headmaster—"

"It's not possible, mind you. Too many students excel to a point where challenging them so they would only be eighty-five percent successful in their ventures would stifle those students who are in jeopardy of failing. I think it's in society's interest and the school's interest to bring the laggards up more than continually challenge our brightest and most powerful. It's a lucky thing that in your situation, we get to do both at once." Amythist smiled so sweetly that it changed the taste of Kylara's sip of tea.

"So you're crippling my ability to defend myself because it aligns with your educational philosophy?" she demanded, her tone a little belligerent.

"Yes! Although that's not the only reason. There are the gates to the pixie realm to consider as well. The fact that there have been no more gates implies that maybe the cuff is working."

"Headmaster—educational goals aside—I did not open those gates. I did not lose control of my magic. I swear it to you."

"And between you and me?" Amythist leaned forward over her cup of tea, looked around conspiratorially, and wrinkled her nose. "I believe you."

"Then why keep her shackled?" Jasmine demanded, her tone as fierce as Kylara's had been. "She needs to practice her control and the other dragons will only benefit from her being more powerful."

The headmaster nodded at this. "You're right about the other students. I hadn't considered that but it does make sense to push them. You know what? You two have convinced me."

"Truly?" Kylara almost hopped up out of her seat.

"Yes, but there's more. I'll set up a special class for you—a tutoring session that will be one on one. I'm not sure if Professor Sharra will be available but maybe it can be...oh, never mind. I'll work through the logistics and we'll have you set up to begin next week. With direct, targeted instruction about your powers and abilities, you'll learn how to use them despite having the bracelet."

"Wait, but...I thought you said we convinced you." Kylara felt deflated.

"I do believe you. I assure you, I truly do. But you being tutored will only help and in the meantime, we must keep up appearances, must we not?"

"Wait, you believe me, but..." She paused, then continued "You want to keep the bracelet on me to keep up appearances?"

Was this whole charade more about laying a trap for whoever had opened the portals rather than about constraining her powers? Anger bubbled in Kylara's chest at the thought. Was she merely being used as bait?

"We must," Amythist insisted. "We truly must. We'll check in after a week, yes? If all seems well with this tutor—I do think Professor Sharra would be best because of her time living with shackles... Anyway, if the professor or whoever we choose approves, then we take it off!"

Kylara was waiting for an all right? Or a sounds good? Or some kind of confirmation so she could say, *No, no that isn't good at all, you haven't listened to a word I said!* But the confirmation never came.

Instead, the headmaster gestured to the door, and Jasmine stood and escorted Kylara back to class.

The rest of the day was as brutal as Magical Theory, if not more so. She was drained after the exertion of trying and failing to lift a book a couple of measly feet off the desk.

It was insane, quite frankly. Turning into a dragon was still tiring with the cuff but not nearly as limiting as her shadow powers seemed to be. She wondered if her plant and storm powers were the same but didn't dare to test them. It took all she had simply to make it through class.

When she finally returned to her dorm room after a hasty dinner eaten early and alone, she found that Tanya wasn't there.

That was a bummer. Kylara had looked forward to seeing her friend and telling her how unfairly and horribly the headmaster had been treating her. She was secretly hoping Tanya could talk her down from the edge, but it was a comfortable relief to be able to sit and not have to socialize for a few minutes.

She stretched on the bed, took a few deep breaths, and let herself relax. A scant five minutes later, however, the general untidiness of her room began to irritate her and she set about restoring order. She was happy to be living with Tanya again. Despite being from different worlds, they understood each other, which made for a simple and very pleasant friendship.

Living with Jasmine had been much more trying. The two didn't see eye to eye on anything and despite both of them being in financially precarious positions, Jasmine was not one to empathize. But wow, could that girl clean a room. She had even cleaned Kylara's side, almost always without asking and always without complaint. Her telekinesis had enabled her to sweep, fold clothes, and make the bed, often simultaneously.

Kylara and Tanya had to rely on more pedestrian means of living quarters upkeep, and as a result, the two inhabited a kind of nest.

One side of the room contained a barrage of Tanya's dresses. All of them had multiple parts, be it accessories, corsets, slips, or petticoats, as well as appropriate shoes and leggings. All these things got dirty at different rates that—as far as Kylara could tell—were only discernable to Tanya. The result was that the young dragon's clothes were usually tossed anywhere and everywhere.

Because of this, Kylara had few concerns about offending her roommate. Her collection of jeans, tops, boots, and jackets was flung about in what she thought of as organized chaos. Her mom would have no doubt called it a disordered, grungy mess.

Normally, she didn't mind, but something about her room right now seemed…off. Her mom had long said that if your living space wasn't right, clean it.

With a sigh, she put her clothes away and threw out homework and assignments that had been graded and returned. She made her bed and was about to turn her attention to her tiny, built-in desk when she noticed a letter placed on top of the clutter with one corner weighted down with a piece of turquoise.

Immediately, her hand jumped to the pendant at her neck. It was made of turquoise as well, as was the matching one her aunt wore around her neck.

The mess forgotten, she picked the letter up and began to read it frantically.

Dear Kylara,

I wish I was writing under better circumstances but alas, good times are a luxury I fear only one of us can afford.

As you most likely surmised, I took Galen with me after the debacle he caused last semester. His powers are unique and I didn't want to see what the dragon establishment would do to him for unearthing something so unusual.

Alas, I was misguided in my efforts. The boy has progressed but he is now beyond my ability to control. He has left me and headed for somewhere in the Rocky Mountains. I can only assume to raise more dragons. I tried to stop him, but was unable to do so as I did not want to hurt or kill the boy as I am unsure what his powers would do upon his death —a hard truth to tell you but I promised you I would not lie.

I tell you all this because I need your help. He is under the belief that you and he are destined to work together. I told him I could arrange a meeting, an idea he rebelled against. He does not trust me anymore, Kylara. He thinks I only wish to use his powers for my benefit and curse it all if I don't understand how he feels.

I was hoping to wait until you finished your schooling before I contacted you again, but there is simply not time. Even leaving this letter instead of sending one of my elementals was a risk, but I thought this best. I do not mean to pressure you again, my niece, but if there is a solution that does not involve violence, I believe it begins and ends with you. I fear that if Galen is not convinced to throttle back on his abilities, he will be completely lost and that you are the only person who can convince him of the perils of unfettered power.

Aunt Cass.

Below that was a string of numbers that Kylara recognized as GPS coordinates.

CHAPTER THIRTEEN

Even before she finished reading the letter, Kylara had already committed the coordinates to memory. It wasn't a decision of if she would go so much as when. Tonight or in the morning?

There were questions of course—so many questions—but none of them changed her gut screaming at her to simply do it.

Still, she knew she couldn't rush off and had to think this through. She knew she couldn't gate there, not with the shackle on her wrist, and she couldn't fly either, which meant...a bus? Hitchhiking, maybe?

She honestly didn't know but she started to pack her bag with warm clothes, just in case.

The dragon mage knew that her professors would tell her that she should have gone to them but she wasn't having it. All they would do was show up and threaten Galen and then, if they did capture him, he'd be shackled for the rest of his life. That was what they had done to her, so why would they be any more lenient on Galen?

Kylara knew he had caused some problems but he was still a kid like her. He didn't deserve to have his power stripped away because Aunt Cass had promised him something she couldn't deliver.

But maybe she had delivered. Perhaps she had taught him how to open gates like Tanya and Sam had thought. Or he might have some kind of link to the pixie realm and was able to go there at will. If that had happened, it would make sense why he had turned on Aunt Cass. She would have wanted to go there to get powers of her own. She knew the woman well enough to be sure of that. Perhaps the idea had frightened Galen?

Or maybe this was unrelated to the gates. A pixie could have opened the portals as a way to get more attention. The little beings were weird like that. Diamantine had always said you couldn't trust their logic any more than you could trust a dragon to give gold up. There were a million things to learn, and she knew that if she told her professors or worse, the headmaster, she would be denied the opportunity to learn any of them.

It wasn't like Kylara was afraid of Galen. He was something of a wimp before he had learned his powers—she felt bad thinking of him in those terms but it was the truth—and she was certain that even in her weakened state, she could take him physically. There were the hordes of skeletal dragons to worry about, of course, but that was why she had to go alone.

She couldn't risk Galen becoming frightened and losing control. Her somewhat vague plan was to talk to him about it and if she failed to persuade him, she would get out and call for backup. She snatched her phone and charger up and crammed them into her backpack. On second thought, she took her phone out and went ahead and plugged the GPS coordinates into her maps app.

It took only a moment to pull a coat on, throw her backpack over her shoulder, and peek into the hallway. It was deserted, and she snuck out into the cold night.

Without the team of mages led by Amy Williams, the security was nowhere near as tight as it once was. It was much easier to slip past the few remaining guards than it had been the last time Kylara had done this. She didn't even have to use her shadow powers to conceal herself. Thank goodness for that. She wasn't at all certain that she could have made herself invisible if it came down to that, anyway.

When she finally exited the grounds, she hiked up and over the ridge. By the time she was on the other side, she was breathing hard but it felt good. She was still stronger than a human and a nighttime hike through the snow felt great.

She turned to her path through the snow and called upon the weather to create a gust of wind to blow snow over her footprints and hide her passing. The winds kicked up and a few flurries later, all signs of her passage were gone. She noticed that her head didn't hurt nearly as much after using her storm magic. Did different magics call for different levels of power? It had never felt that way before but she felt that acutely right now.

Kylara took to her dragon form and headed toward the nearest town. She loved flying as much as ever and had always found it effortless. Now, however, it was like swimming through concrete. She had to flap vigorously simply to stay airborne, and it felt like the muscles in her chest kept tearing every time she pumped her wings.

Until this moment, she had never realized how much her magic helped her to fly, restoring muscles and generally making flight possible. The dampening bracelet made the difference painfully clear.

It took almost everything she had to glide to a nearby town. She landed well off the highway and changed into her human body before she walked to the interstate and hooked a thumb out. It wasn't long before a trucker slowed to a stop to give a lift to the wayward young woman with a bag on her back and her thumb asking for help.

Kylara knew that as a young woman, hitchhiking might not have been an option to her had she been human. But she wasn't a normal human. If the man driving the truck with his flabby beer belly, helpful grin, and outstretched hand wanted to try something, she knew she could crack his fingers before he even knew what was happening. She had practiced many hours—thousands of hours—of aikido with her mom. That meant big people didn't scare her.

She climbed in without hesitation, thanked the driver, and let her mind wonder about all the people who could most certainly kick her ass. Although she told herself she was going away from most of them, damn if her gut didn't have something else to say about that.

CHAPTER FOURTEEN

"Hey, Ky, I didn't see you in the dining hall, so I snagged some of those zucchini muffins you like so much even though they taste like nothing without chocolate chips and nuts on them. Ky?"

Tanya paused and looked around her dorm room as if it were possible for Kylara to hide inside the tiny space. She smiled when she realized that her friend could, in fact, hide in a place like this. "Ky, if you're wrapped in shadow or whatever, you can come out now. I know classes sucked today, but you've made your point. You're still the toughest dragon in this dorm. Or mage. Or whatever you are. Ky?"

But her friend was nowhere to be found. Stranger still, the room was clean. Well, not clean, but cleaner. That was odd. Her roommate had spent the last week plotting with her on how the two of them could somehow convince Jasmine to pay them a visit and then be convinced to clean their mess.

Never one to be ashamed about getting into other people's business, Tanya gave Kylara's half of the room a quick scrutiny.

It didn't take her long to find the letter on the desk where it perched beneath a hunk of rock that looked much like the pendant Kylara always wore around her neck. Tanya snatched the note up and recalled that Cassandra had worn a similar pendant.

Her gaze skipped to the end of the letter first to check the signature. It was signed *Aunt Cass,* and a string of numbers was provided below the name. A phone number maybe? She dialed the numbers but her phone refused to register the string of digits as something it could use.

The young dragon read the note hurriedly. By the time she had finished, she was already walking toward the headmaster's office. It was exactly like Kylara to go and do something like this, but dragonfire save her if it wasn't freaking annoying.

She understood that the note said Galen would only listen to Kylara, but that was foolishness. Tanya had been there when he learned his powers. She had saved his life and he had saved her in turn. If anyone could talk him down, it was her. It was exactly like her roommate to think that she and she alone could solve a problem like this.

Both irritated and concerned, she knocked on the headmaster's door. After a moment of what sounded like papers being shuffled about, the door opened, although Amythist was still seated at her desk.

"Miss Fastwing, please, come in. Would you like some tea?"

"Not now, Headmaster, no thank you. I need to tell you about something."

"Oh? Not a problem with your power, I hope. I must admit, the ability to control plant growth absolutely fascinates me. I had quite a garden at my cottage in Michigan and haven't quite mastered the climate down here yet."

Even given the stakes of the situation, Tanya couldn't help but think that was adorable. "I can give you tips about what the plants like, but there's something more pressing."

"More pressing than hyacinths?" The ancient dragon winked at her. "Do tell."

In silence, she retrieved the letter she had found and handed it to the headmaster. Part of her was worried that the raw clutter of the office would simply engulf the missive like an ocean wave would a drop of rain, but it managed to stay in the headmaster's hands long enough for her to read it.

"If young Miss Diamantine were bringing me this, I would say that it was…interesting. But given how you are bringing it to me, despite it being addressed to our mutual friend I'm…concerned. Please tell me that Kylara is waiting outside or talking to the Silver Bullet."

"She's gone," Tanya confirmed.

Amythist cursed with such force and color it would have made historians from across the ages blush. "The foolish dragonling of a girl! I cannot believe she flew off on another of her… her adventures. Do you have any idea about the coordinates that are mentioned? The bottom of the letter is torn."

Tanya had been preparing her aura for this very moment. She pumped confusion and a sense of loss into the air in hopes of disguising the fact that she knew exactly where that strip of paper was. Namely, in her pocket.

"No, ma'am," Tanya replied, as straight-faced as she could manage. At least now, she knew the numbers were coordinates. She had speed-read the letter so quickly she had missed that detail. All she'd been certain of was that they were important.

"Very well. Thank you for bringing this to my attention," the old dragon said formally. "Now, please, back to your room. I have many people to call so we can track this student and chain her to a wall."

"You won't seriously do that, will you?" Tanya asked.

"If Kylara calls? No, we won't do that. But between you and me, the girl can't read auras to save her life so yes, I might chain her for a day or two. It used to be common practice."

Tanya nodded and hurried out of the room. Had Amythist known that she was trying to fool her with her aura, or had the mention of it merely been the slip of the tongue? The young dragon was so worried that the headmaster would overhear her phone call that she almost didn't eavesdrop as she left the office.

Despite her haste, she paused when she heard Amythist's voice. "Yeah, Brian? It's me. I have a wayward dragonling and hoped you could run a trace. No, I don't know where she's going. That's why I called. Wait a second. Tanya, get to your dorm room *now*!"

The young dragon swallowed hard and headed toward her room. She had almost entered the building when the feeling in her stomach forced her to change direction. How far had Kylara already gone? Despite it barely being six in the evening, it was already dark due to the long winter nights. Tanya knew she couldn't do anything to bring Kylara back, not at night. She was a dragon but her plant powers relied on the sun. It was a good thing she had two friends who had no such limitations.

At the entrance to her building, she turned and hurried to the training fields. She was hardly surprised to find Sam and Karl there, fighting as usual.

Both boys were in their human forms, honing their skills in their weaker bodies. Sam looked like a spotlight from heaven itself was shining on him. Tanya couldn't see Karl at all, but she knew he was there as tendrils of dark energy lashed constantly at Sam from the darkness.

"Show yourself, coward!" the golden dragon taunted.

"My ability is shadow powers, you dolt. Showing myself is not part of my strategy." It was Karl's voice but it seemed to come from all over. A neat trick, for sure. "Besides, you're the coward, hiding inside your stupid cone of light."

"It's a cylinder." Sam sneered, although he said nothing about being called a coward. "And dropping it is not part of my strategy." The last words were delivered in a fairly weak impersonation of Karl Midnight.

As weak as it was, it was still enough to goad the other dragon to attack. A great mass of dark tendrils was launched at Sam from outside his cylinder of light. It was like watching a thousand greasy rags attack at once or a net full of jellyfish covered in spilled oil. The light burned away the outer strips of darkness, but Karl had wrapped himself in many layers. He powered into Sam and extinguished the cylinder of light as he smothered him in hundreds of threads of shadow.

It was obvious that Sam was still in the fight, for the mass of ropy darkness rolled constantly from one side to another and the two boys' grunts could be heard from within. A beam of light burst through the dark strands and was quickly throttled and choked out. Another beam burst through, then another. More and more followed and blazed through the darkness, evaporating Karl's magic little by little until there was nothing left.

"Ha!" The golden dragon pumped his fist in triumph.

But—like a human magician's grandest trick—Karl was nowhere to be seen.

"Nice job, dingus! You escaped," Midnight gloated.

Sam growled annoyance and looked for the source of the voice.

Tanya saw her opportunity and pulsed her aura at the two dragons so they could sense her concern. Both of them turned to her before she spoke. It was pleasant to receive that kind of response. Sometimes, Tanya forgot how hard it could be to talk to Kylara because she couldn't feel anyone's emotions but her own.

"Tanya!" Sam said.

"We were just wrapping up," Karl joked and emerged from the shadow.

"What's up?"

Tanya had always had a gift of the gab. She could talk quickly and in great detail. She had never thought of it as a strength but now, confronted by these two dueling dragons, she drew on every ounce of gossiping power she had under her control.

It meant that less than a minute later, the boys were filled in on every detail.

"What are we waiting for?" Sam asked. "We have the coordinates. Let's go after her."

"It's amazing that someone with light powers can be so dim." Karl sneered at him.

"What? Are you scared?"

"Do you think we can simply race off after her and hope to leave the campus undetected?" Karl waved his hand dismissively. "That's not gonna happen. We'll be seen, especially since Tanya went to the headmaster first."

"I went to the headmaster first because she has access to the resources to help Kylara," she shouted at the two battling numbskulls. "But we're her friends. We should do something too."

"No way. I won't go after her. We'd get busted."

"You could use your shadow powers to hide us, tough guy," Sam said.

Karl nodded thoughtfully, which suggested that he hadn't considered this. "You know what? I'm in. Let's go now."

She nodded. "Do you both think we should?"

Her friends nodded.

"That's because they're high on adrenaline and testosterone and because they both like her," Jasmine Patel said as she emerged from somewhere nearby. Tanya hadn't sensed her at all and it irritated her. She was a mage, though, so her aura wasn't as easy to discern as a dragon's.

"Jasmine? What are you doing here?" Tanya asked.

"I make a habit of watching the best duelists on campus. Well, second and third best in this case. My family—despite the Steel Dragon's new rules about equality—still believe in serving dragons."

"Wait, which one of us is third?" Sam asked.

Karl scoffed. "You, dumbass."

"It didn't look like that earlier," the golden dragon retorted.

"See? They're jacked up on hormones," Jasmine said dismissively. "It would be the height of stupidity to rush off in the middle of the night after Kylara. She's far stronger than any of us. We'd be lucky to catch her tail and we'd never stop her."

"I don't want to stop her. I want to help her," Tanya replied.

"I think we all agree that helping her is our goal," Sam said. Tanya noticed that he was taking deep breaths and that his aura had shifted. He had worked himself up and now tried to calm himself.

"I agree with the pretty boy," Karl said.

"Don't call me that."

"No problem, ugly."

Sam ground his teeth. Tanya could not help a smile. He had set himself up for that one.

"But if we don't follow her, how are we supposed to help?" Tanya asked.

"You already told the headmaster, so we can assume they'll have a plan that involves a deeper, more accomplished team than us."

"How did you know that?" Sam asked. "Tanya just told us. Did you tell Jasmine first?" he asked Tanya.

"I came straight here."

"One of a mage's primary responsibilities is anticipating a dragon's needs," Jasmine said. "That often means listening very closely…even when the dragon doesn't know you're listening."

"You were spying on me," Tanya said.

"Technically, I was spying on Sam and Karl, so when you explained everything to them, I caught it all."

"That's impossible," Karl said. "I had a web out fifty feet in every direction. If you had stepped on it, I would have known."

"And yet, here we are, all talking about a conversation I heard that the three of you thought was secure."

Tanya smiled and began to understand exactly what this mage was capable of. "What are you thinking, exactly?" she asked.

"Like I said. They'll send someone after her. If we rush off, we'll either get in the way or worse, go on a wild goose chase once they get fresh intelligence."

"So you think we should simply sit here on our hands?" Sam asked. He didn't sound pleased at the idea.

"Sit on our hands and listen," Jasmine said. "We find out what the official response is, assess their plan for holes, and fill the gaps."

"Okay…that sounds good," Tanya nodded. "We all agree not to tell anyone else, right?"

Everyone agreed to that. Unfortunately, they now had the unpleasant task of waiting and a great deal of reconnaissance ahead of them.

CHAPTER FIFTEEN

Kylara's first impression of the trucker turned out to be accurate. He never once so much as reached across the seat toward her. The most aggressive thing he did was sing along to show tunes on the radio a little too enthusiastically. Not that she wasn't singing along too. She loved show tunes.

After a few hours and quite a few musicals, he pulled into a truck stop and looked apologetic even before he spoke. "I wish I could take ya farther, I honestly do, but... Well, if you're heading up there into the Rockies, you need to go west. I'm headed east from here."

"It's no problem, Jim. Thanks for your hospitality."

He tipped his hat at her and smiled although there was concern in his eyes. "Look, Lara, I want you to understand that I didn't ask you no questions about what the hell you was doing out on the highway alone in February weather, but I can't guarantee everyone out here will be as nice as me."

"No one could be as nice as you, Jim."

His serious face was in evidence. She had learned to recognize it when he started ranking musicals by song versus production values. "I'm serious, Lara. Damn serious. There are way too many roughnecks out here—people who wouldn't think twice about taking advantage of a young, pretty girl like you."

"They're welcome to try," she said sweetly.

Jim raised an eyebrow at that and something seemed to click. "You wouldn't know anything about that dragon school that's supposed to be hidden around here somewhere, would you?"

"The what?" She batted her eyelashes and he grinned even more broadly.

"Ah, jeez, and here I was thinking you were singing along cuz you was afraid of me. You could've kicked my butt, huh?"

Kylara shrugged even though the answer was a resounding yes. "I'll be careful." She reached into her pocket and pulled out some cash. "This will cover the gas, yeah?"

"You're crazy if you think I'll take money for you tagging along for a few hundred miles. You didn't make no difference to an eighteen-wheeler loaded with more beer than some towns see in a year. Keep your cash. You might need it."

The dragon mage nodded, understanding the logic of his gesture and also the kindness of it. "Thanks, Jim."

Her mission to help a fellow student now uppermost in her mind again, she crossed the blustery parking lot to the wide windows of the diner beneath a glowing sign that read simply, *Get-yer-Eats*. Kylara smiled inwardly. She had never seen anything like it in real life before and yet it was immediately familiar—like something from a movie set in small-town America.

Red vinyl booths were pushed up against the windows. Square tables with rounded corners stood on a black-and-white checkerboard tile floor between the booths and the bar. At the counter were chromed round stools with red vinyl tops that matched the booths. She was almost certain there would be a jukebox inside, and probably hokey signed photos and posters of the American southwest.

She pushed the door open and was greeted by the exact smell

she had imagined. Perfectly fried bacon and slightly burnt coffee vied for dominance, while fried eggs, fries, and sizzling burgers all tried to add their signature to the tantalizing aroma.

Kylara had expected it to be empty given the late hour, but she was wrong. Most of the booths were filled, as were about half the tables. At the bar, a few people hurriedly scarfed plates of food and downed cups of coffee—more truckers, she assumed.

This didn't appear to be the kind of establishment with a host to take patrons to their seats, so she found a place at the bar where she wouldn't bump elbows with anyone and sat.

Despite seemingly being ignored when she walked in, the woman behind the counter was there in less than a minute. She smiled and revealed the faintest trace of lipstick on her teeth.

"Hi, hon. Are you here for food, dessert, or simply want some coffee while you wait?"

"All three, please!" She grinned. "What do you recommend?"

The woman smiled knowingly. "Oh, well, it's not every day I get asked about our specials. We serve breakfast all day, so that's always popular. Bagley knows his way around eggs, so you can't go wrong there. My favorite is the Denver omelet, even though I can't stand the city myself. If you don't do eggs at this time of day, we have a burger with grilled onions and hatch chilies—I know we're not in New Mexico, but we're dang close—and that's real popular. For dessert, your choices are apple or cherry pie. Both are excellent if I can pat myself on the back."

"It sounds great. I'll take all of it and a cup of coffee please, Janus." Kylara had noted the woman's faded nametag when she'd first approached.

"You mean you want the Denver omelet and the uh…both slices of pie?"

"No, ma'am. I'm sorry I wasn't clear. I would like the omelet, the burger, both slices of pie, and also a side of bacon and fries if they're fresh."

"Are you meeting someone or something?" Janus asked and didn't even try to hide her scrutiny of Kylara's slim figure.

"I'm refueling before the next leg of hitchhiking," she replied.

The waitress frowned, confused by the order. Realization slapped Kylara across the face. She had ordered far more than humans would have. Still, she was hungry. "I'm uh…bulimic."

Janus raised her eyebrows at that but it seemed to placate her. Perhaps bulimia was as common as the movies and TV made it seem to be. "All right, then, dear, but…uh, none of that in our bathroom, all right?"

"Of course not, ma'am," she replied, still smiling.

The woman hung her order on a metal wire with a clothespin above the cook's head. He barely glanced at it before he dumped peppers on his griddle and dropped an order of fries into the deep fryer.

Kylara, hoping that Janus wasn't the type to gossip but also knowing that she was guaranteed to be, turned on her stool to take in the other diners. She had slipped away but she wasn't naïve enough to forget that she might have been tailed. It was a good thing that she took the letter with her.

The letter. Her heart sank when she realized she had left it behind. She rubbed her face in frustration.

"Is everything all right, hon?" Janus asked as she placed a cup of coffee in front of her.

"Yeah. Yeah, it's fine. Thanks," she said noncommittally.

The woman nodded, used to minding her own business when she needed to, and ambled away with her pot of coffee. Kylara followed her transit through the diner and acknowledged that the chances of her being tailed were higher than she'd realized.

Still, she saw no obvious mages or dragons. There were no oddly shaved heads or geometric tattoos in this bar, and no men or women with perfect features wearing perfectly fitting suits or dresses. That did not mean that she wasn't being pursued, of course, but she didn't know how else to tell a dragon or a mage. She couldn't read dragon auras but at least she had her pendant to protect her from dragons trying to read her.

After a brief but thorough scrutiny, she didn't see anyone who looked out of place. Most people were seated in pairs or trios and involved in conversations about their lives. The few people at the bar ate hurriedly, their focus on their plates. None of them even looked up when Janus deposited two large plates of food in front of the dragon mage.

The only people who looked at all odd were a woman who sat alone at a booth and a man, also by himself, two booths over. The woman constantly looked around nervously, which honestly wasn't that weird for a woman if she didn't have dragon powers. Kylara had caught the man looking at her when her gaze settled on him, but that wasn't exactly evidence of him tracking her. After all, she was looking at him too. Still, there was something probing in his eyes. If he followed Kylara when she left, she'd take note.

But for now, she seemed safe and the food in front of her smelled great, the concentrated version of the aroma that had greeted her when she'd walked in.

She tucked in immediately and ate a little of everything at once. This was genuine diner food, she reminded herself. She had never had food like this before. As a kid growing up in isolation on Hester Diamantine's homestead, their food had all been survival-style. Great hunks of deer served with black beans, greens from their garden, repeat. The school was the opposite. Every mouthful there was perfectly calculated to tantalize the refined tastes of the dragon students.

This meal was right in the middle. It was survival food for people who liked salt and weren't concerned about eating too much fat. The burger was great, fried on the griddle so the outside of the patty got slightly crispy. It could have been spicier but hey, they were no longer in New Mexico. The omelet was surprisingly good as well, and the bacon and fries didn't disappoint in the least.

While she ate, she considered her next move. She was closer to where Aunt Cassandra had asked her to meet but she still had a long way to go. It was too far to fly in her weakened state, and she didn't want to risk opening a portal. She knew that she hadn't accidentally opened one to the pixie realm, but she wouldn't simply ignore everything Amythist and her professors had said. If she did have something to do with the pixie realm, opening magical gateways of any kind seemed particularly unwise. Plus, she wasn't sure she could open one while still bound by the silver cuff.

Which left hitchhiking as her main option for transport. She had lucked out with Jim. How did she go about finding another ride? The men at the bar trying to shovel food down their throats seemed like the logical choice as they were most likely the truckers, but was there an etiquette to hitching? Was it considered impolite to ask while they ate or preferable? She was used to the formal world of dragon interactions. Hester had drilled it into her but somehow, the dragon's instruction had missed the nuts and bolts of hitchhiking.

Kylara had turned to her slices of pie when she noticed a group of three men stand and head toward the back of the diner. She hadn't made a note of them earlier because they were all drinking beer by the pitcher and when they had looked at her, the only thing in their eyes had been the petty arousal of men who thought ogling young women was their right. They weren't tracking her, so she had ignored them. Now, however, they sat at the table with the woman who had been eating alone and who looked unmistakably nervous.

One of them said something in a low grumble that made the woman's brown skin darken and the other two men laugh uproariously.

"Is there a problem here?" the patron who had been seated

alone said to the three men loudly enough for the entire diner to hear.

A brief moment of silence followed during which everyone familiar with the three jerks held their breath. The man didn't blink.

"No problem. We're reminding Becky here that we paid her tab last time and that she owes us."

"Ma'am, I'll get these three tonight, all right?" the man said to Janus, who nodded quickly.

"Your tab's all paid up, Tony. Do you want a pitcher on the house?" she asked.

"Yeah, that'd be great, Jan," one of the goons said. All three stood and returned to their booth. One of them slapped the man on the shoulder and winked at him as he passed. "Thanks for the meal, buddy."

"You got it."

The three sat and the chatter of the bar resumed, although it was slightly more subdued. The woman waited maybe twenty seconds before she stood and hurried out into the cold night.

Kylara sighed, glad the woman was going home and that the moment of tension had passed.

The three men remained at their table, chatting to each other until Janus brought them their promised pitcher of beer. She poured them glasses and, as one, all three of them pounded their beers before they stood and followed the woman into the parking lot.

"Janus? I'd like to pay my check please."

"You haven't touched your pie."

"Something came up. Does forty cover it?" Kylara put two twenties on the table.

"Forty's too much, hon. Let me get your change."

"There's no time, Janus. This was the best diner food I've ever eaten. You and Bagley deserve the tip."

The woman nodded and took the money. "You be careful out

there, hon. All right? Becky has a car. She knows to get in and lock the doors. We have security cameras up. They won't risk breaking her window again, even if Dobbs' brother is a cop."

Kylara had heard more than enough. She straightened. "I'll be careful but you don't need to worry. I'm not bulimic."

Janus glanced at the two empty plates of food. "Oh, I knew what you were the moment you walked in, honey. The cameras cover the handicap spots and the front, but we're saving to get eyes on the dumpster." She winked.

Kylara thanked her and followed the men outside.

CHAPTER SIXTEEN

Drew was at an impasse. He knew exactly what kind of assholes the three goons messing with poor Becky were. Also, he knew for certain that he could handle them, especially since they were drunk and his nausea from passing through Amy William's teleportation ring had passed. What he didn't know was what Kylara Diamantine intended to do.

Her disappearance from campus had been noted almost immediately if the GPS evidence could be believed—and given that he had intercepted her path, it could be. When Amythist had first called Kristen's brother Brian, there had been something of an uproar about what to do if the girl used her ability to teleport. Once it became clear that she was traveling at trucker speeds, Drew had been tapped to tail her.

He'd loaded his truck, driven across the parking lot, and like a scene from an eighties movie, a swirling portal had opened and swept him across space and time. Well, timezones, but he still thought it was damn cool, even if it did make him feel like he would lose his lunch every damn time he did it.

Brian had put a fancy GPS tracking app thingy on Drew's

phone. The plan had been to use it to follow her in his truck and find out where she was going. He was only supposed to make contact if necessary, but that plan hadn't lasted long. No one had expected him to arrive at the same diner where she had stopped to eat dinner. When the truck she was in had pulled into the parking lot and she had stepped out, he had taken note. He had noticed her notice him but he thought his cover had stayed intact.

Depending on how the next couple of minutes went, he was entirely aware that all their plans of him tailing her from a distance were about to go up in dragon fire.

He had thought that when the three dickheads had followed poor Becky out of the diner, he would have to blow his cover. Drew had been in law enforcement for over a decade because he liked helping people. He certainly would not sit by while someone was mugged or worse merely so he could protect a dragon mage who didn't need protecting. When he moved to stand, however, Kylara had beaten him to it.

He was already impressed. Standing up for others was never easy. Even he didn't want to bust these guys' heads unless it was necessary, but Kylara had gone to help without hesitation. That was even more impressive given that she was operating in a weakened state because of the bracelet around her wrist that she should have done a better job of keeping hidden.

For now, Drew let her take the lead. Once the doors swung shut behind her, he went to the bar, put a couple of hundred-dollar bills on the counter for him, Becky, the goons, and whatever damage was about to be done and followed her out after telling Janus not to call the cops.

He didn't think the young dragon mage was in danger, but he wouldn't be much of a cop if he simply let her go. He knew the bracelets affected dragons and mages in different ways. There was no telling how it would affect her. She might be so weakened that the three men could overpower her. It was unlikely but possible.

It was also possible that her strength wasn't all that diminished and she might inadvertently crack these men's skulls wide open. He didn't particularly want that either, nor did he want her to blow her not so carefully concealed cover unless she needed to.

All this went through his head as he followed the girl out the door. He saw Becky's car—he had seen her park and get out—in a handicap spot. The woman was nowhere to be seen. Drew glanced down the side of the building and caught Kylara's shoes rounding the corner toward the back of the diner.

An enormous crash sounded like a car had driven into a dumpster, and he increased his pace. He slowed only when he reached the end of the diner, where he paused and peered around the corner.

His first instinct was that he was too late. The woman, Becky, was on the ground, crying silently as if she knew the penalty for making too much noise. Her cheek was red and puffy and she'd be bruised in the morning. Two men had their back to her, which was something of a relief. If they had towered over her, he would have moved. As it was, it looked like he didn't have to yet.

He didn't spring into action because he had discovered the source of the loud banging noise. The third man—Dobbs—had been thrown into the metal dumpster with such force that it had been dented. Kylara stood between him and the other two men, who seemed to be trying to determine how the hell a seventeen-year-old girl had flipped a guy three times her size over her shoulder and into a dumpster.

But while the two knuckleheads were faced with a choice to fight and save their friend and whatever they counted for honor or run like the cowards men like them always were, Drew had better options. He could intervene now and together, he and Kylara could mop the floor with these thugs. Or he could wait a moment and see if she could trounce the other two as thoroughly as she had the first.

Feeling a little guilty for wanting to see the young dragon mage in action—but also knowing that if the tables turned against her, he could join the fight in seconds—he settled in to watch from the shadows.

CHAPTER SEVENTEEN

Kylara wished she had been faster. She could have been, even in her limited state, but she had thought a brisk walk would have been enough.

It hadn't been, unfortunately. By the time she'd stepped behind the building—it seemed Janus wasn't the only one who knew about the cameras' blindspots—Becky was already on the ground, sobbing and holding her injured face.

The girl moved toward Dobbs, the leader of the three, and he rushed at her. She let him make the first strike, a clumsy punch that he might have turned into a hair grab if she'd given him the opportunity.

Kylara had trained in aikido for years. She moved only slightly as her opponent tried to land a blow and let him overextend his arm. Then, she caught his wrist, punched his elbow, and broke it inadvertently—something even regular people could do if not careful—and threw her shoulder into his fat gut. She unconsciously drew on her dragon strength, lifted Dobbs off his feet, and hurled him over her shoulder into the dumpster with a clang that was way more satisfying than it had any right to be.

It felt damn good to treat this creep the way he had treated

Becky, but there was a cost. Lifting him had used some of her dragon energy. Already, her breathing was labored and her brow slick with sweat, even in the chill night air.

No matter. It simply meant she had to be quicker and a little more subtle when she dealt with the other two creeps.

"You bitch!" one of the men shouted at her. Why was it that assholes like these never had creative insults?

He barreled forward and swung his fists in punches that were less threatening than Dobbs' had been but also more controlled. He wouldn't let her inside his defenses as easily as his leader had and he had seen what she was capable of.

She let him punch, once, twice, thrice. When he tried to catch her with an uppercut, she retaliated and hammered him twice in the midsection. The man wheezed but stumbled toward her, not to be outdone by a girl. Kylara led him past her, then kicked him so hard in the butt that he crashed into the side of the dumpster and slumped to the ground.

Unfortunately, she hadn't paid enough attention to the third goon. She turned, thinking she had some distance between her and the man and discovering that she didn't.

He swung at her and Kylara raised her forearms to defend herself. Hot pain flared below her wrist and suddenly, she was slick with blood—her blood, she realized with surprise. The douchebag had pulled a knife.

She took a step back to put some space between her and the man who now swung his blade wildly at her. The look in his eye left her shaken. It was the same look wolves evidenced when they knew a deer was almost out of breath—the look of a predator— and seeing it on a human's face and directed at another human disgusted her to her very core.

He continued his frenzied attack and she danced away from him. She was trying to buy time because of her injury and they both knew it. The thing was that she knew the wound would heal, while the attacker probably hoped she would pass out from blood loss or the sight of so much of her fluids being spilled in the dirty snow of the parking lot.

"How's your arm, bitch?" the guy asked and demonstrated that he was, if it were possible, even less clever than his imbecilic friend.

"Not as bad you want it to be," she said, which was technically true on all fronts. He moved constantly while she willed the wound to heal. It did but much too slowly. While she wouldn't bleed out or anything, she didn't have full functionality in her injured arm and she didn't think she would regain her abilities before this fight needed to end.

That meant she had to be careful, which wasn't something a dragon mage was used to. Still, she took a deep breath, tried to slow her movements, and waited for her attacker to overextend himself.

He saw her shift in movement and like a wolf detecting a change in its prey, he altered his behavior. His gaze still fixed on her, he didn't press forward but moved laterally in an attempt to get to her side. She pivoted with him, watched his feet, and minded her own.

The guy shouted a creep's version of a warrior's yell and surged forward. Kylara braced herself to toss him, but before she could, she was grasped from behind.

"You didn't see that coming, did you, honey?" the man asked before she elbowed him in the gut and rolled him over her shoulder and into the dumpster where he belonged.

The man with a knife had dodged his buddy's flight. He wasn't a scrupulous fighter and tried to use the distraction to stab her. His assault was timed to coincide with his friend's attack. She grasped him by the knife hand and he slashed wildly in an attempt to wound her with the edge of the blade. Kylara kept it far enough away that he was unable to do so.

"Drop the knife."

"You're not in any position to make demands," the guy

screeched, which she found dishonest and plain rude, so she squeezed the fragile bones in his hand until she felt some of them crack. He screamed. She took him by his collar and threw him up and inside the dumpster. He thunked against the inner wall with such force that the lid slammed shut. It was quite a satisfying sound, she had to admit.

Kylara straightened and turned to Becky only to find that the fight wasn't done. Dobbs had scrambled away from the dumpster and behind a parked car. He had a gun aimed at the young dragon mage, and despite having a broken elbow, the barrel was remarkably steady. She wondered if he was ambidextrous.

"You move, and I shoot you. Is that understood? My brother is a cop so don't think anyone will come to your rescue. You hurt my friends good. Any injuries they have, I'll do double to Becky here."

"No, you won't," she said as Becky choked out a sob.

She was too far away to reach the gun. Perhaps if she had full access to her speed, she could have managed it, but even that seemed unlikely. The car was in the way, Dobbs was super-focused on her, and there was Becky to consider. Her getting hurt any more than she had already been was not an option.

Which meant it was time to show Dobbs exactly what he was dealing with. While she didn't want to reveal that she was a dragon to diners at the Get-yer-Eats, she saw no choice. If he fired his gun at her diamond scales, it would do nothing. Only dragon bullets could penetrate them, which meant that unless Dobbs was way better connected than she realized, she would be fine and he most certainly would not be.

It was unfortunate to have to blow her cover, but it would be worse if Dobbs continued to get away with whatever this community had allowed.

Kylara was about to transform when a man stepped forward and placed the barrel of a pistol squarely against Dobb's temple.

"What the hell is this?" the thug protested incredulously.

"Finger off the trigger," the man said. She recognized him as the guy who had tried to pay for Dobbs to leave Becky alone.

The bully grumbled but he complied. "It's good you're here, sir. This terrorist was assaulting my friends and—"

He didn't get to finish his nonsensical explanation because the stranger whacked him upside the head with the butt of his gun and rendered him unconscious.

Becky screamed, scrambled into her car, and accelerated away, her tires squealing. The three unconscious men sprawled about the area, while Kylara and the newcomer appraised each other.

CHAPTER EIGHTEEN

Kylara and the man who'd saved her from revealing herself stared at each other across the parking lot as snow began to fall. The thick flakes flickered between neon pink and washed-out blue as they tumbled through the fluorescent lights of the diner sign.

She spoke first. "Who the hell are you?"

"Someone who doesn't like men who treat women like punching bags," the man said as he moved toward the dumpster.

He had clubbed Dobbs and had a gun so she didn't block his passage, but she didn't like his evasive answer either. "I asked what your name was."

"No, you didn't," the man said as he pulled something out of the dumpster. An old extension cord? He retrieved a knife and cut the plug off, then made strips of cord before he scrambled into the dumpster to bind the first man and throw him out. That done, he bound the second man's wrists and heaved him over the edge to land hard on the road.

He walked toward Kylara, then past her. Annoyed, she caught him by the shoulder to get his damn attention.

His response was immediate—and straight out of Hester's playbook. He grasped her, bent his knees, and tossed her over his shoulder in an extremely well-practiced motion. She twisted, landed on her feet, went into a roll, and came up in a fighting stance.

"Do you want to fight, buddy?" she demanded, shocked that he had been able to fling her around so easily and certain that she wouldn't let him get the best of her again.

"Nice moves, and no thank you. I don't like to fight people like you all that much."

"You mean girls?"

The man narrowed his eyes as if he understood exactly how foolish her answer had been. "I mean injured people. That cut's bleeding badly. You should get it stitched and the sooner the better given the source of the injury." He dragged Dobbs to the other two, tied his wrists as well, then set all three men as close to one another as possible and tied them together with a complicated knot that did not look at all fun to untangle.

"I heal fast," Kylara said as she appraised his work. It was a decent solution, she had to admit. If they called the cops, Dobbs had made it clear that his brother would let them off. At least this way, the creeps could wallow in the consequences of their actions for a while.

"I bet you do," he replied and glanced at the injury. Kylara wondered how long he had been watching. Had he seen her receive the wound? If so, he might have seen how bad it had been. There was certainly still considerable blood.

"How did you know how to flip me like that?" she asked.

"How did you flip a guy who must have weighed twice what you do?"

"Practice."

The man smiled for the first time. "My name's Drew, by the way."

"Nice to meet you, Drew. Do you mind telling me what the hell you're doing out here in the snow behind this diner?"

"The same thing as you. I saw you follow these assholes

outside without finishing your pie and assumed you might need a hand. It turns out you didn't until Dobbs got the drop on you, so I stepped in when I knew I wouldn't be in the way."

"Why did you pay for their beers?" she demanded.

"Sometimes, a soft touch is better than a hard one," Drew said and tapped his gun casually. "Do you mind if we go inside? I'm freezing."

"Inside sounds better than this," Kylara said hesitantly. "I'm Lara, by the way."

"Lara, huh?" He half smiled and she thought it might hold amusement but wasn't sure. "Let's go eat some pie, Lara."

Kylara had settled into Drew's booth, finished both slices of pie, ordered another, and was working on a fresh cup of coffee Janus brought to her.

Drew returned from the restroom with his cell phone pressed against his ear. "Yes, sir. Uh-huh. I left them outside. No, sir, thank you." He hung up.

"What was all that about? Did you call the cops on him? He said his brother would simply cover for him."

"It turns out his brother works for what this town calls its police force but he doesn't work for the state. I called the big boys in."

"Is that something you do often, Drew? Call in state police?" She thought it was clever, mostly, but a little suspicious too. How did someone go about getting the number for the state police? Who was this guy, exactly? He carried a gun, was quite skilled in hand-to-hand combat, and knew enough about goons to have more than one strategy to use against them. The obvious solution dawned on her. "Are you a cop?"

He chuckled as he reached for the slice of pie that Janus had brought for Kylara.

Before the waitress could leave, Kylara asked her for another. The cherry was damn good.

"I'm sorry, I thought you had ordered that for me." Drew gestured to the two empty plates in front of her.

"She's a pit, hon—a bottomless pit. I might as well bring the rest of the pie, huh?" Janus suggested.

They both nodded and the woman left with a smile on her face.

"Okay, so are you a cop?"

Drew finished chewing his mouthful before he admitted that he was. "I used to be for years. It was a great job—simple compared to what I do now."

"And what's that?"

He gestured vaguely around the diner. "Consulting work, mostly. Security stuff. It's different all the time, which is a huge pain."

"And being a cop was always the same?" Kylara had always had a fascination with police because that was how the Steel Dragon got her start.

"It was for most of my time in the service. Each day was slightly different, of course, but Detroit was Detroit. I got to know my beat so well that after a while, it was routine. OD over here, domestic dispute over there—almost predictable."

"Wait, wait, wait, hold up. You were a cop in Detroit? Did you ever meet...you know...her?"

Drew stuck a forkful of pie in his mouth before he answered. He chewed and seemed to consider his answer carefully. "Who?" he asked finally.

Kylara guffawed at his response. "Who? Kristen Hall. The Steel Dragon herself. I guess you didn't, huh?"

He chuckled. She liked the sound of his laughter. It was almost well-practiced as if he wished to reassure her that he was amused. She wondered how many alleged criminals had been treated to the same disarming little chuckle. "I was there in the beginning. Before she knew what she was, yeah. That was about the last time being a cop was simple."

"Do you miss it?" she asked, eager to learn more and keep the conversation away from herself.

"I do. I liked being a part of the community. It was hard too, of course. Police have power and power corrupts, and it was a constant struggle against those forces."

"What do you mean?"

"Sometimes, people would do things simply because they could—not because they were trying to be bad, mind you, but because they could. That was the worst part of the job. There was one guy, Jonesy." He smiled and shook his head. "He was a great cop, but Lord, he couldn't control his tongue to save his life. He said the worst damn things to people we were supposed to take to jail. It wasn't necessarily a big deal, but even little slip-ups like that can distort power. You know what I mean? Like, a criminal sees him swear, then they try it and of course are told to mind their language by whoever else is on duty. Then they see the power difference. It's like dragons, I guess."

"What do you know about dragons?" Kylara asked and realized only belatedly that she had asked the question far too quickly.

"Oh, in the grand scheme of things, I wouldn't say I know much. I'm certainly still learning about them. I only meant that a dragon thinks using their fire breath to incinerate a couple of deer is their God-given right. People who don't have that power feel like they are corrupt and that doing it is an abuse of power. It's all about perspective—and specifically, the perspective of the least powerful."

"People like Becky, you mean," Kylara said.

"I do." Drew nodded and took another slice of pie.

They ate in silence for a while. He ate two slices, while Kylara polished off the rest of the dessert. She eventually gave up on moving slices to her plate one at a time and ate them from the tin. It was exceptionally good pie.

They watched as the state troopers arrived and carted Dobbs and his cronies off. Most of the people in the diner smiled when this happened, and Janus approached to tell them that the meal was on the house. Kylara wanted to protest but Drew shushed her with a gesture.

"We ate a whole pie!" she said when the woman left to make another round of coffee refills. "The least we can do is pay for it."

"I understand where you're coming from but she was trying to do us a kindness since we dealt with those knuckleheads. If I was still a cop, I would have said no on principle, but since it was you and me kicking ass, I feel we earned that pie."

"We could still have paid."

"So leave her a good tip and forget about it. She probably has to throw away a couple of slices every night anyway. I bet she was tickled that we polished it off."

Kylara nodded and realized yet again that there were entire cultures she didn't understand. She had grown so accustomed to scrambling to learn how dragon and mage culture worked, how they intersected, and how all of that was changing that she often forgot that the vast majority of the people on earth were neither dragons nor mages.

She had seen regular people before, but only those who lived in the tiny town near the desert homestead where she had grown up. As a result, she didn't understand the etiquette of free pie any better than she had understood the interplay between mages and dragons a few months before.

"Well, I should probably hit the road. My car won't drive to Aspen itself," Drew said once Janus cleared their plates.

"Aspen, huh?" she asked. Aspen was damn close to where she was trying to get to. Could she trust Drew? She felt like she could. He was an ex-cop and had wanted to help poor Becky even before

Kylara realized what he was doing. She didn't think he was a creep and if he was, she could handle him. Yes, he had flipped her over his shoulder, but that was when she was in her human body. If she became a dragon, that would make things a little different. "Would it…um, be possible to hitch a ride in that direction?"

He looked down his nose at her as if he saw her for the first time. She didn't like the examination but it was his truck and his time and he certainly had the right to give her the once-over if he wanted to.

"Are you running from something or searching for something?" he asked.

"Searching for something," she admitted. "A friend who's fallen on hard times, I guess you could say. I'm hoping I can talk some sense into him."

"That's a fairly good reason to travel. Is there any reason you're out here alone?"

"I had to do it alone. Everyone else who knows this guy thinks he's a lost cause."

"But you don't?"

"I don't know, honestly. But he at least deserves a chance."

Drew nodded after he'd thought about her request for an uncomfortable length of time that made her nervous.

"All right, then. I'll give you a ride as far as Aspen. Hell, depending on where this charity case of yours is, I might be able to take you straight there if it's less than an hour or so out of my way."

"Oh, my goodness, that would be wonderful, thank you, Drew! I have cash to throw in for gas and can get food too."

"None of that is necessary. I'm already headed that way, so gas ain't a huge deal, and I'm not about to let a seventeen-year-old buy my meals."

Kylara hadn't mentioned her age. Still, she knew she looked young so maybe that didn't mean anything sinister. "I can't mooch the whole time, though."

"If you have cash, you can pay for your motel room tonight. I'll drive for a few hours but don't want to push too far if the snow picks up again. And I don't want to bunk with no seventeen-year-old girl either."

She nodded. He must have simply chosen that number to make it clear that he thought she was too young for him to see her as anything but a big kid. This provided another reassurance, at least at face value. Kylara followed Drew to his truck and they drove off into the night.

CHAPTER NINETEEN

The next day dawned and was particularly beautiful. The clouds that had brought snowfall the day before evaporated early in the morning, leaving desert scrubland covered in snow that sparkled in the bright morning sun. As they drove, the landscape began to show one or two signs of the transition from scrub to the taller deciduous and pine trees of the upper elevations, although they still had a way to go before it transformed completely.

Kylara loved being up in the mountains. The land that she'd grown up on extended most of the way into the foothills and her favorite days were always spent up high where she could see the world splayed beneath her. It felt better up there. The air tasted cleaner and everything about it made her feel safe.

Drew also helped to distract her from what might have been stressful wonderings.

"So this guy tells me he doesn't know where any of the cocaine is. Meanwhile, it's all over his face." Drew laughed as he drove. "He kept saying we needed probable cause to search his home but he's wearing the merchandise instead of clothes."

"He was naked?" Kylara was shocked. She had heard any number of cop stories from her mom—after all, Hester Diamantine had been in Dragon SWAT for decades—but none of those stories were funny. She certainly hadn't told any stories about naked drug addicts.

"No, no, no. He had dirty underpants on. I don't know what it is with cokeheads and dirty underpants." He shook his head and continued to laugh for a moment before a more somber expression slid across his face. "I shouldn't be talking to you about all this. You're only a kid, too young for this kind of tale. Drugs are bad news, kid."

"Honestly? Telling me about you busting these people does not make me want to do any."

"That's good, I guess," he said agreeably. "But enough about me. It's your turn to tell me more about you. Where are you from?"

Kylara wasn't at all sure how to answer. It was true that he had done most of the talking, but it was also true that almost everything he had talked about had been superficial, isolated stories. She knew he didn't like cheese on his burgers and couldn't stand it when a man hit a woman, but she still didn't know much about him the person. He was frustratingly vague about the exact length of time he'd worked as a cop and what he knew about the Steel Dragon was vaguer still.

"Come on," Drew complained. "Do you want to choose the next restaurant? You have to tell me why you're out here or we'll stop at the first chain we see."

"What? Why? That diner was way better than any of the fast-food we've had."

"Food's food," he said. "Unless you tell me otherwise."

A deep breath didn't help much as she honestly didn't know where to begin. She knew she couldn't reveal that she was a dragon or a mage who absorbed dragon powers, or whatever the hell she was to him. He seemed to have stopped being a cop after the Steel Dragon appeared. She didn't know if that was because he didn't like dragons or was intimidated by them. But whatever his reason, he didn't need to know she was on the run from the Lumos School, Amythist, and likely the Steel Dragon herself.

"I truly am out here for a friend," she began.

"What's his name?"

Kylara didn't see any point in lying and she didn't have something prepared so she went with the truth. "Galen."

"Galen?" For a moment, she was worried that he intended to ask the boy's last name, to which she would have had to lie because *Stormwing* was so obviously draconic. But he didn't press that point. "Galen? Jesus, with a name like that, I bet he's under a ton of pressure from his parents."

She was incredibly relieved. "He is. To make things worse, he has this perfect older brother. Well, not perfect to anyone but his parents, but of course Galen thinks that's what he needs to be too."

"So what changed?"

"Excuse me?" she asked, not sure how Drew was making these connections.

"If you're running away—"

"I'm not running away."

"Fine, sure." He glanced at her out of the corner of his eye but didn't lose focus on the road. "You're running after him, though, right?"

"I guess so, yeah," she admitted.

"Well, if you're after him and you're alone, I can't imagine him still at home, failing to impress his parents. Is he the runaway?"

"I guess he is, yeah," Kylara said, having realized what Galen was only in that moment.

"Kids don't normally do that kind of thing unless something changes. I'm not saying that has to be the case. It's purely a guess."

"Well, yeah, something did change. Galen came into some uh…power."

"Mmmm…" Drew intoned knowingly. "That can be a problem."

"Yeah. At first, I thought he had run off to get a new teacher to help him, but I don't think that worked. I think he ran away from her too."

"So why are you on the job?"

"It's not a job," she protested. "I care, is all, I guess. I understand where he's coming from. I grew up in an unusual situation with a mom who was extremely demanding. Although I get that she loves me and was trying to make me as tough as possible."

"Something that she succeeded in, given what you did to Dobbs."

"I only want to talk to Galen and tell him that he's not alone. I remember what that felt like—being alone. It's terrible."

Drew looked at her and nodded. "It's one of the worst feelings in the world, isn't it? And what's even worse is that when you truly feel alone, it's even more difficult to reach out to others. It's good of you to go after this kid, even if you probably should have told—"

"Drew!" Kylara screamed and threw her hands against the dashboard as a portal opened in front of the truck.

Drew's gaze snapped back to the road and he clenched his teeth and dragged the truck into a swerve that threatened to tip the vehicle and tumble it into the snowy scrub on the side of the road.

Kylara paid no attention to what was happening to the truck. Her gaze was fixed on the portal that had appeared from nowhere.

Her companion regained control of the truck and it barely scraped past the magical gateway.

Her gaze stayed locked on it—waiting, praying, and hoping.

"I've never seen one like that before!" Drew shouted before he uttered a string of curses.

She didn't have time to register what one like that before implied because she was still watching the gate, from which skeletons now poured out into the road behind them.

An eighteen-wheeler jackknifed in an attempt to avoid the gate, which rather effectively blocked the highway from any more cars. It meant the skeletons from the gate had no distractions and could focus on their target—Kylara.

"What the hell are those things?" Drew shouted.

"They're revenants," she responded. "Fast ones."

Despite him still driving at almost sixty miles an hour away from the portal, the skeletons hadn't simply given up. Instead, they communicated with each other in loud screeches as more of their brethren spilled through the gate.

The bones of a horse stepped through, reared on its hind legs, and gave chase. Other smaller skeletons of monkeys or raccoons or whatever counted for vermin in the pixie realm climbed atop its back.

"Do you know how to kill them?" Drew said as he drew his pistol.

"Drew, I haven't been completely honest with you."

"All is forgiven if you know how to kill fricking skeletons!"

"I do."

Kylara unbuckled herself and climbed through the back window of the truck and into the flatbed in the back.

"Lara! Lara, get back in here!" he shouted.

She couldn't, not with the skeleton horse approaching. It was faster than the vehicle. But why not? It had no muscles to tire and no nerves to worry about hurting if it overextended itself.

As it approached steadily, she readied herself. Once it was alongside the truck, she made her hand glow and blasted the creatures off its back with a beam of light. Her light powers didn't seem as affected by the bracelet as her shadow powers were. She hoped her plant powers would listen to her. She called on them when the smaller monsters landed, the scrub obeyed.

Woody, spiny branches entangled them and dragged them into the earth, smothering them with its roots. It was as if the plants could draw on some of the skeletal magic to put them in their resting place, almost like this was the way the magic was supposed to flow.

"You truly didn't tell me everything!" Drew shouted as he swerved the vehicle into the horse and shattered it. Pieces of the skeleton clattered on the asphalt and skidded across the road. Some slid off the road surface and she used her plant powers to bind them into the dirt.

"If you can get them into the scrub, I can bury them," she shouted.

"I just did!" Drew replied.

"That was only a test," Kylara said. He had to keep his eyes on the road ahead of him but she didn't. Her gaze was locked on the gate and the aberrations of bone that continued to spill out of it.

Already, the air was choked with tiny dragons that ranged from the size of a cat to a large dog. They flew on a thin membrane of skin stretched taut between wings of bone.

But despite their numbers, they were not what worried her.

Three great beasts of bone on the ground made her mouth go dry and left her wondering how limiting her bracelet was.

She had seen one of them before or at least something similar. The largest skeleton was that of an elephant but instead of a hole where its blessedly boneless trunk had once been, a long whiplike chain of bone extended with a snapping skull of what might have been an alligator at the end. At least it didn't have monstrous sloth arms like the last mammoth bone monster she had faced.

The other two weren't as big, but each had its individual nightmare characteristics.

One simply looked like a saber-toothed cat, albeit with massively enhanced back legs that enabled it to jump like a grasshopper. As soon as it touched the ground, it leapt forward again, and each bound carried it ahead yards at a time. Kylara assumed it would reach the truck first, as its motion helped it to catch up rapidly.

The third creature was the one she least wanted to face. It

looked like a horse's bones had been used in a necromancer's homework assignment in which he was supposed to have made a centipede. The horrible, crawling, snaking aberration moved far faster than she was comfortable with. Despite its sinuous motion, it was also close to eight feet tall, which she thought was both gross and unfair.

CHAPTER TWENTY

The saber-toothed tiger skeleton was the first to catch up to the truck. It burst out of the growing cloud of dragon skeletons, landed beside the vehicle, and roared as Drew accelerated and attempted to pull farther away.

"It won't miss again, will it?" he hollered from the front seat.

"I don't think so, no," she replied.

The beast crouched on its haunches and launched itself forward again. This time, its effort took it well past the truck and it landed on the road in front of them. Drew tried to swerve around it but it moved across the road and remained in his path.

The centipede horse had caught up to the back of the vehicle. It lifted its front hooves and rained holy hell on the back of the pickup. In a moment, his taillights, license plate, and paneling on the tailgate were all destroyed.

"My insurance plan doesn't cover the undead, so I'd appreciate it if you could do something about that!" Drew hollered. Kylara felt the truck lurch forward as he accelerated toward the massive skeleton still in their path. She had expected him to swerve but then reasoned that the cattle guard on the front of the vehicle had to be used for something.

The expected collision with the monstrous feline never materialized. Instead, it elevated vertically and rose maybe twenty feet to land out of the way inside the cloud of now rapidly approaching undead dragons.

That left Kylara relatively undistracted while she tried to decide what to do with the damn horse-centipede. A gap had opened between the truck and the monster when Drew had accelerated, but the beast now moved faster than ever.

She lashed out with her dark powers before it could power into the truck. The headache came almost instantly and before she could even make contact with the monster, she dissolved the strands.

The horse pounded its hooves into Drew's truck and dislodged his bumper, which clattered noisily across the road.

"Come on, Lara!"

Kylara tried her light powers next, but they did nothing to this beast of bone. She knew her plant powers currently worked better than both her light and dark powers, but she couldn't do a damn thing about that as long as the skeletons were on the cold asphalt. She could try her storm powers too, but that would take time and be anything but precise. Not only that, but she was still working on her lightning's accuracy and this didn't seem like the time to find out how well it worked with the bracelet on.

Besides, she knew a more direct way.

She vaulted from the back of the truck. The wind caught her almost immediately and slowed her relative to the racing vehicle. She flew deliberately toward the horse centipede. The moment her feet lost contact with the vehicle, she transformed. By the time she made impact with the mutant, she was a full-sized, diamond-scaled beast that was already thoroughly sick of this bizarre pursuit.

Her long claws reached easily through the empty space of the aberration's many ribs and she lifted it high. It thrashed and kicked with hooves that were harder than bone, although still much softer than diamond. The creature seemed to realize this and stopped its attack to switch to an obnoxious thrashing designed to wrest itself loose from her hold.

She let it fall in the middle of a field of scrub, grasses, and wildflowers. A quick blast of fire melted the patches of snow, and a burst of her inner magic brought the plants in the area to life. Hungry for this many-legged skeleton beast, a hundred thorny branches of mesquite, cactus, and diminutive pine trees dragged and clawed it into the dirt.

Kylara wheeled and pumped her wings as fast as she could to catch up to the racing truck. It wasn't easy. While her dragon form worked better than any of her other powers did with the bracelet, in moments, her chest was already burning from the exertion.

She would have made it easily, though, if not for the dozens of dog-sized skeletons that were airborne and mobbed her like a flock of angry blue jays targeting a much larger hawk. She lashed out with her diamond-tipped tail. Any of the undead that she struck with the hard, crystalline structures on the tip exploded. Bits of animated bone that had—mere moments before—been in the form of a dragon fell earthward, a far more macabre white snow than what had fallen the night before.

Unfortunately, there were too many. For every one she caught with the tip of her tail or one of her claws, another five dove in to scratch and claw at her. They couldn't get through her scales, of course, but they learned this far too quickly for creatures that were essentially brainless. Instead of trying to scratch and claw, they tried to latch onto her.

Some simply clung to her and ruined her aerodynamics to make it harder to fly in her weakened state. Others crawled across her body to shred her wings, and a healthy dozen of the damn mutants flew around her head and divebombed her face like gnats with their focus on her eyes.

Kylara blasted the swarm near her head with fire and incinerated them. Before they could regroup, she seared another group with her fire breath. The effort drained her, though, and she tucked her wings to return to the back of the pickup truck before her energy left her.

She forced herself to catch up, as hard as it was with the undead creatures all around her. As she moved into position over the bed, she transformed into her human form and tucked into a flip to land lightly in the back. When she began her transformation, the skeletal dragons that had clung to her lost their hold and were caught by the wind to reassemble into a cloud behind the truck.

"Nice of you to join me!" Drew shouted from the front.

"Yeah, no problem."

"And you forgot to mention that you're a dragon," Drew shouted over the wind but he didn't sound angry. He sounded excited, which surprised her.

"I'm not really, but let's get into that later. That mammoth is almost on us. I take it you took care of the saber-tooth?"

"I thought you did."

Something impacted near the front of the truck with an enormous bang and Kylara was tossed upward as the back of the vehicle popped up off the ground and landed again. She hadn't elevated high enough to go over the damaged tailgate. Instead, she landed in the middle of it and was thrown into one corner and then the other. Drew cursed continuously and jerked the steering wheel from one side to the other as needed to keep them on the road, while the saber-toothed skeleton punched holes in his windshield and tried to gut him.

She pushed to her feet, keeping her head down against the wind, and moved toward the front of the truck to dispatch the saber-tooth. The mammoth monster and remaining tiny dragons were a more existential threat, but if the vehicle stopped moving, she knew they were dead. She had to stop the undead feline.

Cautiously, she poked her head up over the cab of the truck

and was confronted by the heavy skull of the beast. It currently used its pair of sword-like teeth to try to impale Drew. She wasn't sure that she could outmuscle it in her human form but she was determined to try.

As she dragged in a long breath to ready herself, a single gunshot rang out and the vicious skeleton was reduced to nothing but loose bones that clattered off the truck and into the road, utterly unanimated.

"What the hell did you shoot it with?" Kylara demanded.

"Special bullets!" Drew replied as enigmatically as anyone could when yelling over the sound of rushing wind and a racing engine.

"Special bullets?"

"We'll talk about it when you tell me how you're not really a dragon!"

"Deal!" she said, ignored the mountains on either side of the road in front of them, and turned toward the horde of skeletons behind them. The mammoth continued to gain on them.

"Have you ever fired a gun?" Drew shouted from the front seat.

"Never!" she yelled in response, oddly shocked that it was true. She had grown up as the daughter of a dragon and had learned to defend herself with her fists, diamond scales, and fire breath. When she needed to hunt, she learned to use her wings and claws. There had never been a need for her to use a gun, nor had her mom anticipated that one day, skeletons might bleed into this realm and that only a gun filled with special bullets would stop them.

"It's not hard. Make sure the safety's off, point, and pull the trigger."

"I don't know—"

But he did. He pushed his arm through the back window, a pistol in hand, and held it out for her.

Kylara, her head still hurting from even attempting to use her shadow powers, took the weapon. It was heavier than she had imagined it to be and cool to the touch.

"Right, so pointy-pointy," Drew shouted.

Cautiously, she raised the pistol and aimed at the mammoth, squeezed the trigger, and frowned as the beast continued untouched when nothing happened.

"Safety! The switch on the side," Drew shouted.

"Right!" She flipped the switch, aimed again, and fired.

She missed and with gritted teeth and a frown of concentration, she tried again.

This time, she hit a dragon skeleton. It shattered but that wasn't exactly cause for celebration when each of the tiny dragons massed less than one of the elephant's leg bones.

The enormous monster was close enough to lash out with its long twisting nose. The alligator head on the end snapped at her and managed to sink its teeth into her forearm.

"Shoot it in the head," Drew shouted, but she had already yanked her arm free. Blood spilled in the back of his mangled truck, but the wound wasn't as deep as the knife wound from the night before had been. A tiny blessing, she acknowledged.

The alligator head reared and coiled the bones that connected it to the mammoth that powered it. In the next moment, it lunged forward. She squeezed off three more shots and managed to shoot the skull with the third one. Or maybe the second. She had stopped counting when she ran out of bullets.

The reptile head disintegrated and the bones supporting it fell away, but the mammoth skeleton continued to race after the vehicle.

"Where's the reload button?" Kylara screamed.

"Reload button? There's no reload button. How did you empty that entire magazine?"

"I don't know."

"Shit!" Drew sounded unimpressed.

"Shit!" Kylara echoed him as he pressed the accelerator as far as it would go and forced the truck ever faster up the road. They now moved between two rock faces that must have been connected decades earlier, before dynamite and the American economy made this a road instead of the middle of a mountain.

"I have an idea!" she said to Drew and studied the landscape.

"If it saves my truck, I support it," he responded.

"I give it fifty-fifty!" She took to her dragon form again and launched herself forward using the wind the truck created to lift her. In moments, she soared up the mountainside, leveled out, and hoped her aim with boulders was better than her aim with firearms

She lashed out with her tail to dislodge rocks and dirt from one side of the road onto the asphalt below.

Drew was already ahead of the rockslide and drove on unmolested, but the mammoth skeleton was not able to continue unchallenged. Boulders and dirt rained on the monster, partially buried it, and broke one of its tusks in half. Despite its temporary setback, it was able to heave itself out of the dirt and move forward. It stabilized itself and immediately tried to gain speed.

Kylara crossed to the other side of the mountain and hurled more rocks and dirt. This section was well ahead of the mammoth, so it didn't bury it but blocked its path.

Before it could run past the rough blockade she'd created, she called on the seeds that had waited dormant on that mountaintop for decades. They sprouted and the piles of dry desert soil flushed instantly with green. The mammoth knew it was beaten. It stopped its relentless chase of Drew's truck, trumpeted somehow despite not being made of anything but bone, and turned.

Kylara braced herself for the dragonling skeletons to attack her next but they didn't. They pulled back and circled the mammoth like gulls around a whale that had forced a shoal of fish to the surface of the ocean.

Despite the burning she felt in her chest and wings from the exertion of maintaining her dragon form, she remained aloft and watched for whatever hellish development the skeletons would attempt next.

It seemed they'd had enough, however.

A portal opened to the swampy area of the pixie realm with its telltale gnarled trees and their dripping limbs. The mammoth vanished inside and the other skeletons followed.

Kylara watched until she was sure the gate had closed, then swooped to land in the back of Drew's thoroughly damaged truck. He didn't slow until they rounded the next bend of the road and he only slowed at that point because he lost traction and almost sent the truck over the edge of the road and down the side of the mountain.

Neither of them commented on how dangerously he was driving. It seemed downright reasonable given what they had encountered on the road.

CHAPTER TWENTY-ONE

For once, Lord Boneclaw wasn't furious with anyone but himself.

Well, that wasn't quite true. He continued to be annoyed with the mage Cassandra and her constant demands. Galen remained a pathetic excuse for a dragon. Right now, however, Boneclaw didn't want to eviscerate either of them. It was once again the Steel Dragon who was the subject of most of his ire. Her and the obnoxious human strays she had taken in and armed with bullets made of dragon bone that he had helped to design.

What infuriated him about the situation was that he'd already had a moment to eliminate the human—Drew, he recalled acerbically. He could have struck when Kylara first met him at night in the parking lot. If he had recognized the human at that point, he wouldn't be in the situation he was in now. He could have slaughtered him and harvested his skull for old time's sake, even though he no longer had a human form to wear skulls as he once had.

Instead, he had watched the entire exchange from the darkness and had completely failed to recognize Drew. If he had struck then, the Steel Dragon could have assumed all kinds of things. She could have thought there was a car accident, or that

Kylara had done something to Drew when she was surprised, or a thousand other options. But now, the man had no doubt made contact with his master. If Boneclaw interfered, Drew might leave clues of his existence. He wasn't ready to face Kristen Hall again—not yet.

He had hoped that opening the gate and flooding the road with skeletons would have done the job, but Kylara and Drew had worked together too well for that to be an effective strategy.

Now, he had to be doubly careful. He knew he could swoop in the next time the truck drove beneath the shade of a pine tree and slaughter the man and maybe the girl, but there were too many risks. With one phone call, his deception might be revealed. He needed Kylara alone so he could draw her into the pixie realm. Drew would make that much more difficult.

He followed them into the mountains and toward the destination he had given Kylara. And to think that she had bought the letter completely. If not for that infernal busybody, she would be on her way toward his trap, unwitting and alone. But instead, she had an ally. A weak one, yes, but also one who wasn't afraid to ask for help and was far more clever than he had any right to be.

Boneclaw knew he had to get closer. He had to get inside the truck to find out what they were talking about. Were they telling each other of their true identities at that very moment? He didn't know. The vehicle was too cramped for him to risk his presence inside. Instead, he jumped from the shadow of a tree, to the shadow of a boulder, to the underside of a fallen log, keeping pace with them and ruminating on how he could kill the man and make it look like an accident.

It was imperative that he remove Drew before Kylara reached the destination to which he had sent her with his forged letter. It would be too difficult to draw her into the pixie realm otherwise. It was truly annoying how much trouble one powerless human could cause.

But the ancient dragon had lived for thousands of years

before the Steel Dragon ended the first phase of his existence. He knew that accidents happened and that even the best-laid plans could fall prey to misfortune. Not even the most suspicious of minds could predict every possible outcome.

The wet and sometimes icy roads that snaked through the Rocky Mountains was the kind of place where such an accident might very well happen. Boneclaw darted ahead of Drew's truck, looking for an outcrop of rock, a clump of trees growing in poor soil, or anything that he could knock down onto the truck. He had to be careful because he did not want Kylara to die, not until he'd taken her power. What he needed was to hurt them both badly so her healing powers could kick in and take care of her. Drew would simply die because he was a fragile human.

A few miles up the road he found exactly what he was looking for. An ancient pine tree had spent the last few hundred years pushing through a pile of boulders. None of them were particularly large, although he knew that even a basketball-sized rock administered to the side of a human head would be more than adequate if wielded correctly. There was a risk that one of these rocks might hit Kylara, but he thought it unlikely. His goal was simply to hit the truck, force them to lose control, and let gravity do its work. Who knew? Maybe he could open a gate and take her at that moment.

He positioned himself and Drew's beat-up vehicle had just come around a bend about a quarter mile down the hill when he felt the tug of Cassandra's consciousness pulling at his own.

"Lord Boneclaw. It is I, your master. Come to me."

"Not now!"

"Do not disobey your master, Boneclaw, or you will be banished from this realm with no hope of returning."

Boneclaw didn't believe she had as much power over him as she thought, but he was less than sure about his plan to crush Drew and not Kylara, so he decided to obey. He transformed into shadow and flowed into the cracks that ran through the mountains. Moving at the speed of darkness, it didn't take him long to travel through a network of fissures in the earth and return to Cassandra's base hidden in a desert cave.

They had left the castle in France as he'd wanted to do, but much to his dismay, their current accommodations were disgusting. The mage and the dragon boy slept on dirty cots on the floor of a cave. What light they had came from candles and Cassandra's fire spirit. It was a filthy, disgusting location, hardly worthy of Lord Boneclaw. He couldn't wait to gain the power he needed to simply take what he wanted once more.

"Lord Boneclaw," Cassandra said when he materialized in his bone form. Unlike the skeletons he summoned, his skeleton was wound by veins of black cords, his spirit given form and purchase in the old bones thanks to the mage. He flexed this dark, veiny mass, hoping to intimidate her. If she noticed, she gave him no sign. "How fares my niece?"

Boneclaw knew he couldn't tell her that he had been about to drop a pile of rocks on the girl. Still, there were things the mage should know. "She's no longer alone."

"Did one of her friends catch up to her? I have met them both before and don't think they will pose much of a problem."

"I wish it were one of the other dragonlings, but no. It's one of the Steel Dragon's minions—a regular, non-magical human named Drew. He is an ex-police officer."

"Then all is lost. She worships the Steel Dragon. If Kylara has her help, we won't be able to change her mind," Cassandra said, clenched her fists, and emitted magic in her fury that made the walls of the cave shudder thanks to the earth spirit who obeyed her so precisely.

"I don't think so. It was hard to be certain, but I believe that this Drew is working incognito. They're probably hoping to test her to see where she's going. If he is still with her when she reaches the destination, it will be difficult to execute the final part of our plan."

"It is not our plan, Lord Boneclaw. I never gave you permission to write a letter using my name, nor did I give you permission to deliver it. And yes, I knew—my spirits are everywhere and keep watch on things that concern me."

"You never forbade it, either."

"It's very odd," the mage said as wind began to blow inside the cave—her air spirit paying attention to the conversation, no doubt. "I never have to specifically forbid any of the other spirits I control from doing things. Yet, you seem to continually push boundaries."

Lord Boneclaw shrugged amicably, a gesture that was lost when performed by the skeleton of a dragon. "You've never summoned a being who lived in this realm for thousands of years before. Those...spirits of yours lack the cognitive capacity to plan in this world. They don't know what time is or how the rest of the creatures here react. I think you should consider yourself very lucky that I behave differently."

"Perhaps if I sank his bones into the ground again, he'd obey," Galen said from his cot.

"And maybe I would cease to exist in this realm and all our plans to better control our new powers would simply unravel," the ancient dragon countered.

"Please, we are all on the same team here," Cassandra said. "There's no need to squabble. When Kylara arrives, she needs to see us working together."

"That won't matter if Drew is still with her. He's untrusting of dragons and more so of me," Boneclaw said.

"But I'm sure that if Kylara is alone, she'll help us," Cassandra said.

"Then perhaps we need to adjust the plan," he suggested. "What if when she gets there she doesn't find Galen at all but a trap?"

"Huh? I thought you wrote her that letter to convince her to come to talk to me," Galen protested. "I thought you were serious about her having insight into my powers if we go to the pixie realm."

"I am serious," the shadow dragon said quickly.

"It might work." Cassandra almost purred with anticipation. "But if this human is there to interfere, she won't be thinking clearly. Instead of talking to you, she'll be distracted by how to look her best in front of Drew, especially if she realizes he works with the Steel Dragon."

"If she realizes that, all is lost," Boneclaw said. "Our only hope is to make contact with her alone before she realizes that you're working with me. The Steel Dragon is toxic and despite an unrefined aura, she is able to change the minds of others with troubling frequency."

"So I should have simply stayed in France?" Galen sounded petulant.

"I suppose so," Cassandra agreed. "This has all become so complicated."

"But it doesn't have to be, not for much longer," Boneclaw said soothingly. "We let them continue to their destination unmolested. I'll stay as close as I can so I can find out if Drew reveals himself. It's something I should be doing right now but cannot since you summoned me here."

"You opened a portal. Of course I needed you to come here to report," Cassandra snapped.

"How do you know of that?" Boneclaw asked. He didn't think Cassandra had any power over him. Well, no power besides the ability to make him hear her, no matter where the two of them were, but he couldn't be sure. Could she sense his actions and his abilities?

"It's all over the news, dingus." Galen chortled. Boneclaw didn't know what a dingus was but he didn't like the tone the young dragon used when he said the word. The boy took his phone out and played a video. It showed a reporter talking animatedly about some new discovery while he stood over the dozen horses that Boneclaw had combined to attack the truck.

They had been pulled into the earth by the desert scrub in a show of power that even the ancient dragon could admit was impressive. Unfortunately, they hadn't been completely buried and had only been pulled maybe halfway under, at which point he had lost control of them. How he longed to make one of the horses thrash out with a hoof and break the vapid reporter's kneecap but alas, the bones had forgotten their place of origin and the being who had released them into this world.

"I gave you no permission to do this either," Cassandra snapped.

"I know you did not, but I assure you that Kylara was never in danger. I simply wished to test their defenses using something that wouldn't raise any more questions for her."

"And you think a cop who works with dragons won't have any questions about a horde of skeletons?" Galen sneered.

"I don't think he'll connect any of that to me or Cassandra, no. It is possible he will think of you, young Galen. That is why we're keeping you around, is it not? To control these skeletons? Even though it seems that I have a level of control with them that you simply lack."

"They don't obey you like they obey me," the boy protested.

"Ah, but yours only obey until they don't," Boneclaw pointed out. "Which seems to be a liability."

"That is quite enough, Boneclaw. Galen is here because without him, you would not exist right now."

"So why not release him into the wild, then?" the shadow dragon asked, his tone on the edge of insulting.

"Because I know how to get through Kylara's diamond scales," Galen said.

"Galen!" Cassandra hissed her impatience.

"What? I do. I saw one of my skeletons do it." The young dragon reached under his cot and retrieved a long, black claw.

Boneclaw had seen its ilk hundreds of years before on the claw of a dragon who had styled himself the Prairie King.

"How did you come into possession of that?" he asked, his tone all kindness now.

"I took it when we left the campus last year," Galen said. He looked as if he was quite unsure about giving it to someone else.

But it was too late for that now. The ancient dragon slithered closer to him and extended his claw. Galen hesitated for only a moment before he handed it to him with a sigh of resignation. Boneclaw shed one of the claws of his right hand and attached this sickle of dark, almost black, crystalline bone.

"This changes nothing, Boneclaw," Cassandra said and glared at Galen. "My niece will help us if we get her alone. We're family. If you hurt her any more than you need to do to press her to pass her powers on, you will be banished from this realm."

"Of course." He was all agreement now that he had a new toy. "Let us focus on the matter at hand. They will be here soon—Kylara in her weakened state and Drew looking to help her. We need to make sure that when they arrive, she feels that she had lost control and that his death was by her hand."

CHAPTER TWENTY-TWO

As they raced up the twisting mountain roads and away from where the gate that flooded the highway with monsters had been, Kylara couldn't help but utter a whoop of joy. It was weirdly amusing, now that the danger was over, that the creatures looked like a necromancer had joined the bones with about the same level of attention to detail as a six-year-old would a set of Legos.

"I can't say I've ever seen someone so delighted to have almost been killed by a saber-toothed tiger," Drew muttered, his hands tight on the wheel as he urged his now dilapidated truck ever higher up the mountain. Even though the engine still ran, the body was all but destroyed. Every section of paneling was dented and every piece of glass was shattered. Still, Kylara saw all that as a win.

"I'm merely happy to be alive," she said, which was mostly true.

"I call BS," Drew said. "The normal response in a crazy situation such as this would be relief or gratitude, or—I don't know, terror? The idea that skeletons can attack a truck driving seventy miles an hour ought to bring up some of those emotions rather than joy. Something else is up."

"You're right," she said, unable to help herself because he was right. Furthermore, he had proven himself to be not only someone who could be trusted but someone who could handle themselves in a potentially deadly situation. "That portal appeared out of nowhere, right?"

"Well, we're in the middle of nowhere so yeah, almost everything out here qualifies as nowhere."

"No, I meant that…well…okay, I haven't been completely honest with you."

Drew laughed at that. "Yeah, you might have neglected to mention that you were a dragon."

"But you don't seem that surprised," Kylara responded.

"Well, when I saw you follow those goons out of that diner, I was a little curious about what your story might be. When you kicked all three of their butts…that's not easy for anyone, especially not someone with your muscle mass."

"Excuse me?"

"I'm only saying that if you were a regular human, man or woman, those skinny arms of yours wouldn't have lifted anyone over your shoulder, let alone thrown them hard enough to dent a dumpster. I assumed you had something special about you. I will admit that I didn't think you were a dragon with what—crystal scales or something? And plant powers?"

"You haven't been completely honest with me either," Kylara pointed out.

Drew shrugged as he kept his hands on the wheel. "Believe it or not, I haven't lied to you."

"What about the special bullets in your gun? You didn't tell me about those. Let me guess—they're made of dragon bone?"

"All right, you got me there but still, I haven't lied. I haven't told you every single detail of my past or about every single thing inside my truck, but that's a little deep for a first conversation with a hitchhiker, don't you think?"

"You still haven't told me where you got the bullets."

"You haven't told me about what exactly you're capable of. I saw something else back there too. Whips or something? It looked like they were made of black rags. What was that about? And then there's your reaction to that portal snapping shut. That grin on your face doesn't look like the grin of survival. That's the face of someone who won."

Kylara leaned forward and appraised him for a long moment. He let her look and kept his eyes on the road while she studied his strong jaw, his stubbly cheeks, and his eyes that remained locked on the twisting road ahead of them.

"Someone blamed me for opening another gate like that." Kylara finally decided to confess. "They said it was related to me being under stress. But we were simply talking when that gate opened."

"About your misguided friend, though. Maybe you found that a little stressful?"

She shook her head vigorously. "Nuh-uh. No way. Last time, the portal closed when I was knocked in the head. This time, it was like something called those monsters here. I didn't have anything to do with that."

"No...no I reckon you didn't," Drew agreed after he'd negotiated another few bends in the road.

"All right, so I told you why I was excited. Now it's your turn. How did you get those bullets? I thought the Steel Dragon confiscated all of them from the technomages who made them."

"That would be impossible," Drew said. "Once tech like that's out there, you can't simply get rid of all of it. It doesn't work like that. But yeah, she scooped up a ton of those munitions."

"So you do know her."

"Not as well as some," Drew said cryptically.

"But enough for her to arm you with those bullets even though dragons hate them?"

"She armed the whole damn Detroit police department with these things precisely because dragons hate them. When she was conducting what is considered to be her revolution, Detroit was a huge target for dragons who were invested in the status quo. She wanted everyone in law enforcement there to be able to defend ourselves. It's not my fault I'm a good shot and don't waste my ammo. That's why I still have a box under the seat."

"So you've met the Steel Dragon?"

"Nuh-uh!" Drew grinned. "It's my turn to ask you a question."

"Fine."

"Why are you out here? Is it honestly about this kid, Galen? Is he a mage or something? And is your real name Lara?"

"It's Kylara. And he's a dragon. How did you know?"

"You said he came into power. It's all starting to make more sense. So what power did he get?"

"The power to raise those skeletons we faced."

"Is that right?"

"He thought he could control it. Last semester, he came to campus with about fifty full-size dragon skeletons to prove that he had mastered it but things got out of hand and he lost control. When that happened, my aunt took him with her. I think she wanted to help him but she failed. It was she who asked me for help."

"I won't lie, that is quite a bit to unpack," Drew said, his eyes wide. "Maybe we should pull over for a minute? I don't think we're being tailed."

"Sure."

He pulled over at one of the many scenic overlooks and they got out of the truck. Kylara couldn't pull her gaze away from how damaged the vehicle was but Drew merely looked out over the horizon and the mountains covered in boulders and trees.

"How do these gates or whatever they are fit into all this? Does this kid—Galen—do those too?"

"No." She dragged her focus away from the truck and decided that the landscape before them was indeed far more interesting than any amount of damage to a vehicle. "Or I don't think so, anyway. He learned the ability to raise and control the skeletons in the pixie realm."

"I thought learning stuff in the pixie realm was the domain of the Steel Dragon."

"It used to be, but the Lumos School is now trying to get all of us to learn new powers."

"So you are a runaway!" Drew turned away from the mountain vista for the first time. "I knew it. You're supposed to be a student at this school, but you're out here being a hero and playing hooky."

Kylara sighed. "I guess so, yeah."

"Oh, don't get all bent out of shape about it. I won't rat on you to the principal or anything. But back to this power. If the kid didn't learn it, who did? Your aunt?"

"I don't think so. She's a mage like me, but she wants to be a dragon."

Drew ran a hand down his face as if he tried to wipe the confusion away. "Wait, so you're a mage who can change into a dragon. And your aunt is jealous?"

"Yes!" Kylara blurted. "But I don't think she would do anything to hurt me. She did kidnap my friends last semester, but that feels like ancient history now."

He chuckled. "If you call that ancient history, I don't want to know what that makes me. But back to your story. If your aunt didn't open the gate and this kid didn't do it, who did?"

"I don't know. Amythist thought it was me. That's why she put this on my wrist." She wiggled her silver cuff for him to see.

"I've seen those on mages. They aren't too pleasant from what I hear. Still, that's within the headmaster's prerogative to keep the campus safe, right?"

Kylara paused. She didn't recall mentioning that Amythist was the headmaster. How had Drew known that? The Lumos School was supposed to be kept confidential from regular people to avoid it becoming a publicity nightmare.

Drew noticed her hesitation but misinterpreted it. "It's messed up that she did that but at least you know it's not you."

"I suppose," Kylara said but wondered more and more who this guy was with his dragon bullets who didn't seem upset that his vehicle had been all but destroyed. "I learned how to open gates from this dimension to the pixie one when I was in the pixie world. As far as anyone knows, I'm the only one who can do it."

"And those monsters were definitely from there? I've seen gates open in Detroit, but I've never seen anything like those bone daddies come out of them."

"Oh, yeah. I had a glimpse through. It's a swampy corner of the pixie realm. Those things were from there, no doubt about it. My friend Tanya saw the little flying cat-sized ones when she was in the swamp, and some of them attacked earlier in the year. It was the pixie realm."

"It sounds like we need to talk to someone who can open those gates," Drew said prosaically.

"We can't. I'm the only one anyone knows who can open them."

"Well, that's not entirely true, is it?" he asked.

"First you have dragon bullets, now you're going to tell me about an esoteric form of magic? Who are you, Drew?"

"Oh, don't get all worked up about me. I'm not talking about some old wizard. I'm talking about pixies. They travel between this world and theirs, right? It's logical that they must. I've seen them here and they obviously go there."

"Oh, my God, why didn't I think of that?" Kylara blurted. "Maybe a pixie is behind those attacks."

Drew smiled. "Have you ever met a pixie?"

"As a matter of fact, I have," she retorted. "A pixie named Petalwing came to my school and took us to the pixie realm. I've met six pixies if you must know." She desperately hoped that he didn't ask her to name any of the others as she would have no answer.

"Me too," he said. "I don't see them often but I've crossed paths with one or two. Do you think a pixie is capable of something like this?"

"Opening gates to their realm? Of course they're capable of that."

"No, not opening the gates but masterminding the different things that have happened. Do you think a pixie would open gates to attack you at school, then close them at the right moment when you hit your head? Honestly, it seems a stretch for pixies. They don't operate the same way we do and don't understand what a clunk on the head means for regular people like us. Well, me as you're not exactly regular, are you?"

Kylara chewed her lip and thought about the pixies she knew. Drew was right. The idea of one of them implementing any kind of plot seemed...unrealistic. Plots and plans and the lies and deceptions needed to perpetrate them seemed to be firmly in the hands of mages and dragons. Well, and regular people too, of course, but a regular person didn't open the gate.

"I admit that the pixies I met don't seem the type to plan much of anything," Kylara said.

"Precisely. I can't imagine pixies being behind all this. And if they are, I bet all we'd have to do is ask one of them and they'd tell us everything. Pixies aren't exactly masters of deception."

"Unfortunately, I don't have any pixie's phone numbers saved in my address book," she quipped. "Do you?"

"As a matter of fact, I do. Well, not personally, but they're a friend of a friend. Not far from here, actually."

"It seems awfully convenient," she said and began to wonder about Drew again now that she was no longer distracted. Who was he? How did he know what he knew? What was his connection to the world of dragons and magic? How on earth could he continue to ignore the damage to his truck? A memory niggled at the back of her mind, something about a person named Drew who she ought to remember, but he broke into her train of thought before she could pin it down.

"I told you I was headed this way when I picked you up. I had business up here, but I like to visit folks when I can. I planned to stop at my friend's house on the way back but we can go there now. If this is a portal to the pixie realm, we might as well talk to pixies about it, right?"

"What about your consulting job?"

He laughed loudly at that. "I used to be a cop, remember? We're all about nesting our priorities on top of one another. And you have to be considerably dumber or crazier than I realized if you think I can simply walk away from a girl who has a horde of teleporting skeletons on her tail. I don't mind taking you. It's not far out of the way and it might help whenever you meet Galen."

"You'd do that for me?" Kylara asked.

"Sure." He turned and strode toward his truck. "Let me make the call. If they're there and don't mind us dropping in a few days earlier than planned, we could be there in a couple of hours."

"But Galen—"

"Is still on our route," Drew assured her as he slid into his truck and retrieved his phone. "If you don't want to go meet these pixies, that's fine. I'll keep driving, but they might be able to crack this wide open—what with it being related to the pixie realm and all."

She nodded and he dialed a number on his phone.

It rang only once before whoever he'd dialed picked up. He turned his back to Kylara while he spoke but she listened shamelessly.

"Yeah, hey. It's Drew."

A pause followed as he listened. She couldn't make out the words spoken by the other party, which was extremely annoying.

"Yeah, I'm fine. No broken glass."

That was a weird thing for him to say given that there was broken glass only inches in front of him.

"No, ma'am. No, ma'am. No, I don't think so. Not yet, anyway. Uh-huh."

Another pause followed and she scowled, no closer to gleaning any information.

"Yes, ma'am. I was hoping you could check to see if there were any pixies at the Colorado Summer retreat. Uh-huh. Uh-huh...I'd say about two hours if that's all right."

Another pause ensued, this one even longer.

"Ma'am, I don't think that's what's happening here, I truly don't. Look, I...uh..." He glanced over his shoulder at Kylara, "I don't want to say too much right now, but I think pixies might be...uh, essential, so to speak."

He shook his head as he listened again, then nodded. "No, thank you, ma'am," he said finally and hung up.

"What's the plan?" she asked, even though she wanted to know what wasn't happening there. She had no clue what he was talking about and that left her feeling very much on edge.

"They're excited to see us. We should be there for dinner."

CHAPTER TWENTY-THREE

As promised, they pulled off the highway about an hour later and turned onto a road that was somehow even more twisty than the last one. After about thirty minutes during which they rose ever higher on switchbacks up the side of a mountain, they began a slow descent into a valley on another set of switchbacks. Finally, they pulled into a dirt driveway lined with massive pine trees.

Kylara was surprised to see wildlife peeking out at them instead of scurrying away. A deer watched their approach, as did a family of raccoons in a tree. The animals didn't seem skittish at all, which both calmed her and made her want to ask even more questions. Top of the list was what the hell she was getting into.

The dirt driveway left the shade of the pine trees and took them into a beautiful mountain meadow. She could immediately see why pixies would live there. It was like the field in their home, the place of flowers and butterflies with the grottos, only this scene didn't have trees ringing it but mountains. She might not have noticed the house at all if she hadn't been looking at the mountains.

It was built into the side of one, so all she saw at first were huge windows and a door.

"Is that it?" she asked and pointed, and Drew nodded.

"It's dug into the mountain," he explained. "It's an awesome little place. The pixies don't let the human who lives with them here trim any of the plants, though, so there are probably still roots poking through the ceiling."

Now that she could use the windows as a reference, she saw that the meadow wasn't as wild as she had originally thought. The space in front of the house was still all wildflowers and tall grasses, but they were planted in patterns and whirls like a geometric mage tattoo but done on the scale of a mountainside. It was beautiful although difficult to discern the pattern at first. She longed to transform and take to the sky to see it from above.

Drew put the truck in park and they climbed out of the damaged cab and stepped into the meadow in front of the house.

Kylara barely had time to take a step before the front door of the house burst open to the sounds of screams. She planted her feet and raised her fists, wondering why she trusted Drew to bring her there when she didn't know his whole story. She had been naïve and too trusting.

Something burst from the open door, then vanished into the grass. Kylara tracked its approach as the grass bent with its passing. Screaming continued from inside the house, but she could hear the words now.

"Rider! Get back here, Rider. We're supposed to have guests soon. Rider, this is an embarrassment!"

She didn't know what a Rider was or why it might embarrass the speaker if Rider attacked her.

Instinctively, she called on her dragon powers and spoke to the grass to tell it to capture whatever was passing through it toward her. The grass obeyed its master and swung downward to try to stop Rider's approach.

A yelp was followed by an animal growling and suddenly, Rider was upon them.

He turned out to be about ten inches tall with oversized eyes and what appeared to be a backpack made of a giant beetle on his back. He sat on the back of a raccoon and held tightly onto its whiskers. The raccoon, free of the grasping grass but now exposed in the dirt driveway, seemed to weigh its options before it decided that first and foremost, it needed to knock the pixie from its back.

"Be still, foul beast!" Rider shouted from his perch, which achieved the exact opposite. The unwilling mount darted toward Drew's truck and flattened itself to go under it. Rider did his best to hang on but that took up all of his attention, so he failed to notice the quickly approaching door of the vehicle.

The raccoon vanished and Rider pounded into the side of the damaged vehicle like a bug that might have hit the windshield when it still existed.

"Are you all right, little buddy?" Drew asked the little creature.

"I am stupendous!" Rider boasted as he peeled himself off the side of the truck. Before he could fall the foot or so to the ground, his beetle backpack opened to reveal a giant pair of wings beneath. They unfolded and fluttered to elevate him seconds before he landed in the dirt. Kylara realized that the contraption on his back wasn't a backpack at all but part of his body. He had a hard, protective shell to cover his wings, exactly like a beetle did.

She was about to attempt to introduce herself but Rider had no time for her. He buzzed to the other side of the truck, berating his mount as he went. "Foolish beast! Return to your master. They will make cartoons about our exploits. Beast! Return to me."

More buzzing sounded from the open door of the house and she turned as three more pixies flew toward them. One of them appeared to be female, although she had to admit that was only a guess. She had a narrower waist than Rider and a hint of a swell to her chest, and her face was prettier and more feminine than his. Two enormous butterfly wings flapped from her back, speckled in a pattern of black and yellow. She wore a dress that appeared to be made entirely of woven grass.

The other two pixies were more difficult for Kylara to sort into either human or insect categories. One of the pixies was so androgenous that she didn't dare to guess its gender although either way, it was quite beautiful. It darted constantly and each time it paused, it hovered in place on dragonfly wings that must have been at least twelve inches apiece.

The third pixie was also androgynous, but it looked less human than the others so gender wasn't the first question that came to mind when she looked at it. It looked like a cross between a human and a wasp. Its eyes were huge and multifaceted and instead of ears, it had long antennae that were somewhat fuzzy. For being a cross between a human and a bug, Kylara was surprised at how cute the being was.

"Mari, it's nice to see you," Drew said, bowing formally to the pixie with the butterfly wings.

"Human!" Mari replied and buzzed around Drew's head to sprinkle him with golden sparks that vanished the moment they touched him. "It is nice to see you."

"Drew. My name is Drew, Mari. Remember?"

"Yes, Drew!" Mari smiled. "And who is this?"

"She is dragon—or mage or...pixie. I do not know. I like her very much!" the pixie with the antennae said. It circled Kylara very slowly like a bee looking for nectar, but instead of probing for flowers, it kept touching her with its antennae.

"Do not sniff without permission, Hound. Humans do not like to be sniffed," Mari snapped at Hound, who ignored her.

"It's fine, truly," Kylara said quickly. She had no desire to piss off these tiny, strange creatures.

"This human is very polite," the dragonfly-winged pixie said. Her voice sounded female and much older than the others.

"Ah yes, that she is. Oda, allow me to introduce Kylara Diamantine. She's who you were briefed about on the phone."

"Ah! I see it now," Oda said.

"I smell it!" Hound chirped.

"Wait, briefed about? What do you mean by briefed?" she asked Drew.

He waved her concern away. "It's a figure of speech. I didn't talk to Mari or Oda on the phone."

"We do not like nor understand your magic far-talky box," Rider added as he glided over their heads, having finally let the raccoon go.

"What did you mean about how I smelled?" Kylara asked Hound and decided that she would regard him as male unless told otherwise.

He merely kept sniffing with a wide smile on his face as if he'd smelled a baking apple pie and wished to nap until it was finished.

"Is Atramento still here?" Drew asked, which vaguely bothered Kylara.

"He is inside, yes," Mari said. "He insists that you humans like a clean house, so he is cleaning it."

"Have you guys made him live in a mess? That guy hated it when someone left a post-it note out of place. I can't imagine what four pixies are doing to him."

"I will do much punishment when I see him next." Rider shouted. "He released the masked bandit before I was ready."

"Maybe we could all have some tea?" Drew asked.

"Ah...tea, yes. This is something we have learned to do well. The old purple one would be very proud!" Mari said.

"I'm sure she would," Drew said.

"Who would?" Kylara asked, thinking of someone she knew who liked tea.

"It's not important right now," he said with another dismissive gesture. "Do you mind showing us around? I'd love to stretch my legs. We've been in the truck for a while."

"It would be our honor, Human Drew," Oda said and bowed

so low she tumbled into a somersault.

Oda drifted toward the house inside the hill, and Drew and Kylara followed. Mari chatted about the flowers and plants as they went as if they were old friends and Drew asked about how they were doing. To the ex-cop's credit, he nodded and asked polite questions that she answered with a smile. "Oh yes, the columbine didn't wish to be trimmed but sometimes, it simply must be, you know?" or "The pine trees dropped so many cones this year! They're happy as you might have noticed."

Rider ran on the ground and darted from clumps of flowers to clumps of grass as if he were hunting another creature to ride. Hound remained extremely close to Kylara, sniffed her with everything he had, probed her with his antennae, and generally made a nuisance of himself.

Mari led them inside a house that Kylara found both familiar and utterly bizarre. She had lived in a house built into the side of a mountain and could feel the weight of the stone and earth behind the back wall, exactly like she had at home. The solidity of the floor triggered her memory and she could see how the stove and sink were positioned carefully to hide their fixings.

But that was where the similarities ended. Her home had been a place of clean lines and tidy surfaces. There had been separate rooms, each with its own feel and purpose. This abode was merely one large space filled with a smattering of tables, chairs, a sofa, and so many plants that it made Amythist's office look tame. Roots did indeed sprout from the ceiling, some of which had been exposed for a long time as they had grown bark and were now being used to hang planters with vines or drying herbs.

Like her home, it was also flooded with light from an entire wall of windows. Despite being partially underground, it didn't feel cramped or claustrophobic.

"Atramento, is that you?"

A mage covered in geometric tattoos from the tips of his

fingers, up his arms and neck, across his bald head, and onto his ears, turned and darted Drew a look of disapproval.

"I was told I would be able to retire in the mountains. This is not retirement." A teapot lifted off the counter next to him and poured fragrant, steaming tea into three cups and four thimbles.

"It's nice to see you," Drew said and shook the mage's hand before he took his cup of tea.

"You as well, Drew. It's been too long since I've been able to have a conversation with someone who understands that time only flows in one direction." Atramento took his cup of tea and sat in one of the only clean chairs available. As if remembering his manners, he gestured and two other chairs were cleared of leaves, twigs, and a thousand other tiny items Kylara could only guess at the composition of.

"I was working on that pile!" Oda grouched.

"I thought you finished it already," the mage said and made no effort to hide his annoyance.

"Ah, yes. That's right!" Oda beamed, the mystery solved.

Atramento's finger traced a circle around his ear as he pointed at her with the other. The playground sign language for crazy seemed appropriate.

"This is her, then?" Atramento asked and nodded at the young dragon mage.

"It is. She is the one. The queen of stink! Never have I smelled such a bouquet," Hound shouted as if the world needed to hear. "Human. Dragon. Mage. I even detect a hint of pixie."

"Are you sure about that?" Mari asked.

"No. Not yet. More smelling must be done," Hound said and buried his nose in Kylara's hair.

"Why do you bring this creature to us, Drew the Human of the Motor City," Mari asked.

"I think it might be best if Kylara explains all that for herself," he said and gestured for her to take the floor.

Despite her initial hesitation, she complied and told the pixies all that had happened since the first portal opened. She told them of her ability to open gates to the pixie's realm, and how she had learned to do so from a pixie. They listened intently while she told them how the portals continued to open all around her, and how she had been blamed and subsequently cuffed to prevent more from opening. She told them of Galen and the skeletons he could summon, and how that ability was also derived from the pixie realm.

When she had finally finished, the first to speak was Hound.

"It's not you!" he said in triumph. "Most certainly not."

"Are you sure?" Mari asked.

"I would not say so if I was not sure!" Hound sounded indignant. "I smell the stinky stank of brimstone that so many dragons have. I smell magic in her veins, coursing and flowing as it does in the veins of those with magic, and I smell other things too. Raw magic. Wild magic. Our magic."

"Could that be what's opening the portals?" Drew asked.

"Do not interrupt me, Human Drew!" Hound roared in the world's highest-pitched and least threatening roar. "And no, I detect no stinky leaks. Although it is hard to be certain with that...that thing!" He gestured at the silver cuff on Kylara's wrist, wrinkled his nose, and twitched his antennae in disgust. "I thought the Steel Dragon made those devices...what is the human term? Eagle?"

"Illegal," Atramento corrected dryly. "And yes, they are no longer used very often, despite centuries of them working admirably for both dragons and mages."

"You don't miss working for the dragons, do you?" Drew asked.

The mage's frown deepened. "Dragons were predictable. These pixies are anything but."

Mari, Oda, and Hound all fell over laughing at his long-suffering tone.

Drew tried not to chuckle while Kylara couldn't help but guffaw at the ridiculous little creatures.

Because of this, she failed to notice Rider drop from the air wielding a kitchen knife until he was already on her.

"Yeaaarrrgh!" he screamed as he plummeted with both hands on the handle of the knife and his feet clinging to either side of it like it was a shovel he intended to drive straight into her wrist.

He didn't hit her flesh, thankfully, and deftly managed to catch only the bracelet on it. With a quick twist and a vicious little snarl, he snapped the cuff. Instantly, Kylara felt her magic surge through her body. It was like removing a stick from a blocked creek. Where once stagnant energy had pooled, searching for somewhere—anywhere—to flow, there was now the gentle trickle of energy growing into a steady rush as it cleared away the detritus and scum that had built up.

She sighed with relief at being freed.

"I'm sure this will be fine," Atramento commented sardonically. "I'm sure there was no reason for that to be on her wrist."

"You got that right." Rider thumped his chest in victory. "Those things are disgusting. Unnatural and not right!"

"Weren't you trying to put a harness on that raccoon only yesterday?" Atramento inquired.

"I am a changed pixie," Rider shouted. "And I'm so sorry about that." He ran from the house and out into the field, looking for the raccoon and shouting apologies as he went.

"Should someone…go after him?" Kylara asked tentatively.

"Naw," Drew and Atramento said together.

Oda shook her head. "This will give us time to speak without being interrupt—"

"You smell better!" Hound chirped from somewhere near Kylara's ear. "That bracelet made it very hard to smell you but you are much stinkier now."

"I'm…sorry?"

"In a good way!" Hound squeaked. "I am still not sure about

the pixie smell, but there is something about you—something particularly good. Like cinnamon, but better. Nutmeg? It is hard to put in words you would understand."

"It is good that the device was broken," Oda said. "I do not believe that you are leaking but we can now properly test you. Tell me, have you ever been to the place that's not a place?"

"Uh...no?" Kylara said.

"Excellent, because then you would have been reduced to your...er, what's the word?"

"Constituent atoms?" Atramento suggested.

"Yes! Your constituent atoms. Come! We will go there now."

"Are you sure about this?" she asked warily.

"Oh, yes!" Mari replied. "Time is a-wasting. Come. We leave now. Atramento will fix us dinner."

CHAPTER TWENTY-FOUR

Tanya didn't understand much about how Jasmine's magic worked. It seemed like the girl had a thousand different ways to call on her powers and none of them was anything remotely like transforming into a dragon or making plants grow. And yet, despite their differences, she could still see how useful the mage's abilities were.

"I don't get it. Are you sure this works?" Sam asked. Jasmine, Karl, and Samuel were all crammed inside Tanya's tiny dorm room. Fortunately, Jasmine had arrived first and cleaned the mess with a snap of her fingers and the briefest of scowls. They all huddled around a tiny ball of air—no, more like wind, maybe, although it was difficult for Tanya to describe—and listened intently. Despite not understanding how the magic worked, Tanya understood what it did. Sam was being more obstinate.

"How can you even ask her such a stupid question?" Karl had given up hiding his disdain for Sam the moment Kylara had left. "We can hear the headmaster's voice. You think—what?—this mage is fabricating the entire thing?"

"No. I only…I've never seen magic like this before," Sam said somewhat grumpily.

"It's something the Patel family invented," Jasmine said while her fingers moved in carefully choreographed synchronization to keep the ball of air spinning. No, that was not right. It was more like it only looked like it was spinning, whereas in reality, it was vibrating.

"When I was called into the office the other day for fighting—"

"Please let me know if you ever need help doing that again," Karl said with a grin.

"I set up an anchor point for the other end of this spell," Jasmine continued as if Karl hadn't interrupted her. "Whatever Amythist hears, we hear too."

"Won't she notice it, though?" Sam asked.

"I hid it in a box marked *grades*. I think we'll be fine," the mage replied.

"Shut up. Shut up—there are voices," Karl said.

It had been a few days and despite monitoring Amythist's office almost nonstop, the group of students had yet to glean any useful information about Kylara. It seemed Amythist was planning a sprawling herb garden for the approaching spring. There were talks of adding a few new teachers in the fall, and that was it. Still, there was something deliciously clandestine about listening to the headmaster without her knowledge.

The students quieted to hear what would be said in supposed privacy.

"Kristen. I'm so glad you finally called," Amythist said to start the conversation.

All four young people stopped breathing for a moment. Tanya knew as well as anyone that Amythist knew an extremely famous person named Kristen. Of course, it wasn't so much a person as the Steel Dragon herself.

"You don't think that's—"

"Shh!!" The other three shushed Sam.

"How are things on campus?" Kristen asked.

"Oh, fine," Amythist replied. "Nothing we can't handle. Honestly, ever since Kylara left it's been especially quiet."

"So you have no need of my mages then?" Kristen chuckled.

The two boys took turns punching each other in the arm in celebration at the confirmation of who this was.

"No, thanks. We don't need any more security here. You'd better use everything you have to track her."

"Eh…I don't think that's necessary yet," the Steel Dragon replied.

"You're letting her run about unsupervised? If she's right about the portals to the pixie realm not being from her, she could be in real danger."

"I didn't say she was unsupervised." Kristen Hall, the most powerful person in the world, sounded chastened by the same headmaster who doled out punishments to seventeen-year-old kids.

"Oh, thank goodness. Is Timeflash with her? I'd be curious what would happen if young Miss Diamantine absorbed her power."

"Timeflash isn't one for subtlety. Given the contents of the letter you shared with me, I wanted someone more discreet."

"Oh, so you have grown up. Who did you send? Not Amy, not if you want subtlety—oh, I guess Kylara already knows her, huh? Did you get Larry to go along with it? One of the new dragons?"

"Drew, actually."

"Drew?" The old dragon yelled so loudly that Jasmine had to restructure her little orb of vibrating air. "You sent a regular old human to protect what may very well be the next stage of magical evolution? What are you—crazy? You are lucky you're not a student here or I would put you in detention so fast that—"

"I'm not a student, Headmaster. I'm head of the Dragon Council and de facto boss of the world." Kristen sighed. Tanya didn't know her except from news clips but wow, did she sound tired.

"Right you are. Right you are," Amythist said hastily. "So what's the plan then? Assuming a dragon doesn't come along and simply eat the two of them?"

"Drew's armed and more than capable of dealing with a dragon or two," Kristen replied. "They're doing well and driving north into Colorado, and have just stopped at the Home in the Hill."

"Oh, that poor child. Those pixies make the ones we have on campus look positively tame."

"It was Drew's idea, but I think it's a good one. Plus, it's not far from Kylara's mom's house, so if anything goes wrong, she'll be close by."

"Amy's portals will be faster than any dragon," Amythist replied.

"You try telling that to a former member of Dragon SWAT who has been laying low in her burned-out home after hiding for sixteen years," Kristen snapped.

The headmaster didn't sound offended or anything, though. She merely clucked her tongue as if she understood how stressful it must be for Kristen. "Well, I'll trust your judgment of course, but if there's anything else you need, let us know."

"Honestly? I'd love the rest of your semester to go as uneventfully as possible if that's not too much to ask."

"I don't know about that." The ancient dragon chuckled. "Kylara has a way of stirring the pot that reminds me of another young dragon who didn't quite understand how things were done."

"Well, make sure her friends don't follow. That one with the plant powers might prove to be the key to all this. I want her safe."

"I'll double the guards on her room as soon as we're done here, all right?" Amythist said placatingly.

Tanya didn't hear any more of the conversation. For starters, it was no longer relevant. The two were going on about someone named Hernandez, joking and swapping stories, but nothing else was said about Kylara. But that wasn't the reason why she had stopped listening. She had grasped the reality that their time of freedom had only minutes remaining.

"What do we do?" she blurted to her three friends.

"Do? What are you talking about?" Jasmine asked. "We discover that Kylara is under the Steel Dragon's protection. We don't have anything to worry about."

"Nothing to worry about? Seriously?" Karl sneered. "She said she was under protection from a regular old vanilla human."

"She said he was armed," the light dragon pointed out.

Karl's scowl was toxic. "Which means what? That he has dragon bullets? Some of us have practiced dodging those, you know. Their existence isn't a secret anymore. What if he comes up against a dragon with an ax to grind against the new world order?"

"Don't you think that's a little paranoid?" Jasmine asked.

"No. I think Karl makes a good point. One human will not be equipped to handle those skeletons coming from the pixie realm. Even if his gun can…I don't know…blast them away or whatever, we've seen so many of them. Two against a horde won't work." Sam rubbed his chin in thought.

"So you think we should go after her?" Tanya asked.

"No," Jasmine replied.

"Of course," Karl countered.

"I don't know," Sam said.

"You heard the headmaster." Karl gestured to the orb of vibrating air still buzzing with gossip. "She'll strengthen the guard as soon as she gets off the phone. It'll be as hard as hell to sneak you three goons off campus as it is. If she doubles the guard, we're screwed. This is it—our final chance."

"Goons? I could get off campus before you could." Sam pounded his chest like he was an ape instead of a dragon. Tanya rubbed her eyes at the sheer maleness of the two knuckleheads.

"What do you think we should do, Tanya?" Jasmine asked.

"Honestly, I'm with you. I don't think we should go, but..."

"But what?" Sam asked.

"But the grounds are about to get locked down and we know exactly where we should go to start—and it's not that dangerous."

"You mean Kylara's mom's house?" Karl asked.

Tanya nodded. "I do. If she gets a call and rushes off to help, it will go better if we're there to lend a hand however we can."

"Except we're students, not a member of SWAT with diamond scales," Sam pointed out, although he didn't sound scared at all. More like he was playing devil's advocate.

"Again, I'd normally agree, but those skeletons are hard to beat without me burying them," Tanya pointed out.

"You've convinced me," Jasmine said. "Let's go."

"Wait, just like that?" Karl asked.

"I thought you wanted to go." Sam snorted. "Now you're scared?"

"I merely want to know what changed her mind." Karl gestured at Jasmine.

Tanya frowned. The two boys were getting better at it but they could both still be dismissive of mages in general.

"Tanya did. She's right. If we let Amythist lock us down, we're out of this when they might need Tanya's powers if something happens to Kylara."

"Plus, we should go to get back at Kylara for leaving us behind," Tanya said. "I cannot believe she did this to us again."

"So we're in agreement, then?" Karl asked and grinned mischievously.

The two girls nodded.

"What about you, lightbulb?" Karl asked Sam.

"I'm not about to let the three of you run off and get killed without me." The golden dragon tried to match Karl's grin, but mischievous simply wasn't part of his nature. He looked like a choir boy forced to compromise his morals, but Tanya liked that about him.

"All right, then. Does anyone need cover?" Karl asked as ropes of dark energy whipped out from his feet and swirled around him.

"That would be appreciated, yes," Tanya said.

"I can handle it," Jasmine said.

"Me too," Sam responded, although Tanya didn't have any idea how a dragon who could make light energy would accomplish sneaking off campus in the late afternoon. Still, she wasn't about to say anything and make the two boys act even dumber.

They left Tanya's room, moved casually down the hallway, and nodded at Ruby Firedrake who barely looked up from her magazine.

Once outside, Karl took Tanya's hand and she was instantly wrapped in his tendrils of darkness. It was insane how different she felt now compared to the first time he had done it to her. He had been threatening her then, trying to expose her for the vanilla dragon she was. Now, her powers might very well be the only thing that could save Kylara and finally put the unnaturally revived bones to rest.

Last time, Karl's tendrils had made her feel claustrophobic and constrained when he'd wound her in them. Now, it felt more like being wrapped in a blanket made of strips of rags, maybe, but still something strangely comforting. With it, he carried them across the green and into the woods. This wasn't unusual in itself and Karl didn't make much of an effort to hide their passage.

Once he reached the woods, he changed tactics and moved them from one patch of darkness to the next. If anyone was following them, Tanya couldn't see them. Karl was too fast and too good at locating pools of deep shadow. In minutes, they were through the woods and over one of the mountains that framed the valley in which the campus had been built.

"You've done this before, haven't you?" she asked once he released her from his shadow tendrils.

"A couple of times a semester, yeah." He shrugged. "The trick is to act casual until you get to the woods, then sneak."

"You did well."

"It might all be for nothing, though," he said.

"I don't think so. I think—at the very least—it will be good to talk to Hester Diamantine about what's going on with Ky."

"That's not what I meant, but do you honestly think that the headmaster hasn't told her?"

"I don't think she has, no. Frankly, I think she's afraid of Diamantine. I've only talked to her a few times but she is intense. Anyway, what did you mean?" she asked, curious now.

Karl chuckled. "Only that we might get busted because I bet that Sam the goodie-goodie light dragon has never snuck off campus before."

Tanya bit her tongue. She didn't want to encourage him but she was worried about the same thing.

They stood there in the growing dark, waiting for their two friends. After maybe a minute, Jasmine appeared beside them as if she'd stepped from a portal.

"Jasmine!" Tanya blurted when she saw her. "How did you get here?"

"I walked." The young mage shrugged.

"You weren't seen?" Karl asked. His mischievous look was back.

"You tell me," the girl challenged, raised her hands, and vanished. Only...not quite. Tanya had been staring at her when she disappeared, and her gaze was still locked on the place where Jasmine had stood. The dragon narrowed her eyes and realized she was still there. She hadn't vanished and only appeared to.

"How do you do that?" Tanya asked.

Jasmine reappeared. "It's a magic shield turned optical illusion. I make it look like no one's walking here—much like a trick camera or a set of lenses that bend the light around me."

"That's…cool." Karl sounded impressed.

"Gee. The greasy-haired dragon thinks I'm cool. Joy."

Tanya couldn't help but chuckle at Midnight's sneer. Despite insulting everyone constantly, he still couldn't take an insult very well. She also knew that Jasmine had only made that joke because she knew that Karl's family wasn't particularly wealthy—by dragon standards anyway—which meant that she didn't want to work for him and could insult him as much she pleased. This might not have been lost on Karl either.

"I'm still worried that Lumos will screw this up for us."

"I don't think so," Jasmine said flatly.

"Why not?" he demanded.

"Because he's right there." Jasmine pointed to a golden dragon who swooped low over them and down the mountainside.

Tanya and Karl shared a look and took their dragon forms. "You can ride on my back, Jasmine."

"Thank you," Jasmine said with a formal curtsy, then used a blast of wind to launch herself onto Tanya's back. *Okay,* Tanya thought, *so it seems Jasmine is considering working for me.* Which was insane because mere months earlier, Tanya Fastwing was a nobody dragon with no powers. Now, though, she was one of two dragons on the entire planet who could control plants. Perhaps the only one, depending on how you did your math.

The two young dragons flew after Sam and caught up to him after a few minutes. They locked into formation and flew west but were careful to remain low and hug the landscape.

"How the hell did you get off campus without being seen?" Karl asked.

"Without being seen?" Sam laughed. "I thought the point was to make sure we weren't followed."

"Answer the question," Karl growled.

"I told Kor that I was going to town for supplies and asked him if he wanted anything. He has a soft spot for chocolate."

"He let you go?" Tanya was shocked.

"Of course he did." Sam turned his golden dragon head toward them long enough for them to see him wink. "I do errands for professors all the time. The headmaster hadn't talked to him yet or if she had, the chocolate was more pressing in his brain."

"Or—check this one out, lightbulb—he knew exactly what you're doing and now, we're being tailed exactly like Kylara."

From Sam's lack of response to Karl, Tanya saw that he had not considered this possibility.

Still, the idea of having backup when they arrived at Hester Diamantine's house uninvited and unannounced, wasn't such a bad thought.

CHAPTER TWENTY-FIVE

After a lively debate about what exactly Atramento was supposed to cook for dinner, the group headed out into the meadow in front of the House in the Hill. Rider wanted strawberry tarts, Hound wanted an entire cow, while Mari and Oda insisted that the guests should choose since they were the only people in the house who needed to eat food to survive.

"Will we be gone long?" Kylara asked Mari.

The pixie flapped her butterfly wings demurely as if they were eyelashes to flutter. "It may feel like a lifetime but little time will pass here. That is the nature of the realm where we are going."

"Wait, what do you mean, the realm?" Drew asked like an overprotective uncle. "I thought you were taking us to the pixie place."

"You're not going anywhere!" Hound snapped. "You stink like musty humans and guns and car grease and also hamburgers. Atramento, can we have hamburgers for dinner?"

"If you think I'll let you whisk Kylara away without even explaining yourselves, you're out of your crazy little mind."

"Hound is right," Mari explained politely. "I do not smell you as acutely as his antennae make possible, but I smell you all the same. If you come with us, your lack of magic and unwashed armpits will attract denizens of the dark that will have you for dinner."

"Besides..." Rider stood on the hood of Drew's mostly destroyed truck, his hands on his hips. "Someone needs to rustle up dinner with me. I think you'll have to do."

"I have told you before and I will tell you again. There is food in the fridge," Atramento protested. "That is, in fact, the very point of a refrigerator. Once you own one, you don't need to hunt to eat for every single meal. There's still more than enough venison."

"The joke's on you. I don't need to eat at all." Rider smirked like he'd bested the mage in a televised debate.

"Venison sounds great," the young dragon mage interjected. It had been a while since she'd eaten the meat she used to cook almost daily when she lived with Hester.

"Then it's settled," Oda said and her raspy, weathered voice brooked no argument.

"It'll be fine, Drew," Kylara told him quietly. "I think we can trust these guys. And if we can't, someone needs to stay here anyway."

He wrinkled his nose at that but he nodded. "I guess Rider can help me with my truck."

"Indeed," the little being bellowed and hopped off the hood with such force that he knocked it loose and it clattered to the ground with a loud bang.

"Couldn't you have flown off my truck?" the man asked. It was the first time he'd seemed annoyed about the state of the vehicle.

"Oh...right, yeah," Rider acknowledged.

"Shall we?" Mari asked as if they were merely popping into town for groceries instead of leaving the world Kylara knew and called home behind them.

She nodded all the same. If these pixies could discover what was happening with the portals—or even confirm that their recent appearances were not her fault—that would mean the world to her. "Let's do this."

Mari, Oda, and Hound needed no more encouragement. They circled her furiously, then moved out in front of her and created a circle of golden sparks as they increased their speed. Soon, Kylara couldn't tell them apart at all. All that registered was the sound of wings buzzing and the bright pops of golden sparks falling—not down per se but toward the center of the circle as if it was a black hole with its own gravity—as the pixies tried to open a gate to somewhere undeniably alien.

After maybe a minute, the center of the circle turned translucent as if reality itself were nothing but a crude piece of art painted on cellophane. It faded even more until all that was visible in the center was blackness.

"Whelp, here we go!" Mari said in a tone that was too cheerful given that Kylara was staring into a literal abyss. Without any further ado, the pixie streaked into the portal.

"It looks worse than it smells," Hound said and vanished into the gateway.

"Come along. You'll be fine as long as you don't touch anything. Or stare too much. Oh, or talk too loudly." Oda gestured for the dragon mage to go first.

She took a deep breath, tried to convince herself that if harm did come to her in this place, at the very least it wouldn't be intentional, and stepped through the portal.

Later, it would prove impossible for her to say what the first thing was that she noticed. Certainly, the cold was immediately obvious, although not all that different from being high up in the mountains in late winter. It made her realize that magic was afoot in the meadow of grass and flowers that wasn't covered in snow given the time of year.

The sound was remarkable as well. Kylara was intimately

familiar with how sound bounced off stone. She had grown up in a rugged landscape of bare rock walls and canyons that could throw sound a hundred different ways in a hundred different steps. This place was the complete and polar opposite. The darkness swallowed any sounds as if it were some demon's sound studio. Smells were completely absent.

And then there was the darkness. It was all around her like she was in a bubble of nighttime that was barely big enough to fit her and the three pixies who hovered around her. There were no stars, no reflections, and no indication that anything existed beyond the sphere around them.

At the same time, however, Kylara could tell where the darkness began. It pressed in from all sides but something stopped it. She took a step forward, a little frightened but also intensely curious. Tentatively, she extended her hand and Hound promptly bit her on the finger.

"Ouch!" She yanked her finger back.

"Are you trying to unravel our insides and turn us into soup or something?" he snapped.

"Is that what would happen if I touched the edge of this... place? Is this even a place?" Kylara asked.

"Yes!" He nodded enthusiastically.

"No," Oda said meditatively.

"The truth is we don't know what would happen if you touch the edge of our bubble."

"We can be fairly sure that we would not be turned into soup," Oda snapped, apparently shaken from her meditative state.

"I don't think you brought me here to talk about soup or metaphysics," Kylara said.

"That is correct. We brought you here so we could smell you." Hound buzzed closer and began sniffing Kylara. He paid attention to her hair, her fingers, her knees, and her butt, which would have been weirder if he hadn't sniffed every other part of her first and if his name wasn't Hound.

"Something is still blocking you," he said and drifted to her face. He sniffed her eyes, her nose, her chin, then finally settled on her neck. "This! I have found the offending stench." He pointed to the pendant around her neck.

"What is that?" Mari asked. "Is it another binding device like the one that was on your wrist?"

"No—or not exactly, anyway," Kylara explained. "It makes it harder for dragons to read my aura and also makes my aura appear to be that of a dragon. My grandfather made it for my mom, apparently. I've had it since I was a baby."

"And you can take it off?" Oda asked.

She answered in the affirmative.

"There is no need to destroy it then," Oda nodded.

"But you'd better take it off. I still can't smell a thing," Hound instructed.

Kylara nodded and unclasped the silver and turquoise pendant from around her neck. She felt no different with it on or off, but the pixies could tell the difference. They buzzed in excitement as if she had removed the lid to a platter of food and flooded the space with an aroma previously hidden.

"Much better!" Hound gushed. He redoubled his efforts to sniff every single part of her and mumbled as he worked, "Uh-huh…mage, mage…dragon…pixie, mage…dragon, yep, uh-huh."

Kylara wanted to ask what he was doing but compared to what the other two pixies were doing, being sniffed seemed to be the relatively normal procedure.

Oda had produced a long, slightly supple twig from somewhere—her dragonfly wings perhaps?—and used it to gently poke and prod at her. But rather than looking at the skin she was jabbing, her eyes watched the stick itself as if she was measuring the bend of it. She clucked appreciatively as she worked and mumbled numbers to herself.

Mari's behavior, though, put the other two completely to shame. She flew to Kylara's face and hovered in place, flapping her beautiful yellow-and-black butterfly wings rhythmically. After a moment, the rhythm of her wings slowed, yet she didn't plummet. Instead, she began to glow and her wings dissolved.

The black edges first broke apart into a fine dust that began to glow as soon as it left the pixie's body. She flapped again and her wings continued to dissolve until instead of two huge butterfly wings, she only had the strong, vein-like filaments that gave the wings strength. The rest of her wing material had become a glowing powder that swished over Kylara's body.

With each flap of Mari's now threadbare wings, the young dragon mage was washed with the butterfly wing powder, then rinsed as all the powder was sucked back into the pixie's wings, only to wash over her again.

Kylara had no idea how long Mari did this. It was hypnotically entrancing and her breathing settled into a rhythm to match the rate at which the dust washed over her. Whatever the other two pixies were doing seemed less important than this. She ignored the pokes of Oda's stick and Hound's probing and sniffing antennae while Mari performed her test.

Finally, after a long time that Kylara could not guess the length of, the pixies declared their work done.

"Well?" Kylara asked when they didn't immediately divulge their findings.

The three pixies buzzed around each other and communicated in a mixture of English, insect chirps, and a language that sounded something like bells.

"We have determined that you are not leaking!" Mari proclaimed.

"Are you sure?" Although relieved, she felt she needed to confirm.

"Indeed! I detected the magic inside you that can open the ways to the pixie realm, but they are not out of place, nor is their flow blocked or drained. It's simply not possible for you to open that kind of gate without your knowledge."

"All right!" Kylara pumped her fist into the air. "This is great news."

"Indeed!" Mari replied. "And that is not all."

"Oh?" She asked hesitantly, not sure if she wanted more information.

"Can I tell her? Please let me tell her. Come on, I want to tell her," Hound begged.

"Tell me what?"

"Go ahead, Hound. Tell her," Mari said.

"You're a pixie!" he blurted.

"I'm sorry?" Kylara said, totally unsure about what she was supposed to make of such a proclamation.

"What Hound means is that you have a little pixie about you," Oda said with only slightly less eagerness than Hound. "I thought I liked you. This must be why."

"But how can I be a pixie?" the girl asked.

"You're not. Well, not completely, anyway," Mari explained. "But you certainly have more than we've ever sensed in a non-pixie before. There is the magic of mages in you as well, and the magic of dragons has taken root deeply inside you, but there is pixie magic too."

"We like pixie magic." Hound settled onto Kylara's shoulder and began to lick the side of her face.

"But…how is this possible?" Kylara asked. "I have a biological human mom. She was a mage and gave me powers like her."

"Like her?" Oda poked her with a stick. "Could your mom turn into a dragon at will? Could she absorb the powers of others or open gates to places outside of the universe you call home?"

"Well, no. I guess not." She had never met her mom but she knew she couldn't do such things because if she had been able to, Cassandra would have told her. "But that merely begs the question of how you could say that I'm part pixie."

"How? How not? What? What not? String? String knot," Hound said and rubbed his antennae together.

"Very well said, Hound." Mari nodded in appreciation.

"Translation, please?" Kylara asked.

"What Hound means is that the how you came to be this way is not very important to us. It's not our way. We were made by mages as weapons in a war we had no stake in. The how of our existence is irrelevant to who we are," Oda said.

"How can you not be concerned with how things work?" the girl demanded, frustrated. "If I didn't ask how, I wouldn't know anything about gaining more powers."

"We are not saying do not ask how, only to ask other questions as well," Oda said.

"Yeah! Like, what's for dinner? Why do flowers smell good? Why do raccoons smell bad? Why does Rider like riding things?" Hound grinned.

"We are much more concerned with what is rather than how things came to be," Mari said. "Perhaps you should be concerned with what is as well."

"But how can I tell what is if I don't even know what I am?" Kylara demanded.

"What you are doesn't matter," Hound said. "All that matters is who you are and what you do."

"What I do depends on how I work," she complained.

"Would you like us to guess?" Oda asked.

"Yes! Guessing is fun. Maybe you are like a doggy that rolls in stinky stuff but instead of stinky stuff, it's magic, and instead of being a dog you're like a human, mage, dragon, pixie...uh, thingy." Hound lost steam at the end, but Kylara couldn't help but smile at his enthusiasm.

"Maybe you absorb more than specific powers," Oda ventured "Perhaps you accrete a little of the nature of magical beings, too."

"Is that possible?" Kylara asked.

"It seems to be," Mari conceded. "Because you are most certainly a dragon, not merely a mage who can change into one. But you're also a mage."

"And also a wee bit pixie!" Hound added.

"But what am I supposed to do with all of that? What does that mean about what I am?"

"We told you. What you are doesn't matter," Mari reminded her. "All that matters is who you are and what actions you take. And, of course, you are the only one who can determine such a thing."

Somehow, that comforted Kylara. She had heard her mom say the same thing hundreds of times, of course—that it didn't matter that she was a dragon. All that mattered was what she did. As a girl, she had thought it was a speech intended to fire her up to train harder. But now that she understood that Hester Diamantine had understood what her daughter was long before she ever had a clue, it made a different kind of sense.

Her mom had been a dragon, but she hadn't let that define her. She had abandoned her career when it compromised her values, had treated a mage as a friend, and had even gone so far as to name her adopted daughter after her. Her mom was a dragon —of course she was—but she was also much more than that. She was a caregiver, a warrior for social justice, a protector, and a mediocre cook if Kylara was honest.

Could she be like her? Was she able to do as the pixies suggested and stop searching for answers about her future in her past? Could she accept what she was? More importantly, could she accept that what she was might change every week or even every day, but that didn't change who she was?

Kylara didn't know. But in this place of darkness, she felt she could at least try. If this was what was outside the universe she lived in, there was nothing out there. That meant her decisions were more important than ever. It was up to her to make the world a better place, to care for the people she loved, and to protect those who couldn't protect themselves.

"Come on," Mari said. "Rider will eat our burgers if we don't get back in time."

"I thought you said time worked differently here," Kylara said.

"It does," Oda admitted. "But now, it's time to go."

They stepped from the place of darkness and returned to the Home on the Hill, nestled pleasantly somewhere in the Rocky Mountains on the planet Earth.

CHAPTER TWENTY-SIX

After the scentless atmosphere of the void, the smell of grilled venison was utterly tantalizing, but dinner would have to wait. Kylara couldn't tell how long they had been gone but it had been long enough for Drew to completely lose his mind.

"No! This is not what I asked for," Drew yelled at a flurry of flowing sparks that darted all over in front of the House in the Hill, dodging the rocks, sticks, and the occasional snowball that Drew hurled at it.

"What's the problem?" Kylara asked.

"What's the problem? *What's the problem?*" he demanded. "Look." He pointed toward the portal she had stepped from.

She turned to see that the portal had closed with far less ceremony than it had been opened with but she only registered that as an afterthought. Far more demanding of her attention was the newly restored truck, complete with silver and purple tiger stripes and a stylized raccoon face on the hood. The cattleguard had been restored, although the rhinestones speckling it was an interesting choice—aesthetically speaking, anyway.

"I don't hate it." She smiled.

"It looks insane!" Drew complained. "Plus, Rider made it a low-rider. What good is a pickup truck with no clearance? It defeats the entire purpose."

"It has adjustable suspension!" The pixie sounded quite offended that his handiwork was not properly appreciated. He snapped his fingers and the truck raised so violently that it went airborne for a brief moment. Everything that was in the back elevated abruptly before it clattered to a noisy landing, mostly landing in the back of the truck. But mostly wasn't good enough for Drew.

"Great! Just great! Now I have a truck that not only has crappy clearance but I try to fix said clearance and I spill everything in the bed. How can you not see that this is a problem?" he demanded of Rider.

"I seriously think it looks way better," the pixie said matter of factly.

The man squeezed the bridge of his nose between a finger and thumb, as if he could squeeze the tension out of his brain. "Can one of you help me?"

"Rider's the master of vehicles," Mari said.

"That's why he's called Rider," Oda added.

"It is?" Hound was delighted to have this question answered.

"You got that right. You humans and your vehicles. This is much better!" Rider said from the other side of the truck.

"Can't you please turn it back to what it was before?" Drew pleaded.

"I can't, no. Sorry," Rider slumped.

"I like it," Kylara slapped Drew on the back and he took half a step forward from the impact of the blow.

He looked at her and smiled wryly. "So you have some strength back, then?"

"Yeah. I suppose I do. Now come on. We can sort out the raccoon mobile later. Right now, let's eat."

Dinner turned out to be as delicious as it smelled. Atramento had ground the venison and mixed it with fatty beef and produced wild-flavored, intensely moist venison burgers that were topped with produce that was far fresher than a house nestled deep in the mountains had any right to have.

They all sat at the table together—Drew, Atramento, Kylara, and the four pixies. While the conversation meandered in various comfortable directions, the young dragon mage couldn't help but feel like a profound weight had been lifted from her shoulders.

She had spent so much time worrying about what she was. As a kid, she'd wondered what it meant to be a dragon. As soon as she thought that she had that all resolved, she had learned she was a mage. She had never been able to reconcile those two identities. It had been made even more difficult given that her adoptive mother had been abducted by her biological aunt.

But now, seated around this table with a mixture of magical and non-magical beings, she was finally starting to see that such distinctions didn't matter. There were good dragons and bad. Some people had committed grave atrocities and others had elevated the human race through their actions. No matter what she was, she had decisions to make. How one acted was the definition of character. For the first time in her life, Kylara believed this.

When the dinner drew to an end, she knew exactly what she needed to do next.

She clinked a fork—unused but still set on the table with exacting precision by Atramento—against a glass of tea.

Everyone stopped talking and turned to her except Rider, who proceeded to shatter his teacup with his fork. Atramento and all the other pixies ignored him, so Kylara did the same.

"I want to say thank you—all of you—for helping me get this far. For a long time, I don't think I understood what was important, but I now have a better idea. It doesn't matter if you're a pixie, a mage, or a businessman who packs dragon bullets. What matters is what you do. Now that I have my powers back, I need to keep going and share this same wisdom with Galen."

"But first, you will stay the night? Correct? The roads are treacherous outside our little valley at night," Atramento said as pushily and politely as Kylara had ever heard anyone ask anything.

"I don't know. Now that I can fly again—or gate—I don't need to worry about the roads. Drew, thanks for getting me this far, but now that the pixies helped me get that bracelet off, I can go on alone. I don't want you to get hurt or waste any more of those dragon bullets for me."

"No…I can keep going with you," Drew replied awkwardly.

"That's nice of you but I know you have business to attend to. I've already taken up a ton of your time. I don't want to impose anymore. Plus…well, I don't want to be seen in the raccoon mobile."

"The raccoon mobile is radical!" Rider shrieked and proceeded to destroy his plate.

"Kylara, I don't mind going on with you, truly. My job is… flexible these days, and I don't want to ditch you in the middle of this mission."

"It's okay, Drew. I'll be fine. Seriously. And Galen might not react well if you're there."

"Wait!" Mari blurted. "I have an idea…yes—yes! I have quite an idea."

"O…kay…" she murmured. When Mari said nothing, she dared to ask, "So what exactly is your idea?"

"I think you should bring this dude with you!" Mari said.

"You do?" Kylara and Drew said together.

"Sure! He might be useful or something. I don't know."

"I agree," Oda added. "Not about the I don't know part but about the useful part."

"Okay, so why do you think I should bring him with me? No

offense, Drew. You've been incredibly helpful. But now that I have my full powers back, it changes the dynamic somewhat."

"I helped with the skeletons," the man pointed out.

"I know you did, and I appreciate it. But now, things are different. With my dark powers, I can bind them and use my storm and plant powers together to bury them. I'm worried that if you're there, you'll get in the way. I don't want you to get hurt."

"Still, you should take him." Mari pounded her tiny hand on the table.

"Why?"

"I don't know." Mari giggled. "Or maybe I do, but it doesn't matter. All that matters is that it feels like you should take him with you."

"I agree," Oda said. "My hunch says you two should stick together."

"My nose agrees," Hound said. "I don't. But my nose does, and I always listen to my nose. So there you go."

"You all can't seriously expect me to take him with me merely because of a hunch? He could get hurt. There's no good reason to take him."

"I'll be fine," Drew said. "Honestly. I've been hurt in all kinds of ways." The unspoken part seemed to be that he'd never been ditched by a seventeen-year-old before.

"Who needs a reason?" Mari asked, talking over Drew. "A hunch is merely another word for following your gut, which is another phrase for following your intuition, which is something pixies do all the time."

The rest of the pixies—even Rider—nodded sagely at this.

"But I'm not a pixie," Kylara protested.

"Oh yes, you are!" Hound snapped. "You smell like one, even now."

"Which means," Mari cut in, "that you should try it."

"Try what?" she asked, having trouble following the pixie logic or lack thereof.

"Use your intuition," Mari, Oda, and Hound answered in unison.

She rolled her eyes.

"No! Not like that," Oda snapped. "Close your eyes and feel. Go ahead. We'll wait."

Kylara, not thinking for a moment that the pixies would allow her to not do this because she thought it was weird, did as she was told.

She closed her eyes and looked inward, asking herself what she thought she should do with Drew. Yes, he might get hurt, but he had also proven himself more than competent in a fight. If Kylara were honest, she wouldn't be there if not for him. He said he could deal with his business affairs later, so that wasn't a concern.

After a moment, she realized that was all her mind trying to logic everything. That was not what the pixies had told her to do. Intuition was felt, not thought, so she tried to let herself simply experience what she felt when she put Drew in her head.

She found that she mostly trusted him. There was something about him that was calming. He was like a guard dog in that way. He wasn't as strong as her—exactly like no dog was as powerful as a competent human armed with even a simple weapon—but he noticed things and thought in ways that she didn't. There was still something that he wasn't telling her—something that was so close to her understanding that she could almost taste it—but she didn't think it was anything nefarious.

"Do you want to come with me, Drew?" she asked finally.

"Sure." The man smiled. "I have nothing better to do. Fighting skeletons and hanging out with pixies is way more fun than the day job. Plus…well, I don't want to be seen alone in that truck."

"The raccoon mobile is legend," Rider screamed.

"The plan is to meet Galen, but now that we know I'm not causing these portals, we know something else is. It's not too crazy to think they will open again. It could be dangerous."

"Danger merely makes life taste sweeter," Drew replied nonchalantly.

Kylara couldn't help but grin. Her intuition told her that was the exact response she needed to hear. "All right," she agreed. "You're in."

CHAPTER TWENTY-SEVEN

Kylara and Drew spent the night simply because Atramento promised a hot breakfast and Hound threatened to ice the roads outside their valley if they tried to drive off in the night.

They loaded up about an hour after dawn with Drew complaining royally about what had been done to his truck the entire time. "It's not right, you know? It was a normal color before. Now, it's two weird colors. And why does it have stripes? Raccoons don't have stripes."

"They do on their tails," Kylara pointed out, which turned out to be the wrong thing to say. After she said it, he stopped talking and started grumpily to tie down everything in the bed of the truck.

Finally packed, she climbed into the passenger seat and he drove off. She hung out the window and waved goodbye. "Thanks for everything!"

They continued for less than two hours before they arrived at the GPS coordinates Cassandra had sent. Kylara had offered to fly them since it wasn't that far but she was glad they had taken the truck. She felt well rested and ready for whatever might happen inside with Galen.

They climbed out at the end of another twisting dirt road. This time, instead of a house discreetly and beautifully tucked into the side of a mountain, they found what appeared to be a mine shaft that had been abandoned long before. The entrance was a maw of dark and dust, framed in roughly cut timber that still held up admirably despite its obvious age.

"This is the place, huh?" Drew asked.

"I think so," Kylara said. Then, feeling a twinge in her gut, she corrected herself. "Yeah. It has to be."

Drew nodded and together, they went inside.

The first fifty feet of the tunnel was exactly that—the entrance to a mine shaft lined with wood every so often to prevent a cave-in, with holes in the walls here and there where miners had tried to chase veins of gold or silver. It was an unremarkable, normal space, with no sign of anything out of the ordinary.

Drew remarked on this, but Kylara knew her aunt well enough to know that she wouldn't make her lair that easy to find.

"I think we should keep going," she said.

He nodded and whipped the beam of his flashlight from side to side, reminding Kylara in that moment of the cop he used to be. The beam of light did little to illuminate the space, though. It was too narrow.

Fortunately, now that she was free of the silver bracelet, she had other methods of illumination at her fingertips. She ignited both her hands with light to bathe her, Drew, and the dank mine shaft in warm, golden light.

"Now there's a neat trick," he commented.

They continued downward, past a bend, then another. She was about to retrieve the coordinates to check if they had the wrong location when she saw evidence to confirm that they were in the right place.

The walls lost their rough texture as if the enormous hand of a massive creature had smoothed them and patted them dry.

"Do you think dwarves did this?" Drew asked when he noticed the oddly organic look to the tunnel.

"It was an earth spirit," Kylara explained. "My aunt can control them. It means we're getting close."

Sure enough, about a hundred yards farther and past another bend, they came to a cavernous room. It had very clearly been carved not by machines or people with clumsy steel tools but by something that understood the geology of the mountains much more intimately than any human could.

No one was in the room, but that didn't mean it was empty. Two cots stood against one wall and a desk covered in papers and three-ring binders on the opposite side. A pool of water in the middle of the room looked clean enough, and a few sacks of dried goods had been found by rats. It looked like a lived-in place but not exactly a fresh one. That was odd because Cassandra's note had said that Galen was currently living there and that didn't seem possible. Based on the wreckage the rats had caused to the sacks of food alone, it looked like it had been weeks since someone had been here—at the very least.

"I thought that Galen kid was supposed to be here," Drew said. One hand scanned the room with his flashlight while the other rested on the butt of the gun in the holster at his waist.

"He was. Or is."

"It doesn't look like anyone's been here for a while," he said slowly.

"I agree. Maybe we should look around?"

"Are we looking for anything in particular?"

"Where Galen might have gone, I guess, or a clue from my aunt. I'll check the desk. The last time she contacted me, she sent a letter."

"Sure. Transform into a dragon if you run into trouble," Drew joked and the statement echoed in the cavern.

Kylara nodded and moved to the desk. It was messy and cluttered with pens, pencils, notes, and diagrams. One of the images caught her eye, a sketch that showed a dragon and a human's silhouette laid over each other. Lines traced between the two that seemed familiar to her. They were supposed to represent inner magic, maybe? Without thinking, she picked up a pencil and added an image of a butterfly with a human head, arms, and legs to the very center of the mage. Something about drawing the pixie there made sense. Was it because dragons, mages, and pixies weren't all that different? Did each simply represent different tiers of the ability to control magic? Or different branches of the same tree?

She picked the paper up and studied the lines of energy moving through it. It was hard to see because the image was so dusty, so she blew across it. A great cloud of dust rose from the desk when she did so. It seemed she'd used a trace of her weather magic to augment her breath with wind.

"Do you see anything?" Drew hollered from somewhere beyond the dust cloud.

Realization struck Kylara like a lightning bolt to her brain. "Galen was never here." How could he have been? The sacks of vermin-infested food, the desk thick with dust. This was not a place where someone had lived a few days before. "Drew, Galen was never here!" Kylara said, her voice pitched louder. "Or if he was, he's been gone a long time. A month at least."

"I thought you said your aunt's letter said this was the location?"

"It did. For whatever reason, we were supposed to come here. There's no way random coordinates could have taken us to one of Aunt Cassandra's actual hideouts."

In the empty, echoing room, the sound of Drew clicking off the safety of his gun was sharp and loud. "Do you think she lured us here?"

Kylara shook her head and scanned the room with an intensity she hadn't before. "I don't think so. She wants my help. I don't think she would lie to me."

"I'm sorry to be rude but writing a note that sends you to an abandoned mountain lair seems like lying to me," Drew pointed out bluntly.

"But if she wanted me to come to this location, wouldn't she be here?" she asked with a frown.

"Maybe I scared her off?" he suggested.

She gritted her teeth and shook her head. "I know you have those bullets, but she has an elemental made of pure stone. I don't think she'd be too concerned. Oh, crap."

"Crap? Crap's never good. Why crap?" Drew pulled his weapon, his gaze on the entrance they came through and the two dark passages that led away from the central chamber.

"My aunt didn't write that letter at all," Kylara said, the words almost painful to say because they revealed how foolish she had been.

"How do you know?"

"She called one of her spirits an elemental in the letter. I've never heard her call them that. It goes against her whole magical philosophy."

"So…someone else wrote the letter?" His flashlight didn't seem nearly strong enough for this room so she increased the illumination emanating from her hands and made the rest of her body start to glow as well. She could feel her inner magic coursing through her, ready to come out. Wow, it felt good to be back to full power.

"Someone else must have. Someone who knew my aunt and Galen's situation well enough to be able to convince me that it was from my aunt."

"But who could do that? If Kristen can't find your aunt, how could anyone else?"

"Kristen? You mean the Steel Dragon?" It was the first time Drew had mentioned the Steel Dragon on such familiar terms. He'd said he'd worked with her, but this was a level of familiarity that surprised her. If she thought he had known the Steel Dragon on a first-name basis, she would have asked him many more questions. "What do you know about her?"

"I only mean that she hasn't been able to find your aunt any more than anyone else has." If Drew was nervous about betraying some level of information, he didn't show it. His gaze continued to scan the room, looking for enemies that weren't visible.

Kylara felt a stab of distrust in her gut. What was she doing there with him? Why hadn't she asked more questions? He was working against her best interests and could even be a murderer. Perhaps he was a dragon killer and used her to track more dragons. He could…he could…

The pendant at her neck felt hot like it would burn her. She put her hand on it and made her fingers ice-cold with the ability she had taken from Ruby Firedrake. The pendant seemed to calm in her hands and as it did so, the sudden wash of paranoia she had felt consume her went away. Still, the question remained.

"Drew, you need to tell me who you are."

"I will, Kylara, I will, but I don't think now is the time."

"Then when is?"

"I think we should wait until we discover what the hell is causing that." He didn't point or gesture but held his weapon aimed at a spot across the room.

Kylara heard it before she saw it—the sound of reality undoing itself as if some infernal beast grasped a zipper on the backside of existence and with a tug, split the world apart as effortlessly as she did up her jeans. This was followed by the sound of stagnant water trickling past sunken logs, of old heavy branches bending, and of things moving through mud.

It was a gate to the pixie realm, and the two companions barely had a look through it into the swampy place that was now uncomfortably familiar to them before the revenant corpses of the fleshless dead began to pour out of the rift.

CHAPTER TWENTY-EIGHT

Kylara—for the first time since these portals had begun to appear—welcomed the monsters they delivered. A swarm of the cat-sized dragons darted out but she was more than ready for them. She sent tendrils of darkness across the floor of the mine. As soon as they were under the flying creatures, she directed threads upward that snagged them and hurled them to the rocky floor with such force that they shattered.

Human skeletons tried to come through the gate next. They ran at great speed and jumped in enormous leaps that would have been impossible if the bones had been powered by muscle and meat. One vaulted through the gate and hurtled toward her. Before it could even cross half the distance between them, Drew put a bullet through its skull. It exploded and the magic inherent in the bullets rent the skeletal body to bones.

Another came through, followed by another. Drew shot each in the skull with practiced efficiency.

"Ex-cop, huh? You're still a good shot for being retired!" Kylara shouted as she batted a few of the flying dragons out of the air.

"Yeah, well, my new line of work isn't exactly a desk job."

Another skeleton was annihilated the second it stepped through the portal.

"Is that right? Does your boss refill your supply of dragon bullets often?"

"Can we talk about this later?" he asked as he fired three, four, five shots at what seemed to be a wall of bone emerging from the portal.

"If there is a later," Kylara replied and turned her attention to the monster coming out of the pixie realm. It wasn't a wall of bone at the front but a hundred pieces all crammed together. Every time Drew shot it, pieces of a shoulder blade or sternum fell away but the bone was so dense and inessential to the skeleton as a whole that it served as a very effective shield.

"What is that?" he shouted as he paused to reload his gun.

"I don't know but it's mine."

The wall of bone pushed through the portal, followed by a long, probing spike on the end of an articulated appendage made of the femurs from who knew how many creatures. Another of these probing spikes came through and planted itself firmly in the floor of the mine. Two more followed and each secured themselves in the ground—which seemed better than attacking until Kylara realized that these were legs and that there were far more than four of them.

"I don't think my bullets will do much against that one!" Drew shouted.

"You take the bats. I'll take the crab," she said when she realized what the bones had been shaped into as more and more of the massive beast pushed through the gateway. Drew had been firing at an enormous claw that the skeletal crab used as a shield, but that wasn't its only tool for combat. It also boasted eight legs, each of which ended with a spike of sharpened bone. Perhaps it was the tusk of an elephant or mammoth?

She decided she could explore the impossible, unrealistic anatomy it took to make a crab out of the bones of other creatures later. To round out its hideous arsenal, the crab dragged its other claw from the pixie realm. This one wasn't the massive slab of layers of bone like the other one. Instead, it was smaller and more slender, with a snapping claw at the end that looked razor-sharp as it clicked and clacked.

The creature didn't seem so keen on the plan to switch combatants. It raced toward Drew, who emptied his entire magazine into its shield claw and barely managed to slow its relentless advance.

Kylara ran toward it and launched thousands of flecks of diamond as she did so to transform inside the cloud of crystalline dust into her dragon body. She placed herself between Drew and the crab barely in time to protect her combat partner.

The crab drove its shield claw into her, hurled her back, and forced her to focus her energy on not crushing Drew instead of fighting back. She managed to avoid the human but in doing so, left her back exposed. The crab took advantage of this and lunged at her with its stabbing claw.

It hurt like hell but it didn't break her diamond skin. The monster pulled back and tried to puncture her again, but like a well-hardened coconut, she resisted being eaten.

Instead, the crab's blade-like claw snapped in half. The monster didn't give her the impression that it screamed in pain but it did scuttle back. That gave her enough time to gain her feet and glance at Drew, who once again eliminated flying dragons like he was a kid at an arcade game he'd played way too many times.

Knowing he had her back enabled her to focus on the crab. She sent her dark energy toward it, using a single rope of darkness to shove a giant teeming ball made up of ropes directly at the crab's face. The ball burst when it made impact and erupted into a hundred clasping threads that tangled themselves around the multitude of bones that made up this undead horror.

Her power unfettered, she called on her inner magic to hurl

the crab into the earth. The ropes of shadow obeyed and yanked the monster to the ground like it was nothing but a marionette.

"Can you do the plant thing?" Drew demanded.

"There isn't enough water in here," Kylara said and stepped toward the beast that now lay bound and powerless. It tried to break free but was unable to do so. She grinned as she used her diamond-sharp claws and the tip of her tail to batter the skeleton relentlessly until a few seconds later, the aberration had been all but obliterated.

Drew picked off a few others as they came through, but there was no doubt that this fight was over. The monstrous crab was the biggest beast in that part of the pixie realm. Whoever or whatever had opened the portal seemed to understand this as well, because the portal vanished unceremoniously.

Which made it especially annoying when a gate to a different part of the swamp opened to reveal another bevy of skeletal creatures.

"There's another big one in there!" Drew shouted. He had a better angle to see into the portal than she did. "A wild boar maybe? I'll try to get a shot."

But before he could, a third portal opened a few feet away from him. Another of the human-shaped skeletons bounded out, collided with him, and knocked him off his feet. The two combatants fought in a tangle of limbs and unrestrained fury. The skeleton attempted to rip Drew's flesh from his bones while he tried to position his pistol against the fleshless skull.

Thankfully, he won. He raised the gun and pulled the trigger. The undead human lost its animating force and was reduced to bone.

Kylara had raced toward Drew the moment the skeleton landed on top of him. That had given the wild boar he had seen more than enough time to push through the gate. It barreled into her back, less intent on cutting her scales than the crab had been and more interested in simply reducing her bones to powder inside her body.

She flashed light at it, which achieved nothing so she bound it with her dark powers. Unfortunately, it seemed like the skeletons were learning. It let some of its bones—the ones she had tried to grasp with her powers—fall away from its body to free itself. Before she could react, it slipped past her and drove into her again. It was smaller than the crab but much larger than it should have been.

"We need to get out of here!" Drew shouted as he fired shot after shot and felled monster after monster.

"We can beat them!" Kylara shouted before she looked around the space and realized that they couldn't. There were simply too many of them. It also seemed that there were more and more of the strange creatures that looked like they'd been put together by a necromancer with a Lego obsession. A giant frog hopped through, as did something like a serpent, albeit one with wings made of taut, leathery skin that let it fly with relative ease. She might have thought that one was cool if it hadn't been over fifty feet long.

"We can't!" Drew shouted between gunshots "Not in here! We need to get back to the surface where you can use your plant powers. Plus, if we can collapse the tunnel, that might work to stop them, right?"

He was already moving as he spoke, firing careful shots to clear a path for them.

"My plant powers are the only thing that binds them."

"No, I don't think so," he replied. He'd already reached the exit and currently peppered the frog monster with bullets so she could get past without it jumping at her. "Cassandra used an earth elemental to bury one of these bastards and that worked too!"

Despite the absolute chaos of the moment, Kylara recognized right away that he should not have had that information. She hadn't told him about the particulars of that battle and when she'd told the pixies, she'd glossed over the details as well.

"How the hell do you know that?" she demanded and seared a horde of skeletons with her fire breath as she raced toward the exit.

Drew began to sprint up the passage the moment she reached him, whether out of fear of the skeletons or fear of getting caught by the dragon he'd been helping despite keeping secrets from her she didn't know.

Even though she was frustrated with this human and his stash of bullets, she didn't follow him immediately. Instead, she poured her magic into her dark powers and used them to create a net across the tunnel to protect their retreat.

She used tiny holes and fissures in the stone to anchor the dark tendrils. Then, like a spider making a web in fast motion, she sent others between these anchored threads, then more between them. One moment the way was open, then there were a few threads, then a net, and finally a wall of blackness.

Already, the skeletons were driving into it. The web held and bounced elastically as more and more of the revenants hurled themselves against it, adding more and more of their mass to push the limits of her power. Kylara turned and ran up the mineshaft, following Drew but leaving a trail of darkness behind her. If it was severed, the net would dissipate in a moment.

It held, thankfully, and they reached the surface and stumbled out into the light of day.

"Can you collapse the tunnel?" Drew demanded, a little breathless.

"It shouldn't be too hard," Kylara replied and launched fire down the tunnel that ignited the ancient timbers lining either side of it.

The horde pursued them through the flame and smoke. Not needing to breathe and knowing nothing of pain, they were relentless—fleshless horrors that seemed to care for nothing beyond adding Kylara and Drew to their mindless ranks.

The young dragon mage finally ran out of patience. She reached into the cave with two ropes of dark power, grasped some of the timbers, and yanked them from the wall and into the center of the tunnel. The narrow space—already weakened from decades of neglect plus the raging inferno that eroded its support—immediately collapsed and trapped the skeletons inside.

She reached out into the atmosphere and called for the wind to concentrate the moisture above her. Despite not liking that Drew knew details about her previous fights that he shouldn't know, he was right about Cassandra's earth spirit being able to stop the skeletons by putting them underground. She hoped that burying them in the mineshaft would have the same effect, but if it didn't, she would summon clouds fat with rain to drench the earth so she could call on the plants to bind the undead.

"You need to tell me how you knew about my Aunt Cassandra right now," she snapped. Nothing from the collapsed mineshaft had moved for five seconds and she decided that was about as long as she was willing to let him off the hook.

"You can trust me, Kylara. You know that, right?"

"Can I, Drew? Is that even your real name?"

"It is! I was told not to use it but I didn't want to deceive you any more than I had to."

"Deceive me about how you're working with whoever is opening these gates?"

"What? No, Kylara. No way. These monsters have attacked me too! I'd be dead already if you hadn't saved me."

"Explain yourself. Now!"

"I truly hate to sound like a broken record but now is not the time," he said and pointed behind her.

She might have thought it was a trick to get her to turn away so he could make a run for the raccoon mobile, but two clues said otherwise. One was that he knew there was no way his truck could outrace a dragon, not anywhere but especially not in this terrain. The other clue was the sound of more portals opening.

She turned and gaped as one by one, another six gates opened.

Already, more of the flying batlike dragons streamed through the tops of the gateways. More of the bone amalgamations that she was thoroughly sick of emerged through two of the portals.

One of the others spewed the flying snake creatures—joy! She hadn't fought one of those yet, she thought bitterly. From the other gate came the body of a boar, but this one's back was covered in horns and antlers taken from who knew how many other dead creatures.

Kylara called on the clouds above her to open and they obeyed and drenched the skeletons and the dirt all around their bony feet. As soon as the water touched the soil, she called on the plant roots that had lain dormant during the winter and the seeds that might have waited for years. A thousand shoots of green burst forth, reached up through the rain, and grasped any tibia, rib, or flange they could touch.

It wasn't enough, unfortunately. There were too many of the flying ones and these ascended into the rain, moving easily above the meager height of the quickly growing plants. She called the wind down on them and struck those she could with lightning but there were simply too many. The wind could knock them aside but it couldn't destroy them. The lightning could, but she could only bring a bolt down once the clouds had time to charge with static electricity.

"We need to run!" she shouted at Drew as she took to the air and sank her claws into a giant mess of bone in the shape of a massive bird. Instead of feathers, it had delicately worked bones. She drove into it with her claws and pieces of bone scattered everywhere as they tumbled earthward.

"We can't run!" Drew shouted, each word punctuated by a gunshot.

"What? You wanted to run when there were way less of these things than there are now." Kylara managed to get on top of the bird-like revenant seconds before they made impact with the earth. A great cloud of bone dust erupted from the crushed creature, only to be washed quickly to the surface of the earth by the rainstorm she had summoned.

She'd shattered this one and ended its time in her realm, but it had allies. More and more of the monsters that issued from the pixie realm now had wings. Bat-like beasts took to the air as well as more birds and creatures made of bones joined in the shape of insects.

"I suggested we run when I thought we could bottle them. We can't do that now. If we run, there's no telling how many people these monsters would terrorize. It's not an option."

"Well, we're running out of options," Kylara yelled as she tried to bind a massive bat skeleton with her dark powers. It shrieked as she wrapped it—a call for help, apparently, as another of its kind barreled into her back. This one understood that it wouldn't break through her diamond skin so it didn't even try.

Instead, it simply clung to her and weighed her down as more of them clambered onto her.

"Hold on! I need to make a call," Drew said and yanked his cellphone out.

"Not to steal your line but this isn't a good time!" Kylara shouted seconds before she hit the ground and the wind was forced out of her lungs.

The skeletons surged forward and clambered over her even as she dragged dozens of them underground using the grass and shrubs under her control. Despite her concerted efforts, she couldn't shake them all off. Another large one—she had no idea what this one looked like, only that it was heavy—bulldozed into her and pushed her face into the mud.

"We'll both be dead if we don't run!" She tried to shout from under the pile but had not caught her breath yet, so all that came out was a weak, raspy wheeze.

The young dragon mage fought with everything she had and used tendrils of dark energy, blasts of lightning, raging winds, and plant roots and branches to pull the horde off her. Nothing seemed to work effectively, simply because there were too many of them. She couldn't defeat them and the only option was to get away, but it was too late for that. The only place that wasn't crawling with revenants was beneath her, and she couldn't slip into the ground.

Except, she realized suddenly, that she absolutely could.

Kylara dragged in a breath, opened a portal beneath her, and plummeted through a different dimension to reappear behind Drew. He had just hung up his phone, although he still looked grim. He resumed shooting at the monsters, even though there were now so many of them that his perfect accuracy had become meaningless. All he had to do was shoot in the general direction of the teeming mass of bone and he was guaranteed to hit one.

They were overwhelmed and the fight was lost, but it seemed their hidden foe had different ideas. Behind the pile of the dead that had swarmed her, another portal appeared and this one dwarfed all the others.

She could think of only one thing to do. With no time to warn him, she took to the air and snatched Drew in her talons. They had to get help or the world was as good as doomed.

CHAPTER TWENTY-NINE

Kylara pumped her wings to gain elevation but she barely got off the ground before one of the winged bird-like skeletons forced her down.

She landed in the mud and managed to stay on her feet by sheer dint of will forced into her diamond claws. Grimly, she turned to face the portal in the full understanding that the fight was lost and she would not walk away from there—or not with the meat on her bones anyway.

But what emerged from the massive portal wasn't more undead monsters. It was a flight of dragons with mages on their backs. At their head was a pair that Kylara knew well. Hell, anyone with a TV would have recognized them.

It was not every day that one saw the Steel Dragon and the world's most powerful mage in combat.

Kristen flew toward the pile of skeletons, drove into them with steel claws, shattered them with her ax blade tail, and breathed fire. Amy was as devastating from her back. With nothing but gestures, she tore skeletons asunder, cracked bones, and made skulls implode.

But they weren't the only ones to join the fight. Kylara recognized the dragon Heartsbane from the news, as well as the mage on her back, a man named Larry Brockton who rumor said talked even more than Tanya. There were others too that she didn't know by reputation. All of them attacked without mercy to destroy, burn, and shred the enemy with powers of both mage and dragon persuasions.

Kylara glanced at Drew, who had dropped his handgun in the mud and now pocketed his cellphone. His gaze wasn't on her but instead, he focused on a group of people who strode through the portal wearing the black and silver uniforms of the Steel Guard. One of them—a woman who had the sides of her head shaved—tossed an assault rifle at Drew.

He caught it with ease. "Thanks, Hernandez."

"I saved the fun stuff for me," the woman hollered and lobbed a grenade into one of the open portals. It exploded and a great eruption of broken bones blasted out of the gate before it slammed shut.

Between the dragons and the Steel Guards armed with dragon bullets, it didn't take long before the undead critters were reduced to nothing but bone shards. More creatures tried to come through, but it was obvious that the monsters were running out of steam—or at least out of bones—to send an effective force.

The mages no longer bothered with the skeletons. Instead, they worked in threes and fours to perform a series of movements and accompanying chants that shut the gateways. It took a few minutes of the mages working on the portals and the dragons and humans taking care of any stragglers but finally, the combat ceased entirely.

The skeletons were inert and the portals closed. The battle was won.

Kylara—despite the terror she'd felt only moments before—was completely overwhelmed by the people around her. These were not only her personal heroes but living legends. The history of the next century would begin with the people glad-handing each other and slapping each other's backs over a job well done.

Kristen and Amy were there of course, but also Heartsbane and Larry working together, and Constance Vigil herself, the mage who could be blamed with both starting and ending the most recent mage war. The armed humans were of special note too. She recognized the sniper who went by the nickname of Butters. He had been a part of Kristen's team when she'd been on SWAT...and so had Drew.

She couldn't believe that she had overlooked her traveling companion's role in the Steel Dragon's revolution. He had been her boss and helped to teach her how to fight hand-to-hand in her human form.

When she caught his eye, she raised an eyebrow in a challenge. It was time to talk now and she hoped he was ready to answer her questions.

He made eye contact, smiled guiltily, then looked at the massive dragon made of steel that stormed toward Kylara through the mud, a scowl on her face.

CHAPTER THIRTY

Kylara was able to make it all of three steps toward Drew in an effort to chew him out for not coming clean with her before Kristen Hall—still in the body of a steel dragon—blocked her path.

"And where exactly do you think you're going?" the most powerful dragon in the world demanded of her.

"To…uh, talk to Drew about being dishonest with me." There didn't seem to be much point in lying to her hero.

The Steel Dragon didn't move an inch. If she hadn't seen her stride forward to block her path, she would have easily believed that this was a chromed sculpture. But most statues didn't wear scowls on their dragon faces, nor did they blow smoke from their nostrils.

"You were going to talk to someone about being dishonest?" Kristen all but growled. "You snuck off school grounds despite being specifically told not to. You scared many people who care about you—including your mother, who is not a pleasant dragon to talk to, I might add."

"My mom knows I'm all right?"

"For my sake, you'd better be. The only way I convinced her

to not race off and start looking for you herself was by assuring her that I had my very best person on the job."

Drew nodded in acknowledgment, although he still avoided Kylara's eyes. That made her both bothered and pleased.

"It's a shame about your friends." The Steel Dragon shook her head. Then, in a great cloud of dust made of flecks of silver, she transformed into her human form. An extremely fit woman with red hair, freckles, and a look of disappointment on her face stood where a massive dragon had been. "They ran off without telling anyone where they were going."

"They're probably looking for me," Kylara interjected.

"That's what we think too. But they had the stupidity—or audacity, depending on your perspective—to leave their phones behind. Once we escort you to campus, they'll be our top priority."

The young dragon mage was not about to let herself be tucked safely away while her friends were out looking for her, but she knew better than to argue the point. "Wait, so...you've been watching me this entire time, Lady Steel?"

"Of course I have. You're an anomaly in the world and my own country and have garnered the interest of an unsavory character. Trouble sticks to you like poop to a shoe, Kylara. We traced your phone at first, then left it to Drew to report in about what's been happening." Her eyes lingered on Kylara's wrist before her eyebrows raised and her face reddened. "But he didn't mention that you had your bracelet removed."

"It just happened, ma'am." Drew offered no more in explanation.

"I thought you hated those inhibiting bracelets! All the reports in the media said you never made Amy wear them and you passed a decree saying mages are no longer required to wear them. Well, I'm a mage. Why do I have to wear one?"

Kristen groaned in frustration. "Didn't your principal put that on for a reason?"

"She put it on because she thought I was opening these gates to the pixie realm that—wait, you already know all about this, huh?"

"Everything except about why yours was removed."

"The pixies did it, ma'am. It was my idea," Drew confessed.

"It was your idea?" Kristen demanded. Drew seemed to flex his entire body so as to not flinch and take a step back. He behaved as if a dragon was berating him, not a human who could turn into one. He had the faintest of sheepish expressions on his face as if he'd been through all this before.

"She wasn't much good in a fight, ma'am. And the pixies wanted to take her to another dimension and all, so…well, I gotta say it made sense at the time."

"That explains it!" The woman named Hernandez spoke loudly.

"Explains what?" Kristen raised an eyebrow.

"Why his truck looks so damn stupid." Hernandez and the other humans all laughed.

"Purple and silver stripes? Honestly Drew?" The woman laughed harder than all the rest. "How could you agree to anything with beings who created that?" She hooked a thumb at his bizarre truck.

"Since you're being rude, all I'll say is they did the truck makeover after Kylara went into the portal. Otherwise…well, you have a good point."

"The whims of pixies are not a good enough reason to endanger yourself and your community," Kristen said at the end of this exchange.

"I was endangering others with the cuff on," Kylara explained. "The gates still opened when I had the bracelet on. It can't be me."

"I agree, ma'am," Drew added. "It's someone else."

The Steel Dragon nodded. "That's as I suspected. Very well. I wish you had spoken to someone first but I suppose Amythist's theory has been disproven."

"So you won't put one back on me?" she asked.

Kristen sighed. "No. I hate those damn things."

"Great. Because I honestly think I can help. I have plant powers and they work well against the skeletons—"

"You can help," Kristen said, "by returning to school. All of this is no longer your problem."

"But my friends—"

"Are our responsibility, not yours." Her tone brooked no argument. "You need to be back in school, honing your powers. Besides, your teachers are worried sick, and if your friends come back on their own, you need to be there or they might take off again."

"I don't mean to be rude, Lady Steel, but that's not a good idea."

"Not a good idea?" Hernandez smirked. "Lady Steel understands your position but you need to understand that she is the highest-ranking person on this continent. If she says you go back to school, you go. This is not a symposium, or a round-robin, or a show and tell. This is us telling you what to do and you saying, yes ma'am."

"No," Kylara said. "Whoever is doing this is targeting me. If I go back to school, they'll attack the school."

"Your school has wards that took years to build. Dragons who know how to fight are located there, as well as mages skilled in every type of defensive magic. It's safe there."

"I won't risk my friends or the teachers so you can pretend I'm slightly safer!" Kylara said a little more loudly and forcefully than she had intended.

"I'm sorry, sweetheart. I understand where you're coming from, but this is not a situation where you get to decide," Kristen said.

"Thank you for your help," she said and took a step back, then another. "I appreciate it and I'm sure you'll find my friends. But I won't go back. Whoever this is has a grudge against me, which means I'll deal with them my way."

Kylara focused on the pixie-style gate she'd been working on behind her. Already fueled with her magic, it popped open as she took her third step back. She vanished into the pixie realm and snapped the gate shut before anyone so much as had the opportunity to tell her to wait.

CHAPTER THIRTY-ONE

"Amy, follow her!" Kristen shouted in frustration.

Drew smirked. He knew the feeling.

"Just a...second..." Amy wheezed. She was doubled over, breathing hard, and rubbing one side of her head.

"Amy!"

"Cut her some slack, Steel," Hernandez protested. "She must've tossed a hundred of those beasties into the portals. Plus, she closed them."

"More like...two hundred...but...who is counting?" Amy said between ragged breaths.

"Can you follow her or not?" Kristen asked, but her tone was gentler. She could be a tough boss—Drew had taught her well—but she knew better than to push her people past their limits.

"I don't think so, boss," Amy said and her breath caught. "She opens those pixie style gates way more easily than I open mine. But even if I wasn't tired, I don't know how to trace mage-style teleportation spells, let alone pixie ones. I don't know what else to tell you."

"Are you saying you can't track her?" Kristen's skin flickered to steel and back in her frustration.

"She's saying that Kylara is gone, Kristen," Drew said.

"Sorry, boss. I'm wiped, or I might have tried to get a bead on what was on the other side of that gate." Amy shrugged. It wasn't exactly professional but it was the truth.

Kristen sighed. "We're supposed to stop her from opening portals to the pixie realm and we lost her to one? How will that look?"

"Catching her wouldn't have stopped those gates, ma'am," Drew pointed out. "It definitely wasn't her making them. It's a bummer that she got away, but I'm not surprised she ran. She's a sharp kid and probably pissed that I lied to her about who I was."

"Then why are you smiling about it?" the Steel Dragon asked pointedly.

"Because I'm impressed with her. She has a good handle on her powers and doesn't lose her head in a fight. She doesn't like seeing other people get mistreated and only ran off because she wants to make this right herself. You shouldn't have been so hard on her, Kristen," he said.

"Is that right?" she asked. "By the way, you still haven't explained why you're smiling."

"I'm smiling because Kylara reminds me of a certain rookie cop who was tossed onto the SWAT team when she was barely a graduate from the police academy. Y'know, one with a solid sense of justice and a knack for giving her superiors more headaches than they knew what to do with?"

Kristen laughed at that, and the tension that had been building outside the now collapsed mineshaft dissipated like the clouds that had rained on them only moments before. "I guess I ran off once or twice, and all I had to protect me was steel. At least she has diamond scales."

"And, like, shadow whip powers!" Keith gushed. Drew could not comprehend how the man still sounded like such a rookie after so many years on the force, but he did and seemed unlikely to move past the propensity.

"Those were bitchin, as were the plant powers." Hernandez grinned. "I'm still waiting for a dragon with bomb powers, though."

"You'd better hope we don't find any more dragons with weird powers. Kylara is more than enough. Plus, there's Tanya and Galen to worry about—and whoever is opening these gates." Kristen bit her lip in thought.

"You agree it's not Kylara?" Drew asked.

She shook her head. "I'm not about to doubt your judgment, Drew. You spent days with her and I've barely met her. But you being right is a worst-case scenario."

He nodded. "You mean because if it's not her, it has to be someone targeting her?"

"Precisely," Kristen agreed. "There have been no reports of these rifts to the pixie realm opening anywhere but near Kylara Diamantine. That bothers me."

"Me too. What bugs me most, though, is that none of this makes much sense. Whoever can open these gates or whatever you want to call them is also able to control these skeletons, right?"

"It seems obvious to me," Hernandez agreed while Kristen only nodded.

"That's an incredible power," he continued. "Whoever is behind this could open these in civilian areas, military bases, dragon mansions, you name it. But they aren't. Instead, they're harrying Kylara for some reason and hardly doing any damage."

"I don't know. This place looks screwed to me," Hernandez said and pointed at the collapsed mineshaft and piles of bones scattered throughout the area.

"This last one was worse, yeah, but it was also the place to which Kylara was lured," Drew said. "All the others were shut fairly quickly, and even this one didn't cost us any lives, thank God."

"But that doesn't sound so bad to me," Hernandez said.

"Except that it points to these gates having a purpose," he pointed out grimly.

"A purpose we don't understand." Kristen nodded.

"What we have is a new power that doesn't match any of the known magics anyone on our team has experience dealing with." Drew's voice was hard. "This is something new—someone new. And that scares the crap out of me."

CHAPTER THIRTY-TWO

Boneclaw had been so close to finally forcing Kylara into the pixie realm. He hadn't foreseen her removing the bracelet as he hadn't been able to go anywhere near the home of the pixies she had visited. But even with full powers, the fight had been on the side of the revenants—until the Steel Bitch appeared with reinforcements.

As soon as she and her band of horribly shortsighted dragons arrived, Boneclaw knew he would have to wait for another day to take the girl's powers from her. He had watched the fight, hidden as a shadow, but as soon as the mages closed his gates, he had fled. He was not naïve and knew the Steel Dragon would search for the source of the portals. Although he couldn't be sure that she would be able to find him, he couldn't risk the possibility. Not yet. Not until he had become what Kylara already was.

His current form was powerful in ways his living body simply had not been. Pain was no longer a consideration, nor was fatigue, hunger, or any of the other inconveniences of mortality. Furthermore, the steel skin of the Steel Dragon would no longer be the impediment it once was. With the black claw Galen had given him, he could slice into her flesh like a knife into a loaf of bread. He wanted to so badly. To watch her bleed out while he stood above her would be sweet indeed.

But this body had its weaknesses too. He was little more than a fleshless corpse and thus no longer possessed the healing power he had enjoyed while living. If the Steel Dragon shattered his bones, they would not mend. He had to be careful—tediously so—as he proceeded.

Truthfully, not being able to confront the Steel Dragon yet did not bother Boneclaw at the moment. Her time would come, and he was nothing if not patient. What bothered him currently, what felt like a bone lodged in his throat, was the fact that Kylara had slipped into the pixie realm and when she had done so, he had lost track of her. He had no idea where she was and could not even tell if she was in the pixie realm or the material one.

So, beaten by his failure to anticipate the movements of a teenage girl, he returned to Cassandra's hideout.

"Ah, Lord Boneclaw," the mage murmured from her perch atop a chair made of the same sandstone as was every other part of their desert lair. "You return with good news, I hope?"

Much as it pained him, he bowed so his dragon skull was lower than hers. She had taken to ordering him to do this and he was not yet ready to betray the full extent of his freedom. He told her the story of all that had transpired, ending with Kylara's swift exit through a portal. "She has given me the slip, my lady. I had lured her to one of your lairs, as I told you."

"Even though she didn't tell you to do that," Galen pointed out petulantly.

"The lady and I have discussed this, Lord Galen. It will simply take too much time to explain my every move and action," Lord Boneclaw retorted.

"She did not attempt to enter the portals and use the plants there to restrain the skeletons?" Cassandra asked. She had long grown tired of the constant bickering between the revenant and the aspiring bone lord.

"No, my lady. I believe it's because she was with one of the Steel Guard, that obnoxiously clever human I spoke to you about. I think she stayed in this realm to ensure his protection. I told you this would happen and that you should have eliminated him with one of your spirits."

"Then my niece would think I'm working against her. It is unacceptable," Cassandra said.

He had already had this argument with the narrow-minded mage. It would end nowhere, as it always did. "I apologize, my lady. I am frustrated at being thwarted by the Steel Dragon."

"You may rise, Lord Boneclaw. I understand your frustrations. The Steel Dragon is as unyielding in pursuing her goals as the metal skin that protects her. Do not feel beaten because you could not unravel the magic of teleportation. It is next to impossible for a dragon or a mage to make sense of how space and time twist."

"Then she is lost?" he asked as he rose to sit on his haunches.

"To a lesser mage, almost certainly." Cassandra's eyes gleamed. One thing she and Boneclaw shared was a passion for power. "But I have unearthed magic that mages have overlooked for centuries. There is magic in the blood, you know—magic that runs back thousands of years. It is the magic of history, the magic of families, of fathers and sons and mothers and daughters. It is a magic that Kylara and I share. Her mother was my sister and thus, she cannot be lost to me."

"Then are you wasting your time, you worthless heap of a human?" Lord Boneclaw wanted to say but did not. Instead, he raised an eyebrow—a gesture accomplished by moving the black strands of his spirit that choked the dragon skeleton that gave him form. "Do you know where she is? Even now?"

Cassandra nodded. That was something of a relief. At least the mage had already tracked the girl and not completely wasted their time.

"I felt when she vanished from our realm and when she reappeared. She is at her old home, probably visiting the woman she thinks of as her mother, Diamantine."

"Shall we proceed there now?" Boneclaw asked. "With this claw, I can slay the mother. In her grief, the girl will come to us and beg us to make her stronger." Boneclaw would have salivated at the idea if he still had saliva glands.

"You will stay here with Galen." Cassandra clucked with all the smugness of a farmyard hen. "Your plan to lure her into the pixie realm failed, but that does not mean all is lost. She fled from Lady Steel. We can count that as a small victory."

"How can running away ever be a victory?" Galen muttered. It was a fair question from the coward who had spent most of the time Boneclaw had known him running and hiding.

"Every animal in the world knows that running away is the difference between being someone's meal and living to eat another," Cassandra replied.

Lord Boneclaw was pleased he did not have lips anymore, for even he would not have been able to hide his grin at the truth of this statement. The woman did not even know that the fox was already in the henhouse.

"Her running from Lady Steel suggests that she feels at least some distrust toward the dragon leadership structure. That is an exceptionally good thing. The last thing we want is for her to try to ingratiate herself to Kristen and what we know to be her false vision of equality."

"And her running to her mom—a former cop—is better?" Galen asked. Oh, how Boneclaw loathed the impertinence of this brat.

"It is. It makes sense for her. Plus, Diamantine and I have a… relationship. It is preferable to her returning to the Lumos School. That would make it much more difficult to persuade her to help us."

"And you can reach her there?" Lord Boneclaw asked.

"I can and I will. You two will stay together and await my

message. I will call you when I'm ready for you. Do not come before then. Understand?" Before they could respond, her earth spirit wrapped her in stone and pulled her away, leaving the revenant alone with the brat.

Boneclaw turned and appraised Galen. The whelp was on a sofa he had begged—no, demanded—that the mage bring for him. His feet were already up and he held some kind of television with games on it in his hands. He was a waste of a dragon—or he had been. Now, finally, his potential could be realized.

"What are you staring at?" Galen snorted. "You heard her. Leave me alone."

"That is not what she said at all, Lord Galen," Boneclaw all but purred, all kindness now. He had been denied an augmentation of his powers but that was not the only reason the day had been a failure. He had also been unable to test his theory of power acquisition. When he entered the swampy area of the pixie realm where Galen had been given his powers, he felt certain he could accomplish what he wished. He wasn't, however, one to put much faith in feelings or hunches.

"Tell me, Galen, what do you think of your powers?" he asked quietly.

"I wish I had never used them to bring you back. That's for sure," the boy said, full of bravado. The fool must still believe Cassandra could protect him.

"You regret having them?" Boneclaw asked. He ignored the slight and reveled in how dramatically the boy's fate was about to change.

"No...not really," Galen straightened. He was always desperate to talk about his powers. "I merely wish I had more control. I can't even control you."

The shadow dragon nodded sympathetically. It was what the boy expected, fool that he was. "What if there was a way to strengthen them?"

"There is, obviously. But I can't go back to the Lumos School, not after what happened."

"I am not speaking of homework and memorization, you infantile excuse for a dragon. I am speaking of the way I learned my powers."

"The powers that got you killed, you mean?" Galen retorted.

He smiled his lipless grin. Oh, he would enjoy every moment of this. "The powers that let me live for thousands of years. Those that made me so infamous that even in death, I was brought back to this world to save it. That is what you wish, is it not, young Galen? To be respected? For others to see your true value?"

Galen nodded despite not wanting to. Boneclaw could see the desperation in his eyes and smell it on his aura.

"Then come with me and together, we will show the world what we can accomplish with your power."

Before the young dragon could respond or turn to his television game, Boneclaw opened a portal to the pixie world. He had planned this for a long time so knew the perfect location. The portal opened to a pond so placid and deep that the surface was blue instead of the muddy brown of most of the swamp. Around the banks, magnificent cedar trees grew, their branches heavy with moss and lichen. On the banks sat skeleton creatures of the pixie realm. He had signaled to them that he was coming and what he wished of them. They had delivered and the bones of a deer, rabbit, and a few squirrels all looked at Galen and turned their heads toward him. The rabbit even cocked its skull to the side in curious invitation.

"Cassandra said—"

"She said to stay together and not follow her until she called for us. She did not say to stay here, nor did she say that you must remain powerless despite your abilities for the rest of your life. Although I'm sure that's what she plans." Boneclaw kept his voice level, as difficult as it was. He knew that if he still had a tongue, he'd be salivating for what was soon to come to pass.

That encouraged the boy to push off the sofa. He peered into the pixie realm at the idyllic scene beyond the portal. "Do you honestly think I can gain more mastery there?" he asked.

"I am certain that from this pond, a master will arise," Boneclaw assured him.

Galen nodded and walked through the portal.

The ancient dragon followed and closed the gate silently behind him.

For a long moment, the boy stood in the pond and looked at the skeletal creatures all around him. They moved and pantomimed eating as if they were ready to return to life. "Are you doing this?" Galen asked. "Making them behave this way, I mean?"

"I am. And you can too. All you must do is kneel before me, Galen, and I will share what I learned with you in the place beyond life."

Galen—hesitant, cautious, but ultimately desperate for better control—knelt.

"Very good. Now, lean forward, put your hands into the silt at the bottom of this pond and reach out through it. Feel for the body buried at the bottom."

The young dragon leaned forward and sank his hands into the mud. "I...I feel it. It's...powerful. So powerful."

"It was here long before the pixies found this place," Boneclaw explained. "And unless the Steel Dragon truly upsets the natural order of things, it will be here long after the pixies are gone."

"What is it?"

"The source of your power, Galen. It is that which gives me, these skeletons, and this swamp itself life."

"That power is what I'm using?" Galen sounded appalled. "But it's...it's evil." He gasped.

"Well, yes," Boneclaw said, then he acted.

The roots of the cedar trees bound the boy's ankles and wrists under the surface of the pond. Galen screamed as they began to pull him deeper into the muck.

"What are you doing to me?" he asked.

"I'm not sure what the verb is anymore, but I suppose consuming you does the trick." Boneclaw put a claw on his chest—the one with the black talon that the young dragon had given him—and pushed him deeper into the mud.

The plants bound the boy and tightened their grip on him not because Boneclaw told them to but because the plants there had been made by the creators of this place to bind the sleeping behemoth deep beneath the swamp. Galen—poor, stupid Galen—had the same power coursing through him.

"Please! Please don't kill me!" The young dragon sputtered as the thick silt he had kicked up with his pathetic struggles flooded into his mouth.

"I wouldn't kill a dragon, boy, especially one of your pedigree. But it has become clear that you need to be taught a lesson in trust."

"But I do trust. I trusted you."

"That is why you must be taught a lesson," Boneclaw said and leaned closer to him, his dragon skull barely inches away from his face. "Trust no one."

Without warning, the shadow dragon shoved Galen underwater. Immediately, he felt his powers begin to leave. The pond and this entire swamp could take powers, just as other parts of the pixie realm could grant them. The powers were supposed to dissipate into the water but Boneclaw, of course, had other plans.

As soon as he felt some of Galen's magic start to seep away, he latched onto it but with no success. It was like trying to catch a small mouse with the claw of the dragon. And the vines that had grasped the boy now wound themselves around him as well. Terrified for the first time since he'd been resurrected, the revenant panicked. Not wanting to let the power slip out of the boy, he attempted to plug the place from which it exited. In his haste, he used the black claw he had been given.

To his utter delight, the magic poured into the claw like a

lightning rod. He drank it thirstily and added it to himself, laughing with glee.

The skeletons around the pool launched an attack on the vines that bound him. They had never truly obeyed him before. They had attacked at his command because he had convinced them that Kylara had stolen from this realm, but they had never truly obeyed. But with Galen's power, that changed. The skeletons responded to his unspoken command. They focused on defending him from the plants that tried to bind this new source of necromantic energy.

It was a pity he could not control the plants in the same way he could the skeletons, but it no longer mattered.

The ancient dragon ripped Galen out of the pond and tossed him against a tree with enough force to crack some of the boy's bones. He would heal and Boneclaw had not had quite enough time to steal the boy's dragon powers. But that would not matter, not for much longer anyway. He would soon have the powers of a far more formidable opponent and this way, he would keep his promise to the boy to not harm a dragon.

He picked the young dragon up, opened a rift, and hurled him through. Galen tumbled across the floor of Cassandra's lair and came to a stop against his precious couch.

Boneclaw stepped through and sealed the rift behind him. He took a deep breath, pleased by the sensation. While he had not taken all the boy's powers, he had taken more than he had realized in the pixie realm. He had flesh once more, tight and leathery as it was, and scales, although they were the same inky darkness as his spirit had been when it had been forced to cling to his bones. He had lungs too, a heart, and even something like the glands needed to create fire. None of it did anything for him, as he was still mostly a revenant given intelligence via his spirit, but it was a step in the right direction. A step, he thought smugly, toward immortality.

He exhaled slowly, enjoying the sensation very much.

What he did not enjoy was the sound of Galen's laughter.

"You truly are an idiot. I always knew you were, ever since you thought you could defeat the Steel Dragon, but this clinches it."

"What are you speaking of?" he demanded and wondered if he should simply slaughter the boy, dragon be damned.

"You let Cassandra get away, you moron." Galen laughed and spat blood. The shadow dragon had hit him harder than he had realized. "So, you have more skeleton powers. So what? They're not as strong as Kylara is. Hell, they're not as strong as Tanya. And now, Cassandra went off and left you here. Do you honestly think she'll call you one second before she wants you there?"

It was Boneclaw's turn to laugh. He threw his head back and did exactly that—loud and long and clear. Oh, but did it feel amazing to have lungs again. "Ah, Galen. There was the briefest of moments where I felt something like remorse for taking your powers from you, but this only proves how much you had been squandering them."

The young dragon stopped laughing.

"Cassandra summoned my spirit and thought to bind me with her voice. An unfortunate side effect is that I can always hear her talking and I always know exactly where she is."

"No!" Galen shouted and pushed to his feet. "No, you bastard."

But Boneclaw was already fading into shadow and sank into the rocks of this hideout. The young dragon fell to his knees and pounded the floor where the shadow dragon had vanished.

"Come back here! Come back here!" He tried to transform but only managed to do so halfway to become a winged mongrel and not a true dragon at all. Boneclaw left him in the desert. If he could not survive on his own, he didn't deserve to.

The revenant laughed as he raced toward Cassandra, his theory proven and his body ready for more power.

CHAPTER THIRTY-THREE

Kylara was in the pixie realm for a scant few seconds before she opened another gate to her reality. She had not considered a destination, only that she had to get away before the Steel Dragon slapped another dampening cuff on her or Amy wrapped her in magic and kept her there.

She didn't want to spend much time in the pixie realm, but she was beginning to understand that her teleportation worked by moving through it, sometimes for mere millimeters before moving through another gate into her world. Part of her wondered where else she could take the gates, but then she was back in her world, somewhere both safe and rich with memories.

Relieved, she stepped from the gate and into a familiar place. She was home on the piece of land where she had spent her entire life until she and Hester Diamantine had been attacked by her aunt's fire spirits.

A sense of homesickness she had not been consciously aware of lifted from her shoulders when she saw the familiar skyline. She knew these mountains like the back of her hand. She knew their peaks and ridges and even the outcroppings of boulders and often the creatures that called each place home.

But there were changes too. Horrible changes. While she knew the land had burned, she had not yet had a chance to survey how bad the damage was. She had been there once since the attack and had spent all her time inside her home. This time, she had arrived outside and in the light of day, the charred remnants of the forest were almost painful to see.

Trees that had taken hundreds of years to grow tall enough to provide even the scantest of shade had been reduced to charred stumps. Swaths of chaparral that had been home to rabbits, coyotes, and at least a dozen varieties of birds were gone. Wildflowers had attempted to colonize the incinerated landscape, but she knew the creatures of the area well enough to know that a few measly leaves and flower stems were not the same as a thorny shrub when it came to habitat.

It would be years before the mountainside returned to anything resembling normalcy. Decades, if the weather stayed drier than usual.

Although that, at least, she could help with. She closed her eyes and took a deep breath before she summoned the winds of the desert to gather what moisture was in the air. Slowly, she built a great cloud above her land. Before it could grow into a full-sized storm cloud, she squeezed its gray puffs of vapor together, condensed the droplets, and forced them to fall to the burned ground as a gentle drizzle.

Kylara knew that the wildflowers would flourish in the rain, so she ignored them and focused instead on what survived of the larger, woody plants. There were not many still alive, but those that were reached to the sky with fresh, slender branches and sprays of tiny, waxy leaves. Cactus put on new arms and pads that would normally have taken years to grow.

But there was only so far she could push the landscape. These were still desert plants, after all. Their game was the long one. She had bought them maybe a year of growth but didn't have the control needed to make the new shoots and stems harden as they would have to do if they were to survive the desert sun.

With the gentle rain falling, Kylara started up the hill toward her house—or what was left of it.

The last time she had been here, the house was little more than a charred husk, a nightmare of a memory made real by her aunt.

That, at least, had changed.

No one was working on the house at the moment, but it was obvious that work was being done. The charred interior had all been ripped out and was piled in a massive tangle of wood, wire, and pieces of her former life.

Kylara did not let herself linger on the pile of wreckage. She had already moved past her home being destroyed. Plus, the wreckage was not the only pile of materials on the mountain. Stacks of two by fours were piled high near pallets of sheetrock, buckets of paint, and fresh panes of glass to rebuild the wall of glass that had made up the only side of the house that wasn't buried into the mountainside.

Still in the rain, she felt her breath catch in her throat as her mom came out of the hole where all the materials were to be used, looked at the rain, and began to grumble as she dragged tarps over the construction materials.

"One day, the crew's not here—one day, and it rains," Hester complained.

"Here, let me help you with that," Kylara said and closed the distance between them to take hold of the opposite corner.

"Kylara!" Hester dropped the tarp and rushed to her daughter, wrapped her in her arms, and lifted her off the ground. She squeezed so tightly that despite the girl's abundance of dragon powers, she was left breathless.

"I missed you too, mom…" Kylara wheezed. "Now, if you don't mind letting me breathe…"

Hester released her, caught her by the shoulders, and held her at arm's length to study her. "I'm so glad to see you. You don't know how many times over the past few days I almost flew off to find you myself."

"I can take a guess," she replied.

Her mother did not laugh. She never laughed, but her eyes crinkled—which for her was an acknowledgment of humor. "The only reason I didn't go looking for you was that Amythist said one of the Steel Guard was with you. Is that true? If that dragon lied to me, I swear I'll burn her damn garden to the ground."

"You don't need to do that," Kylara assured her mother, despite finding herself once again annoyed that everyone had known she was being tailed except her. "Drew was very helpful. He helped me get that magic cuff off me."

Hester took her arm and held her wrist up. "You devious little mage!" she teased. "Now, let's get out of this rain. You have much to tell me."

Kylara nodded and followed her mother inside. The interior of the house was little more than the carved out interior of the mountain, framed here and there with the very beginning of what would soon make it into a home. The only part of the house that showed much progress was the kitchen. Hester had already put in a great slab of granite that looked like it had been cut from the mountain itself for a kitchen counter. There was a sink, a coffee maker, and a stove with a pot of what smelled like black beans simmering. Kylara also noticed a cot and a small pile of clothes in another corner of the place. Hester had never been one for creature comforts.

"So?" her mom asked. "The last I heard, you were at a pixie house and off to a rendezvous with Galen in the morning. Did you find the kid?"

She shook her head. "It was a trap, Mom." She launched into a play by play of her trek, not sure what details Drew had shared with Kristen and which of these had been passed on to Hester. She tried to be as accurate as she could when describing the rifts, what came out of them, and how they had appeared and vanished. Her mother mostly listened and only asked clarifying questions now and then. "So, what do you think?" she asked when she finished explaining the situation.

Diamantine drummed the scarred fingers of her burned hand against the granite countertop for a moment before she spoke. "If this was a case for Dragon SWAT," she began, "I would say that you are almost certainly being targeted. The notion that you were somehow responsible for these rifts or holes or whatever they are has been disproven. That means we're dealing with someone with a vendetta against you."

"Do you think it's Cassandra?" she asked. She didn't think it was but it would be the simplest explanation.

Hester shook her head. "Not a chance. The letter you described sounds like a fake. Cassandra is many things, but she—much as it pains me to admit it—cares about you. When she held me prisoner, that was something I never doubted. She wants you to respect her and trust her. Even if she did somehow gain these powers, I don't see any conceivable reason why she'd used them against you and not someone like the Steel Dragon."

"So we're back to square one." Kylara sagged. She had hoped that her mom would tell her she was wrong and that it must be Cassandra because at least then there would be a clear path to the end of this madness.

"Not exactly." Hester drummed her fingers again. "We know that whoever did this clearly wants you alone and not surrounded by others. That tells us that this isn't a mage versus dragon plot, nor political maneuvering gone wrong. I don't want to say this because I don't want you to be scared, but—as a former cop—I have to say that this seems personal to me. Someone is either interested in your powers or your past."

"My past?"

The woman shrugged. "To beings as powerful as us dragons, knowledge can be more valuable than gold. I think that you're being targeted but don't want to guess at the why until we know more. Although, honestly, if it was about your past, I would think whoever has been doing this would have come for me already."

"But no one has."

"Right. Which makes me think someone is interested in what you can do, not what you did."

Kylara nodded. That made sense to her as well.

Diamantine bristled, then hardened her gaze as she turned away from her to look out the open window frames at the front of the house.

"It seems that you've been followed," she said.

Kylara nodded. She saw them too—three dragons on the horizon. "Come on. I can open a portal and get us out of here. Where should we go?"

"We will not run away from our home. I don't ever want to abandon this place again."

"We shouldn't stay here. If this is whoever is behind the portals, we can't take them alone."

To Kylara's surprise, Diamantine's rock-hard expression softened. "Look again."

A little anxious still, she complied. Now that the dragons were slightly closer, she could see that it wasn't only three. There was a rider on one of their backs as well. But that was not all she noticed. One dragon was gold, without horns or tendrils on his chin, which made him look handsomely young. Besides him was a black dragon. The membrane on this one's wings was torn as if it were made of rags, but also dark as an oil spill. He had a mane of long black hair, that—even in dragon form—looked greasy. It was Sam and Karl.

The third dragon was Tanya. Her turquoise color was an unmistakable shade of the sea and the delicate, paper-thin membranes on the three ridges down her back and stretched between her slender wings was a recognizable characteristic. The mage on her back could only be Jasmine.

"Like I said, no portals." Diamantine winked. "Open one now and they might rip me limb from limb."

CHAPTER THIRTY-FOUR

Kylara ran out into the gravel driveway in front of the house to greet her friends. She stood among the piles of hastily tarp-covered construction materials and waved excitedly while she told the clouds to clear. Her heart was not into the magic—she was too excited to see her friends—so instead of completely dissipating, the clouds merely parted.

Sunlight burst through onto her, making the three dragons seem to glow as they circled overhead and swooped in to land. By the time the third one had shaken the water droplets from their scales and tucked their wings away at their sides, a rainbow had formed. Kylara had never seen one at her home before. Not ever. How appropriate that she had never had friends over before either.

"Did you miss us or something?" Tanya asked, hardly waiting for Jasmine to climb off her back before she transformed into her human form, opened a parasol against the last few droplets of water still spitting, and ran to embrace her friend. They hugged until Karl catcalled that they were making out behind the paper parasol.

Tanya stuck her tongue out at him. "You wish, oil-spill."

Sam hugged Kylara next and held his broad arms wide until he could wrap her in them. The moment he enveloped her, she felt a pulse of light energy flow into her from him.

"I'm fine," she said.

"A little healing never hurt anyone," he replied with a wink. He pulled away to reveal a sheepish looking Karl rubbing a foot through the damp gravel at their feet.

"Tanya was worried about you," Midnight said. "It was pathetic."

"It's good to know my friends have my back," Kylara said and hugged him. He did not return it, not with his arms anyway, but tendrils of black emerged from his skin to check her for wounds.

"Did you get your powers back?" Jasmine asked. It was always all business with her, not that Kylara minded the sharp-tongued mage. She hugged her despite Jasmine's body language saying it was fine if she didn't.

"She'd better have them," Karl interjected before Kylara could reply. "Her bracelet's gone." A chord of dark energy whipped back to his hands from her wrist.

"Why? Is something wrong?" she asked.

"You mean besides our friend ditching us after totally promising not to?" Tanya asked. She glared meaningfully at her.

"I shouldn't have ditched you guys," she conceded. "It was this letter from my aunt and…well, I thought it was from my aunt…"

"We found the letter," Tanya said. "and the coordinates. Although I will admit, I thought it was a phone number at first."

Karl snorted and made no attempt to hide his amusement at the other dragon's ignorance.

"That's why we came here. The coordinates weren't far from here. We were hoping to find you and here you are!" Tanya beamed.

"You kids probably have a load of questions for your friend, huh?" Diamantine asked.

"No kidding." Karl snorted.

"Yes, ma'am," Sam said much more respectfully.

The woman led the group inside and served them all bowls of beans and cold mint tea from a cooler tucked away in the kitchen. Kylara told them much of what she had told her mother, although she did focus more on Galen and how worried she was about him.

She had almost finished her story and was about to gloss over how sternly Kristen Hall had lashed her with her tongue when the ground began to rumble.

"Kylara, I guess we need to get you a landline because your friends need to call before they come," Diamantine joked, but her tone was all business. She'd already stepped out of the house and into the gravel driveway, where her dragon form had room to spread its diamond-encrusted wings.

Kylara glanced at her friends but they were as ready for battle as her mom was. Jasmine was spinning a shield of magical energy, Karl had tendrils of darkness spreading from his feet, and Sam's eyes glowed. Tanya's eyes were on the plants beyond the driveway, and one hand was clenched into a fist at her side. Kylara wondered if her friend had taken to carrying seeds of the most useful plants for combating the skeletons.

She stepped outside the open window frames and turned into a diamond-encrusted dragon like the woman beside her who she had taken the power from when she was but a baby.

A sphere of earth rose out of the earth in the center of the driveway. First, only the rounded top poked through before it widened to reveal its full diameter of almost eight feet. It finally came to rest on the ground, balanced on a piece of earth no larger than a pebble. A crack formed down the center of it and each side pushed away to create a split that Aunt Cassandra stepped from like a freshly hatched reptile.

"Please, I come here as a friend." Cassandra dropped to her knees the moment she emerged from the egg of stone, threw her hands up in the air, and waved them like miniature flags of surrender.

"Friends come invited," Diamantine snapped from where she hovered above her.

"I know. That's fair. But I couldn't wait any longer. Please, I must speak to you, Kylara."

"Do you expect us to trust you when you simply barge in here?" Sam demanded.

"I'm not barging in!" Cassandra protested. "Please, if I wished you harm, my earth spirit would make quick work of burying your home in the very heart of the mountain. If I didn't wish to be seen, my air spirit could keep me far above the clouds. I know I have not been kind to any of you. All of you have proven yourself through your commitment to my niece. I never should have treated any of you the way I did."

"You can say that again," Tanya responded acidly.

"I will. And I'll apologize as many times as it takes to be a part of Kylara's life."

"You can't simply appear here and expect me to be happy to see you." Kylara didn't like the desperate look in her aunt's eye.

"I know. And I wouldn't have come if I didn't need help. I know you need time to heal after the events a few months ago but I can't wait any longer. Kylara, please, how can I prove myself to you?"

Kylara didn't know what to say. A part of her knew that she shouldn't trust her aunt. She had kidnapped her mom and her friends and had burned down the house they now stood outside of. And yet, she wanted to trust her. More than that, she craved it. She was her last living link to her past—the only person in the entire world who could tell her about her parents. This was a mage who would die before she put a silver cuff on her niece.

"You'd better start talking about why you came here then," she said gruffly.

"Ky—" Tanya frowned.

"Do you still have your pendant?" Diamantine asked.

"Yes, ma'am," Kylara said. She could always feel it in this form, incorporated into her dragon body.

"Good girl. She shouldn't be able to do anything to you," her mother said.

"She's right!" Cassandra blurted. "My father—your grandfather—made that to protect our families from dragons. As long as you're wearing it, you'll be impervious to mind tricks." Cassandra pulled a matching pendant out of her leathers and unclasped it from the back of her neck. She tossed it on the ground at Kylara's feet.

"What's this?"

"A token of my trust," the mage said and looked at the dragons in their human forms who stared out of the house at her while Hester circled above. "Now all these dragons can read my aura. They can tell that I only want your help."

"We can overpower her emotions too," Karl murmured. "Make her so overcome with guilt that she collapses to a pile on the floor."

"If you insist," Cassandra said. "But I fear we don't have the time for that. Please, Kylara, if I could have only an hour of your time. There are a few tests I would like to perform. The dragons can watch if that would make you more comfortable. I'll tell you what I'm doing for every step of the way."

"What are you talking about?" she asked.

"Yeah, you're not making any sense," Tanya pointed out cheekily.

"I must become a dragon, Kylara. You must show me how you take your dragon form. Please!"

"You know as well as I do that I don't know how I absorb powers," she said cautiously.

"I know, but I can't help but think that if I can see you in action, I might be able to discover something. I think it comes down to letting your matter phase through another dimension while you transform. Is that right, do you think?"

Kylara pursed her lips and tried to study her aunt's appearance. She still wore layers of thick, home-sewn leathers, but there was something about them that seemed ragged—as if she had stopped repairing them, perhaps. There was also a disheveled look about her hair and haggard lines around her eyes. She looked like someone who had been very deep in research for an exceedingly long time. Some of the mage students approached something close to that look around finals time.

"I just don't know how I can help you. It's all instinct," Kylara said weakly. Even if she could help her aunt, the poor woman looked like she needed a nap first.

"I think you are what I need!" Cassandra said quickly. "I found someone—a teacher of sorts—who I thought could teach me the theory I needed, but he's convinced that you're a part of this. That if he can get you into the pixie realm, you could use your powers and teach us how to realize some of the amazing things you can do."

"Who is this teacher?" Diamantine asked from her position above them.

"He is incredibly wise but he constantly insists that Kylara is essential to the process. I...I could not wait any longer. I'm so sorry..." The mage began to weep.

"I think she's being honest," Karl said, although his lip was curled in disgust at the woman's tears.

"Please! I don't want to die, Kylara! I'm getting older every day. If I could only have access to the dragon healing power, perhaps I could last long enough for us to treat each other as family one day, but I'll never make it that long unless you help me now." The sobs came loud and hard.

"Who is this teacher?" Diamantine demanded again.

"Wait..." Kylara said before Cassandra—still trying to pull

herself together—could answer. "You said his plan is to get me into the pixie realm?"

Her aunt nodded and wiped her tears on a sleeve of her leathers.

"Has he already tried this?" She all but snarled the question.

Cassandra swallowed hard and glanced at the dragons all around her, who read every twitch or shift in her emotional state.

"He did, yes, but she was always opposed to it," a voice intoned from inside the house.

Karl, Lumos, Tanya, and Jasmine all scattered out into the yard as a cloud of darkness even deeper than the ropes and tendrils Kylara and Karl could make poured out of the shadowed corners of the construction site.

The smoke took the form of a dragon, but as it coalesced, the skin and muscles of the beast shrank and tightened until all that was left was a skeleton wrapped in the stringiest of muscles and tied together with sickly looking tangles of black veins that hugged the bone.

The faintest line of muscle formed lips around its maw of jagged teeth. It smiled and spoke again. "She wasn't a particularly good student, but then, perhaps it was my teaching. We were both quite lost without you."

Kylara's mind raced. How was this possible? All the skeletons that Galen had brought back had been mindless creatures. They had sat, flown, or fought, but little else. This dragon not only spoke but moved its body with the subtle grace of the living that the rest of the revenants had lacked. Plus, Galen was nowhere to be seen.

"Who are you?" she demanded, already convinced that it was not a what speaking to them.

"Forgive me. I had assumed that Lady Cassandra had already told you about her mentor." The dragon bowed slightly and gestured to the mage with a hand on which one wickedly long black claw stood out among the other white bones. Kylara recognized that claw. It had belonged to the body of a dragon known as the Prairie King, a dragon that had already been defeated. "If it wouldn't be too much to ask, I would be honored if you would introduce us."

"But of course." Cassandra tried to bow her head in an attempt at a show of respect that failed to because of her nervousness. "This is Kylara Diamantine, my niece, a mage with the long-forgotten ability to become a dragon, as well as many others. Kylara, this is Lord Boneclaw, former leader of the Dragon Council."

"A pleasure." Boneclaw bowed deeply to Kylara, although the scheming grin of his almost fleshless lips did not slip an inch.

The young dragon mage swallowed hard. She recognized the name, of course. Everyone knew that he was the dragon who stood in the way of the Steel Dragon's revolution. He had killed Sam Lumos's grandfather and controlled dragon society from the shadows for millennia and now, somehow, he was back?

Karl was the one who summed up his reemergence the best. "Shit."

CHAPTER THIRTY-FIVE

"But how?" Kylara asked and turned to her aunt, hoping that the mage had a satisfactory answer, as impossible as such a thing seemed to be.

The ancient shadow dragon answered for the woman. "Lady Cassandra and the young Lord Galen did it together. His newly discovered bone powers, plus the mage's mastery of spirits made me what I am today."

"Aunt Cass—how could you?" she asked. This was unbelievable. Boneclaw was evil. Pure evil! He had worked to keep mages enslaved to dragons for all of history. "How can you trust him?" She hadn't meant for it to slip out in front of the dragon skeleton, but there it was.

"He is no danger, Kylara. I promise you that," Cassandra explained. "Galen raised his bones and I bound his spirit to them. He must obey me or his spirit will be ripped from his bones and sent back to the place of rest."

Kylara shook her head in disbelief. This was painful to hear. "This was a stupid plan, Aunt Cass."

"Agreed," Diamantine said from above. Kylara glanced at her friends. They were all frozen, ready for combat, their muscles as tight as steel and their faces as hard as stone. It was almost hard to believe that the four of them were only students.

"It was the only choice I had!" the older mage said pleadingly. "I must become a dragon, Kylara. I must. I would have come to you but I knew you were angry with me. There are precious few dragons who gained new abilities, and I knew of only three living ones—who would all say no to me. Plus, there are rumors that Boneclaw was not born a dragon but a human."

"Lies, I assure you," Boneclaw growled.

"Quiet," Cassandra said and gestured at the dragon skeleton wrapped in twisted veins like he was nothing more than a yapping chihuahua. "He taught me that it was the pixies who gave him his powers, which made getting you into a position in which you would speak to me all the more important."

"Getting me into position?" Kylara asked, terrified to clarify yet unable to resist.

The woman nodded too quickly. She was obviously at her wit's end. "We knew you wouldn't talk to me as long as you were surrounded by Amythist and her narrow-minded staff. We had to get you away from school so I could ask you for help. That's why I'm here now."

"So it was you all along? The breaches? The attacks from the skeletons? The fake note?"

"Most of that was me, actually," Boneclaw answered. "Galen's power allowed me to open a path to the pixie realm, which I saw the value of when Cassandra did not."

"What you did was use a loophole to undermine me," the mage snapped. "You never told me about your power until after you had used it. Otherwise, you would have been forbidden from enacting such a dangerous plan."

"And the note?" Kylara asked and tears pricked her eyes.

"He wrote it." Cassandra sounded ashamed. "And delivered it, but when he told me about it, I did nothing to remedy it. You must understand how desperate I have become, Kylara. It became increasingly clear that Boneclaw did not intend to help and that his advice always boiled down to the same thing—to get you into the pixie realm and then you could teach us."

The woman turned to Lord Boneclaw. "In fact, you've never made any claim to being able to help me. You have made it plain that Kylara is the key. Now that we are speaking, your services are no longer needed. Return to the lair and await my return. Do so without complaint and perhaps I will let you reside in this realm a little longer."

The ancient dragon threw back his head and laughed loud and hard. It was a horrible thing to witness. His muscles twitched and contracted with his dry cackle, and the outline of his lungs could be seen, deflating and inflating with each guffaw.

"Stupid mage," the skeletal dragon finally managed to say and wiped a nonexistent tear from his eye. A gesture the dragon must have done thousands of times while alive seemed bizarre now.

Cassandra rose from her knees. Slowly, with fire in her eyes, she turned to Boneclaw. She faced him, her shoulders square, her back as straight as a spear, and one fist clenched while the fingers of her other hand worked in complicated patterns.

"Return to my lair, Boneclaw. With the power in my blood, the power in my voice, I command you to leave this place and return to my lair, where you will await your punishment." As she spoke, the ground quaked, wind kicked up, and a tiny stream of water began to flow around the mage's feet.

The shadow dragon swatted her away with his tail like a horse flicking at a fly. She was knocked off her feet and slid through the mud.

He only laughed harder. "Did you honestly think you could control someone as powerful as me?" he demanded. He didn't wait for an answer from the dazed mage, who struggled to lift herself out of the mud.

Instead, Boneclaw lunged at Kylara and before she could so much as take a breath, his skeletal form drove into her. His single long back claw was extended and stabbed into her chest as if her diamond scales were nothing but bologna.

She screamed in pain as she was thrust back to pass through a portal. In the next moment, she splashed into a filthy pond surrounded by cypress trees. She was still in pain from the claw digging into her chest.

Boneclaw's weight settled heavily on her before she could right herself. "Your aunt brought me back because she had dreams that she was too weak to realize." He caught her by the throat with his other claw and pushed her head back into the water.

"I will not waste my time in this realm as she has done," he declared as he continued to apply pressure so she sank into the mud. "I will take your powers and your magic for myself. I will absorb these gifts you have no right to possess and will use them to purge this world of the insipid, disloyal dragons who have made friends out of mages instead of slaves. Thanks to you, young Kylara the mage with a stolen dragon's name, I will take every power of every dragon in this world. I will start with you but will never stop. I no longer tire. I no longer sleep. I will not tarry until I have the power to burn away the filth that the Steel Dragon has introduced to this world. You will die in this pool, Kylara, and you will be remembered as the child who sacrificed herself to make a god!"

Boneclaw forced her head underwater and Kylara began to drown.

CHAPTER THIRTY-SIX

Kylara was trapped beneath the surface of the water. She could feel the roots growing at the bottom of the pond pulling at her as they tried to drag her deeper. When she told them to stop, they hesitated and halted their encirclement of her limbs. That proved to be all the time she needed.

Suddenly, Boneclaw's weight was gone. She surged out of the water as her mom yanking the shadow dragon out of the pixie realm by his wings. She had already ripped one of them with her claws and had her jaws locked on the other. Behind her, the portal he had created shimmered in the air, still open. Her mom had come to save her.

"Foolish mortal!" the ancient dragon railed before he swung his tail into her face. The force of the blow knocked her teeth loose from his wing but he did not injure her. Diamond beat bone.

"Kylara—this way!" Tanya shouted.

She didn't need to be told twice. In seconds, she raced through the portal and onto the land where she grew up.

"I thought that seemed too easy," Boneclaw said. Six more portals opened. He laughed as chimeras of bone poured through each one. He must have been massing them in other parts of the swamp, waiting for this moment. She was coming to realize that he had vastly outmaneuvered them.

Back in what Kylara considered the 'normal' dimension, the first thing she did was to bring the rain clouds. Tanya would need the water.

Already, Karl, Tanya, Jasmine, and Sam worked in coordination to knock the larger skeletons to the ground so Tanya could bind them with plant roots and drag them beneath the surface of the earth.

Hester Diamantine was busy with Boneclaw himself, but she was not doing well. She struck him constantly with blows that Kylara knew from experience were powerful enough to break skin and sever flesh. Unfortunately, he had neither. He let Diamantine hit what paltry amount of desiccated flesh he had, completely oblivious to the pain.

"You have no place in this world!" Hester growled between strikes and dodges.

"Which is why I plan to make one," Boneclaw replied and slashed her across the chest with the black claw. A line of blood—starkly red against her cool blue diamond scales—appeared, although she did not let it slow her. All she did was spit and keep fighting.

"Ky, we got the skeletons!" Tanya shouted and forced a thorny shrub of some kind to lash out and bind what looked like a buffalo with the skull of a lion. "Help your mom!"

Kylara didn't need to be told twice. She waited for Boneclaw to lunge at Diamantine, then struck decisively and reduced some of the bones in his tail to powder.

He turned on her, a cruel rictus on his strange, half-skeletal face. "I wondered if you would let me slaughter your mother or if you wanted to try your hand against a true foe."

Boneclaw leaped at her but before he struck, he puffed into a cloud of dark, inky smoke. She'd had practice fighting dragons with shadow powers, however, so opened her mouth and unleashed a great beam of light on the shadow dragon. He coalesced in the light and collided with her diamond-tipped claws. She ripped savagely at the veins and few pieces of muscle and flesh he had in an attempt to rip his spirit free of his bones.

"I got this, mom!" she shouted. "Help my friends!"

Her mother didn't answer in words. She surged toward the skeleton of what had to be a pterodactyl and forced it to the ground, where Karl proceeded to bind its ungainly wings with his shadow powers so Tanya could finish it off.

"Ah, the arrogance of youth," Boneclaw said before he lunged at her again. He tried the same tactic he had used earlier and turned into a dark cloud as he barreled toward her. She responded as she had before and released a beam of light into the very center of the cloud that made up the shadow dragon's body.

She missed, unfortunately, as her adversary somehow flowed around her beam of light. Claws emerged from the smoke, and one of them—the black one—speared through her shoulder. She was able to pivot and send Boneclaw past her so she didn't end up pinned to the ground, but it was a close call.

"You do know I killed Lumos? One of the greatest dragon warriors to ever live?" Boneclaw growled and lunged toward her again. She retaliated with her dark powers and threw up a hundred strands of darkness in front of the black cloud that approached. He flowed effortlessly through them. Again, he materialized seconds before he powered into her. This time, he didn't even bother to try for a lethal blow. Instead, he stuck his black claw through her forearm. Seeing it go in one side was not so bad, but when it came out the other, Kylara had to scream.

"This is fun!" he said when her scream ceased and she was back on her feet. "What other powers do you have?"

She roared defiance and thunder boomed overhead. Lighting surged inside the giant thundercloud above them before it finally lanced out and struck Boneclaw. It did not hit him, though. He turned to smoke—all except for the black claw—which he left planted in the soil. Lighting struck it and flowed into the earth and in the next moment, he was back and swung his claw across her face.

"Your aunt almost made me believe you would be some kind of change in the world. I see now how wrong she was. To think that you possess the power to absorb the powers of other dragons and you waste it on these parlor tricks?"

Kylara made her entire body flash with light, which was enough to force him off her. Hoping this was the edge she needed, she pushed her attack while her skin still glowed. Boneclaw didn't seem to be able to slip into shadow as easily while she reflected the light and he couldn't vanish to shadow when he struck. He remained a skeleton and matched her blow for blow. Normally, she would be more than willing to brawl with almost anyone. Her diamond skin gave her a huge advantage in hand-to-hand combat, but this was not a normal opponent.

If her strikes failed to break a bone, they were useless. The ancient dragon felt no pain. He suffered nothing like nerve damage and the only way to hurt him was to break one of his bones, which was not easy. He knew this and let her waste time and energy beating his mostly visible skeleton. This kept the fight in close quarters, where he could poke and stab at her as and when he wished to do so.

"How long can you keep this up, Kylara?" Boneclaw asked. He wasn't even winded. "Your friends are overwhelmed and the sun is setting."

A glance confirmed that he wasn't lying about either point. The sun was already kissing the top of the mountains. They had maybe fifteen minutes of sunlight left. Already, the shadows had begun to creep out from the chaparral that she had made regrow.

Hester and her friends were vastly outnumbered. Before, Hester and Sam had been airborne to knock down any of the skeletons that could fly so the other three could finish them off. But the sheer number of monsters had forced them to change tactics. Now on the ground, they fought tooth and claw against hundreds of revenants. Tanya was between them and buried those she could with her plant powers. Karl and Jasmine—fully understanding how important Tanya was to all this—focused all their attention on keeping her safe.

"If you want me," Kylara said to Boneclaw, "fine. I'll follow you to the pixie realm, but let them go!"

"I want everything, you foolish girl. I simply need your powers first," he replied.

Which was just as well. She was not about to sacrifice herself anyway. While she had been talking, she had opened a portal high on the mountain, directly beneath one of her favorite—and one of the largest—piles of boulders that dotted the mountainside. The boulders had fallen through the strange sky of the pixie dimension and gained speed as they fell ever closer to the swamp beneath them. They never reached the murky water, however. Before they could, she opened a gate directly above Boneclaw's head.

Boulders poured out of it. The first caught him directly on the skull. The next pounded into his shoulder blades. He didn't cry out but simply planted his feet and let the avalanche crush him—or attempt to do so. Despite the fact that each of the rocks was large enough to flatten a horse, the ancient dragon shrugged them off.

"I was waiting to see if you could use the gates," Boneclaw said as he strode toward one of his open gates. "And I'm not surprised that you wasted even more of your potential. That, at least, is a power I've already mastered."

To prove his point, he strode to one of the portals into the swamp part of the pixie realm, grasped the edge with his claws, and pulled hard. The gate ripped even wider as if reality were nothing more than a piece of butcher paper holding back the home team at a football game.

Boneclaw cackled with glee as water poured from the gate and flooded the sand, dirt, and grit of the desert. He wasn't infallible, then, and didn't seem to realize that Kylara and Tanya could use this water to fuel more plants to bind his skeletons.

Unfortunately, the water was already fueling something else. It spread from the portal and moved across the surface of the gravel driveway. In its wake, strange plants sprouted that had no place in the desert. The fiddleheads of ferns battled the thick, waxy leaves of orchids for space as vines popped up from the water and began to claw for somewhere to grow.

Carnivorous plants—their flowers covered in balls of sticky resin—of a size that begged the question of what they could not eat, rose and stretched to locate the infinite space in the desert. After these first heralds of the swamp came the true denizens. Tiny cypress trees—almost indistinguishable from ferns at first—emerged from this thick groundcover and reached into the rain. Their trunks thickened and strengthened as they grew shaggy with bark.

Water flowed past Kylara's feet and the ground beneath her changed as well. No longer was it the hard-packed earth of the southwest desert atop massive slabs of granite. The pixie realm had changed all that. Her feet slipped in the mud. Roots from the swamp plants snatched at her claws, her tail, or anything they could reach to slowly and inexorably dragging her under.

She called upon her plant powers and shared her magic with the plants as she told them to stop. To her immense relief, they listened.

In the next moment, however, the skeletons attacked.

Kylara hadn't been paying attention to the clash of dragon versus bone taking place all around her, but when one of the skeletal revenants collided with her and shoved her sideways and into the mud, her attention had a way of focusing on the animated bones.

She landed hard and smacked her head on a mid-sized boulder that had clattered off Boneclaw's shoulders. It did far more damage to her and struck her head so hard the world spun.

The young dragon mage reeled as she tried to regain her bearings. Her mom fought against some massively oversized ape-like skeleton. Hester managed to pick apart its laughable defenses, but she took too much time. While she waited for the ape to attack, something like the skeleton of a bobcat with too many claws jumped on her back, followed by two more. She shook furiously like a dog trying to rid itself of pool water, but the creatures held fast, even when Karl snatched them with his ropes of dark magic.

Sam and Jasmine were doing better. He went toe-to-toe with a bear of such size that polar bears would have been embarrassed to weigh in against it. He did well enough but even in Kylara's dizzy state, she could see that he wasn't able to dodge very well. Every time the bear tried to slash his flesh, a shimmering blob of energy appeared and blocked the attack—Jasmine at work. Sam finally toppled the bear and Tanya—waiting and ready—forced thorny vines to wind around it and pull it into the dirt.

Kylara tried to roll over—her head was pounding—and scramble to her feet. She had time to see her Aunt Cassandra, also back on her feet and in the fight again, before Boneclaw swiped across her arm with his wicked black claw.

"A marvelous turn of events, is it not?" The shadow dragon sneered at the young dragon mage as he attacked ferociously and forced her to back deeper into the swamp water. She had difficulty defending herself and discovered that she normally didn't have to dodge. Her scales were too tough to cut through. Boneclaw's stolen claw made her diamond skin ineffective, though, which meant she had to fight more cautiously. It was not something she was particularly good at.

"I thought I would have to get you in the pixie realm to take your powers, but no." Boneclaw created another portal and more swamp water poured out. This time, it ran down the hill in front of her house and transformed it from a field of wildflowers to a fern-choked waterfall that emptied into a stagnant pond instead of a dry arroyo.

The shadow-dragon spun and used his body to add momentum to his tail strike to drive it into her. She knew how to fight dragons, however, and dodged his tail, calculated the length of his reach easily, and stepped into the waiting coils of a serpent made of bone.

Thick coils of pointed ribs immediately entwined around her to bind her and squeezed her arms and legs against her body so she fell in the mud. Furious at being duped, she lashed out with dark magic to shred the monster from within.

Boneclaw only laughed as he sent a wave of skeletal creatures washing over her. They slashed at her with claws, bit at her with teeth, and beat her with bones whose purpose was no doubt supposed to be more innocent. None of the claws or teeth could get through her diamond skin but that didn't matter. Their purpose was not to make her bleed so much as to hold on. They continued to climb on top of her and those that couldn't find purchase simply clambered onto their undead compatriots. With the weight of each creature, Kylara sank deeper and deeper into the mud.

Through the bones of a thousand bodies, she saw him. Even in this storm of skeletons, Boneclaw stood out. He was the only skeleton with black veins stretched across his bones and pieces of muscle adding definition to the bone structure he had been reduced to in death.

He struck through the massed creatures. His black bone claw launched out like a lance to pierce her in the chest and drag a scream of pain from her. That didn't bother her nearly as much as the cool sensation of the mud she was once again sinking into.

Despite her constant struggles, the increasing weight of the packed monsters continued to force her into the muck.

"Where were we?" Boneclaw asked as his minions parted so he could look her in the eyes before he took everything away from her. "Ah, yes. With your power, I will be all-powerful or something like that? Let's cut to the part where you die, shall we?"

"There's one problem with that," Kylara said before her face was forced underwater.

He smiled indulgently. "And what is that, little dragon of such wasted potential?"

"You forgot that my aunt is a way meaner bitch than my mom."

He had barely enough time to look up, which she counted as a huge victory. There was something incredibly rewarding about the dragon's mostly desiccated face as he watched his pile of skeletons being ripped away by a tornado that then lifted him into the air as if he were nothing but a piece of trash.

CHAPTER THIRTY-SEVEN

"How dare you disrespect the mage who restored you to this realm!" Cassandra screamed, her voice pitched perfectly to be heard over the roar of the tornado her wind elemental spun around Boneclaw.

"Release me!" he responded, his tone edged with fury.

She did not dignify his answer with a response. Instead, she raised her hands high, then brought them down in a swift motion.

The air elemental obeyed. The ancient dragon rose higher in the column of spinning air and suddenly, the tornado was gone and the resurrected dragon seemed to hang motionlessly beneath bruised clouds.

The air elemental had not vanished, however, and merely repositioned itself. Before he could spread his ragged wings—honestly, Kylara wasn't sure if they could even hold air, given the condition they were in—a column of air punched through the clouds and struck the dragon with sufficient power to force him hundreds of feet back to the earth.

A half a second before he landed, a pillar of rock rose to meet him like a hammer. The force of the blow not only cracked half the skeleton's ribs but careened him upward and back into the clutches of the air spirit.

"Kylara, are you all right?" her aunt asked and turned from the action to look at her. Despite being free of the pile of skeletons that had climbed on her, she was still stuck in the mud. She wasn't sure if it was skeletons or the roots of plants that held her, but either way, they didn't want to let her go.

"We'll get Kylara free," Tanya said to Cassandra and immediately focused on the plants around her friend. Karl was in place too and used his shadow tendrils to haul the dragon mage out while Sam, Jasmine, and Diamantine defended them against the skeletons that had fallen from the tornado and now began to knit themselves together again.

"Very well," Cassandra said, her tone almost polite until she turned to Boneclaw who had once more been driven onto a table of stone that had appeared in time to crack more of his bones.

He pushed himself weakly to stand. Even from her position, Kylara could see that the dragon was severely injured. Most of his ribs had been reduced to broken nubs edging his spine. One of his front legs was completely gone—not the one with the black claw, unfortunately. His tail looked like something a hamster might be proud of but it was most certainly an embarrassment to a dragon.

"You have lied to me!" the old mage shouted. "You have not been bound by my voice at all. You treacherous, scheming reptile!"

Boneclaw sneered at her and made it very clear that he didn't appreciate the insults. He crouched in preparation to leap but before he could, the earthen platform he stood on molded around his feet and locked them in place.

The shadow dragon roared and Cassandra smirked. "I do not like being made a fool of," she explained as she spun and twisted her arms in strange patterns.

"But you make it eas—"

Before he could finish his petty insult, a torrent of water shot into his face. It didn't drown him but it drowned his words out, which seemed to piss the dragon off fairly effectively.

The water elemental flowed through the skeleton. At first, Kylara thought that all this did was to prove that water elementals weren't particularly useful against beings that couldn't breathe. She soon noticed, however, that even this attack managed to pull away tiny bits of bone.

"That should do it!" Tanya said as she encouraged the roots around and beneath the dragon mage to raise her to the surface.

She'd barely finished the words when Kylara was released. She joined her friends and her mother and they fell into the familiar rhythm of fighting together. Diamantine and Sam brought skeletons down. Kylara and Karl bound them, and Tanya —and sometimes Kylara—buried them with plant roots. All the while, Jasmine ran interference, protecting the fighters from the undead that breached their perimeter.

Compared to fighting Boneclaw, it was almost mindless. It was dangerous, yes, and demanding, but the skeletons essentially did the same thing. As a result, even though she was involved in a battle against what must have still been over a hundred revenants, she could watch her aunt deal with Boneclaw.

The torrent of water no longer washed over the shadow creature. Still locked to the table, the skeletal dragon stood and spluttered like a wet cat. He looked more streamlined now. Instead of like a skeleton covered in strips of flesh and veins, he merely looked like an extremely skinny dragon. Almost all the exposed bone had been washed away. All that was left was covered in veins or traces of meat. Rather than making him look weaker though, it made him look deadlier—as if only the parts most necessary for cruelty were still attached to his nightmarish body.

He was still trapped in the stone, however, and try as he might, he couldn't pull free.

"I told you that we would never hurt Kylara," Cassandra chastised the dragon like he was a dog who had gotten into the garbage. "If I knew you were planning to drown my niece, I would have done this a long time ago, Boneclaw."

"You should have," he growled as the tiniest sliver of shadow reached from the very tip of a mountain, all the way across the Diamantine homestead, up the platform the earth elemental had raised from the earth and used to bind Boneclaw, and onto his claw.

In one moment, a dragon made of bone and darkness was bound by Aunt Cassandra and in the next, he was nothing but shadow.

"Oh no, you don't!" Cassandra cried and gestured for her air elemental to lift the billowing cloud of darkness into the air again.

But the wind did nothing to dissipate the smoke that flowed inexorably into the shadow of the mountain.

"Impossible!" she blurted.

"These clouds are not made of air any more than they are made of matter," Boneclaw intoned from somewhere inside his cloud of darkness. "You cannot blow me away any more than you can blow a shadow away."

A plinth of stone erupted from the earth where Boneclaw appeared to be. The dragon merely laughed. Another thrust of stone was followed by another, but each of these passed through him as easily as they would have a mist.

"I will make this right, Kylara," Aunt Cassandra said, turned to her niece, and made eye contact through the chaos of bones shattering around them. She reached into her pocket and pulled out what appeared to be a tiny tinder box. When she opened it, a flame leapt forth and moved on the wind until it landed on a recently regrown bush.

"No!" Diamantine screamed, but she made no effort to stop the fire elemental. She couldn't as she was entangled with an aberration of bone put together in the general shape of an octopus. As the flames began to grow, she ripped off its tentacles one by one.

"It'll be okay, mom!" Kylara said, as much for her mom's benefit as Cassandra's. "Tanya and I can regrow everything when this is over."

"When?" Boneclaw laughed. "When? Do you think this is a when and not an if I decide to let you all live?"

"Stop talking and come stand where I can see you," Cassandra commanded and gestured for her fire elemental to obey.

It leapt forward and moved from bush to scrubby tree to clump of wildflowers, growing as it did so. In the end, it wasn't a creature of flame that attacked Boneclaw but a raging inferno of a beast.

And it didn't even need to touch him.

As soon as it drew close, the light emanating from the fire spirit—far brighter than the soft light of the remaining daylight—forced the ancient dragon to materialize out of his shadow state.

He cursed and blasted the fire spirit with his fire breath but it did nothing to the elemental. Kylara didn't think the beings of pure essence laughed but it certainly seemed like the fire spirit did so as it surged at their enemy.

The ancient dragon held his forearms up to defend himself. At that moment, the earth spirit launched out of the earth and took the form of a wall that powered into Boneclaw's hands and face.

Unfortunately, it also cut him off from the light from the fire elemental.

He immediately puffed into a cloud of shadow and flowed into the dirt.

What followed was difficult to track, even though Kylara knew what was happening. She focused on putting as many skeletons in the ground while the earth elemental and the revenant tried to outmaneuver each other. Even from her position, however, she could tell that the earth spirit wasn't winning. Boulders thrust through the earth in a dozen different places, followed by pillars of dirt. The soil split and rejoined itself. Boneclaw laughed at all of it.

"What? Don't you know how to hunt a shadow?"

The pattern of boulders and pillars of dirt launching out of the ground shifted. While before, it had been in a field that was mostly empty, the ancient dragon now led the battle into the mass of skeletons. The earth elemental didn't mind, of course. It merely continued to thrust pillars of stone and dirt in an attempt to destroy the wisps of blackness that Kylara couldn't even see more times than not.

Finally, Boneclaw seemed to tire and he solidified not ten feet away from the young dragon mage. The earth spirit was ready and drove a massive plinth of stone out of the ground and into the shadow dragon. It shattered ribs that he wasn't supposed to have anymore and that he had regrown.

"It's a trap!" Sam yelled far too late.

The shadow dragon had moved the black, crystalline claw to the tip of his tail, also newly reforged. He'd used scraps from the defeated bone creatures to restore himself and now applied the black claw to slice through the base of the stone pillar that had only moments before been used to pulverize his ribs. It cut through the rock like it was made of cheese. In an instant, he disappeared and reappeared at the edge of the stone. He pushed it into the waiting hands of his skeleton minions.

"It's in there, no?" Boneclaw shouted at Cassandra as he carved off pieces of the pillar, first from one end and then the other. The core became smaller and smaller until it was nothing more than the size of a baseball. A skeleton caught it and ran into the pixie dimension.

"No!" Cassandra screamed furiously.

"You should have been more careful about how loudly you speak about your theorems," Boneclaw snapped like a disgruntled teacher. "An earth spirit is only as good as the earth they're connected to."

"Burn him!" Cassandra shouted and the fire spirit attacked. It hadn't avoided the fight with the earth elemental and merely increased its strength. Now, it took the form of a dragon, flapped wings of flame, and struck with white-hot claws.

Boneclaw shrieked and retreated into the swampy water that had now swallowed the area that had been desert not ten minutes before. He exhaled a blast of fire that Kylara thought was a waste of energy until she noticed that he had burned away all the plants between him and the fire spirit.

"You are not safe from me in there. I will bind your spirit to a toad and torture you for a decade!" Cassandra threatened.

The water spirit burst out of a pool behind Boneclaw. It surged toward him but was too slow. The ancient dragon dodged and moved closer to the fire spirit.

"Aunt Cassandra! It's another trick!" Kylara shouted, but she could tell that this fight was no longer in her aunt's hands.

The two spirits didn't have the understanding of how to work together that they needed. When their adversary dodged a spray of water from the water elemental, it extinguished much of the flame elemental.

Boneclaw took the opportunity to leap from the water and grasp the fire elemental in his claws. The flames blackened his bones and made what flesh he had burn, but the dragon felt no pain. He and the elemental stabbed and clawed at each other before they tumbled into the pond. The fire spirit vanished.

Cassandra looked afraid now. Her eyes were wide and her face gleamed with sweat as she tried to tell her air elemental what to do next.

"It's too late, you pathetic mage," the revenant said and changed easily to his gaseous form each time a gust of wind threatened to make him airborne.

The water spirit also proved to be ineffective. He was too good and too slippery and air and water couldn't hold shadow. Earth and fire might have been able to, but he had spent his indentured servitude dissecting the nature of the elements that he couldn't simply slip away from.

Cassandra wasn't ready to give up yet, though. One hand was wrapped in electricity and the other in ice. All around her, pebbles and brush began to levitate as if whatever power poured off her was more powerful than gravity.

Unfortunately, she never had a chance to show her combat skills.

Boneclaw simply slipped inside her defenses and ran her through the chest with his stolen black claw. The monster didn't even bother to pierce her heart. Instead, it was a still living Cassandra that he lifted off the ground like he was preparing for a barbecue.

"Bastard," the mage managed before she spat blood in his face.

"But I missed your heart. Can't you use your healing power to heal? Oh, that's right. You're nothing but trash."

He grinned as he throttled her and tossed her lifeless body over his shoulder like it was nothing but a worn-out rag doll.

The elements mourned her passing. A tornado formed around her body and lifted her a few feet off the ground as an earthquake shook the world beneath everyone's feet. A platform rose, a resting place for the mage. The tornado was then sucked into the air, torn apart by its own forces no longer animated by an air elemental. Water surged from the wet ground to wash the dirt and blood from the mage's body to leave her looking clean with slicked back, wet hair. In the next moment, calm descended around them and Kylara understood that the elementals were gone, exactly like her aunt.

All that remained of Cassandra was the fury in her niece's chest.

CHAPTER THIRTY-EIGHT

Kylara powered through the skeletons she was fighting as if they were nothing but confetti. Bone splintered and sprayed as her diamond scales made short work of the revenants. She was enraged. Boneclaw had killed her only blood relation and he would pay—and not tomorrow or sometime in the future. She would claim her debt now.

He laughed as she approached, arrogant jerk that he was. She blasted him in the chest with a beam of light, then called down a bolt of lightning from the storm clouds above. It struck him exactly where her beam of light had, directly in his solidified chest.

The shadow dragon catapulted back with the sound of a thunderclap. Even as he hurtled in free-flight, he tried to dematerialize into his shadow form.

Kylara had no intention to let that happen. "Are you going somewhere?" she shouted and seared him with another beam of light that forced his body to take shape seconds before he collided with a boulder. Even though she heard bones crunch, he didn't cry out in pain.

He didn't double back to attack either, though. Instead, he tried to turn into his insubstantial cloud of darkness. She blasted him with light again but this time, it didn't work. He had already flowed out of her path and currently forced his clouds of darkness into a crack in the stone.

She could not let him escape. Spurred on by fury, she lashed out with tendrils of dark energy. A hundred threads of darkness worked into the crack that her adversary attempted to flee into. To her shock and delight, she discovered that she could feel his shadow form with her shadow power. But why not? She could feel Karl's powers. Boneclaw's couldn't be that different.

Without wasting time to think this through, she wound the tendrils around part of him and dragged him out of the crack in the earth like a fisherman fighting a shark.

"Are you so desperate to die?" Boneclaw demanded angrily as he became substantial again and lunged into her. She had anticipated his attack with his piercing black claw and blocked his strike with her tail. He was unable to pierce her scales, although he certainly tried with the rest of his appendages. Kylara felt herself bruise beneath her diamond scales but she could weather those.

"Only because it would be such an honor to take you with me," she replied and lashed him to her with tendrils of dark energy. He tried to pull away and she used the opportunity to shatter his regrown ribs with methodical and calculated blows.

He laughed. "Hold on to your stolen powers while you can, mage scum. While we fight, your friends and family die."

Kylara thought he was bluffing, but she couldn't risk it. She glanced over her shoulder and scowled when she realized he was telling the truth. The purple and blue sky of dusk was riddled with holes into the pixie realm. There were already too many for her to count, and more were opening at every second.

More skeletons issued from each one—small ones in the

shapes of rodents and reptiles and big ones that would have made any paleontology museum proud. Some creatures were familiar but many weren't. Humans, dragons, dwarves, and other bipedal, big-skulled beings that Kylara could only guess at all poured into the swampy water and the choking vines that had begun to take over this little patch of desert.

"I don't want to lose this world to the malaise of this pixie swamp and the beast that sleeps beneath it, but I will if you're unwilling to sacrifice yourself!" Boneclaw whispered before he slipped out of her clutches.

Kylara cursed herself but she let him go. There were too many skeletons and too many of her loved ones fighting below.

She hurried to them, hating herself for it but also knowing that she couldn't lose anyone else. Already, she had lost her Aunt Cassandra, the only blood relative she had and possibly the only mage who would ever be able to teach her the full extent of what their bloodline could do. She landed beside her mom and fell into the familiar series of moves she and Hester had run through a thousand times.

Diamantine dispatched a mammoth skeleton while Kylara battled against something like a huge beetle made of skulls. She defeated it easily and used her shadow tendrils to rip its carapace of human heads apart. The victory felt empty, however. She had let Boneclaw get away. None of this was her fault, she reminded herself. It was his. He had always known he could open more gates and had held that power in reserve in case the tide turned against him. With sly intelligence, he had played his cards closer to his chest than she had thought possible and because of it, she was stuck fighting his minions while he fled to regroup.

"I thought these skeletons would be gone when you beat him," Karl shouted. He was tangled with a spider made of bone that constantly snapped his threads of dark magic with precise clips from the claws at the end of its eight legs.

"I didn't beat him," she said and shifted her focus to a group of human skeletons that threw rocks at her.

"Kylara, you have to. We got this," Jasmine said.

"I can't abandon you. You need my plant powers."

"We don't, honestly," the mage insisted.

Kylara was about to point out that they most certainly did when a great pillar of light surged from the sky to illuminate Sam Lumos. She expected the greatest blast of light she had ever seen to be unleashed from his eyes, his mouth, and hands, and hell, based on the size of the pillar of light, she expected his hair follicles to become weapons.

But rather than use his powers to attack, Sam placed his hands on Tanya's shoulders and his light flowed into her.

The young dragon raised her arms and the landscape responded. A thousand plants erupted from beneath the swamp. Desert flowers, mesquite, cactus, and a dozen varieties of thorny shrubs grew through the mire and grasped thousands of bones.

Even the airborne skeletons weren't safe from this attack. Some of the plants grew flowers that fell away, thickened quickly into seeds, and rocketed skyward where they sprouted the moment they came into contact with a drop water of still falling from the rainclouds Kylara had summoned. These aerial plants grew white roots that latched onto bone as greedily as most plants reached into soil.

What followed would likely be immortalized in the fossil record for millions of years. A great mass of plants and skeletons plummeted from the sky to crush those already on the ground and create massive mats of vegetation and bone.

And yet the fight still wouldn't end. More of the undead continued to pour out of the gates.

"Kylara! You still have a chance." Her mom pointed up the mountainside.

The young dragon mage could not immediately explain what

she saw next, but that didn't stop her from taking flight and soaring up the mountain.

Boneclaw was part of it, that much was obvious because of the billowing clouds of blackness, but she could only guess at the identity of the other figure.

It appeared to be a human male—or mostly human anyway—but dragon wings sprouted from his back and a tail ended in a barb. What arrested her the most about the figure, though, was that he appeared to stop the shadow dragon. Every time he tried to dematerialize and vanish into the stone of the mountain, the figure lashed out with a limb that ended in an amalgamation of a claw and a human hand. What was shocking—what made her mouth go dry—was that this being was able to take hold of Boneclaw's clouds of shadow.

He was able to grasp his clouds as if he were nothing but a plastic bag or an old piece of cloth. The ancient dragon could tear away from the hold of this half-human, half-dragon, but he couldn't get far enough away before he was snatched again.

"So you're not the pathetic little coward I took you for after all," the shadow dragon raged at his opponent. "To think that all it took was losing your power over bones to grow a spine."

"This is for what you did to Cassandra!" the figure replied and lunged after Boneclaw, using his wings to carry him thirty feet before he powered into the cloud of shadow and deflated it into a dragon like he had crashed through a tent and knocked it to the ground.

This exchange meant that the figure could only be one person—Galen! It had to be. Cassandra had said he'd been essential in bringing Boneclaw back, and Kylara had only gone on her wild goose chase because of him. But what had happened to him? Why did it look like he was trapped in mid-transformation?

It was great that he managed to slow their adversary, but if he was there to help, why not stop the skeletons with his powers? In the next moment, the realization of what Boneclaw had said, along with what he had been planning to do to her set in. The ancient dragon had taken Galen's powers for his own and left him as this half-human, half-dragon mongrel.

"Did she give you this power?" Boneclaw fumed as first one clawed arm, then another pulled itself from the mess of clouds beneath his opponent's feet. Even Galen's presence on top of him was enough to hold him.

Kylara drew closer and pulled on her inner magic. She would only have one chance at this and had to make it count.

"You gave me this power, you stupid old fart!" Galen yelled at Boneclaw as he stamped on the smoke beneath him like a child attempting to destroy a nest of ants. "When you took my power, you left a…a mark on me! I can feel you, you sick monster. I can feel what you did to me. You can't escape."

"The Steel Dragon and her mongrel horde will be here soon. Even those morons won't fail to notice the magic here, but I suppose I shall have to make time for you to die before I depart." Boneclaw growled belligerently and knocked Galen aside with the back side of one of his claws. In doing so, he gave Kylara exactly the opportunity she'd been waiting for.

She plunged from her slightly higher position and ignited every diamond scale she had with light magic. As she plummeted, a hundred scales began to glow with blinding white light, then a thousand, then ten thousand. She sparkled like a nuclear-powered chandelier as she fell directly toward Boneclaw.

"This again?" the ancient dragon fumed, unable to slip away into shadow because of the light but also unafraid of fighting Kylara in hand-to-hand combat.

She bulldozed into him and ripped into his chest with hooked talons. With her tail wound around him, she bit his neck with her teeth and refused to let go.

"You do realize that all I have to do is open a portal and my revenants will peel your dead corpse from mine?" Boneclaw snapped and moved his black claw into position to puncture her heart.

"It's my turn to open a gate," she said and opened a portal beneath him. Tangled and unable to free themselves, both she and her adversary plunged into another dimension.

CHAPTER THIRTY-NINE

Once again, it was the nothingness that struck Kylara. There were no smells of desert plants and rain there, no odor of rotten swamp, and not a trace of bone dust.

There was, quite simply nothing at all. That wouldn't work, though. She knew that she couldn't defeat Boneclaw in a vacuum. Those weren't her powers so, while he fought to free himself from her, she used her weather powers to bring air and water droplets through her portal into this bubble in the void.

"You have no idea what you've done!" the shadow dragon shouted and managed to break free because she was distracted by redirecting air. Half-dragon and half-shadow, he partly swam and partly flew toward the only landmark in the void—a rip in the darkness that showed the purple sky and clouds that served as a backdrop for the battle left behind in the desert of New Mexico.

She closed the gate and plunged them into darkness.

Boneclaw roared and lashed out. At first, she thought it was nothing more than a poorly aimed attack, but then she realized that he must be trying to escape. "There's nothing beyond the bubble we're in. The pixies told me as much. But you know that, don't you? You were trapped in this non-place when you tried to ruin Kristen Hall's peace talks."

Kylara changed into her true form—her human form—and used her weather powers to make wind that righted herself so she faced him. She made her skin begin to glow. Not much and certainly not an attack, only enough to illuminate the claws and billowing clouds of darkness that made up Boneclaw's shadow form.

It was funny in an oddly perverse way. In New Mexico, he had seemed to be made of pure darkness—something darker than even the shadow powers she had taken from Karl. But there, compared to the absolute nothingness of the void all around him, he was merely a shadow.

Boneclaw's skull and twisted lips appeared in the middle of his churning, billowing clouds of darkness. "This was your grand plan?" He snarled disdainfully. "You thought to take me—a shadow dragon—to a place of perfect darkness? Have you changed your mind, then, and wish to sacrifice yourself to someone more worthy of your powers?"

"You're not the only shadow dragon here." She lashed out with tendrils of darkness that plunged into his amorphous body and forced it to coalesce into bone again.

"Your powers are but the darkness of early evening, while mine are the black of nightmares."

"Maybe," Kylara agreed and pulled Boneclaw in different directions to force more bones to drop out of him like a chemical reaction. "But I'm not only a shadow dragon." She called upon her light powers and unleashed a beam directly into his smug face. The light burned away most of his lips to leave little but ragged shreds connected to his skull. "I'm a light dragon too."

"What you are is a thieving mage!" Her adversary growled in fury and lashed out with his tail.

She let the blow land and didn't remember until too late that he had put the black, crystalline claw at the tip of his tail. Her thigh burned where it stabbed her, but she caught hold of it with both hands, wrapped it in tendrils of darkness, and held it tightly.

"Thanks for the reminder, by the way," she said through clenched teeth. "I am merely a mage."

It was easy to make her eyes blaze with light as she had seen Sam do. She released that energy into Boneclaw to sear some of the black veins away and reveal the brittle bone beneath.

"Do you want my powers? Here they are!" She took her hands away from the claw in her leg but kept it bound with her shadow power. Before he could react, she grasped his tail, made her hands heat with the power she'd taken from Ruby Firedrake, and turned the part of the appendage that connected to the claw into nothing but ash.

Boneclaw screamed and pulled away. He attempted to strike but she called on the air and moisture she'd brought into the bubble to release the energy that had been building in hidden clouds. A bolt of lightning lanced out and cracked toward the shadow dragon with blinding energy.

He dodged easily and laughed as he did so. "Lightning?" He sneered at her. "Do you think you could defeat me with lightning? Do you know how many weather dragons I have killed?"

"I didn't miss because I wasn't aiming for you."

Boneclaw turned to see the angry blister on the bubble behind them. She had never seen a skull show shock before, but one did so now. The paltry muscles he had where his eyebrows should be seemed to raise in alarm and the ragged remnants of lips yanked into a terrified grimace. "No, you idiot! You'll kill us both."

Kylara ignored him, and commanded the wind and water vapor in the space to move faster. As the molecules brushed past each other, their electrons reacted in jerky movements to charge the air with electricity. Lightning was usually hard to control. It jumped whenever it had an opportunity to do so, but in this place of nothing, there was nowhere for it to go except where she directed it.

The ancient dragon wasn't defeated yet, however. He rose, looked into her eyes, and roared. Kylara stared curiously at him. It seemed like he had expended a great deal of energy but had accomplished nothing. Confused but undeterred, he roared again.

"Are you done?" she asked.

"How is this possible?" He fumed. "You should be a whimpering mess on the floor. You should be slitting your wrists to escape me. No mage can resist my aura."

"What about Aunt Cassandra?" she demanded and withdrew the pendant she always wore around her neck—one identical to the one her aunt had always worn and which was intended to block dragon auras.

"Impossible!"

"This is for her," Kylara said.

Leaving him no opportunity to ask what she meant, she brought the lightning.

Boneclaw didn't dodge this time but took the bolt full in the chest in a desperate attempt to stop it from striking the wall. He failed, however, and it didn't stop but seared through him as she had directed it to do.

It struck the weakened place on the wall and blasted a hole in the bubble that protected them from the void.

The air in the room was immediately sucked toward the hole as if they were in a spaceship and the void outside was simply outer space. But space had stars. There was nothing out there.

Boneclaw screamed as he was sucked back, his billowing form not impervious to the hunger of the void. He thudded into the hole and his shadow form was suddenly a weakness instead of a strength. It was sucked through almost instantly so only his skull and his two front limbs remained. They grasped the edges of the bubble and held on desperately as air rushed past him.

"If even one of my bones survives, if only a speck of me makes it back, I will end you, mage!"

"My name is Kylara Diamantine!" she said, took the form of a dragon, and let the wind suck her into Boneclaw. She made impact and her diamond-encrusted body thrust the pitiful remnants of bones that were all that remained of him into the void. He didn't fall into the distance or plunge into a liquid. He simply vanished and the utter darkness swallowed his cries as if they had never existed.

Before Kylara could meet the same fate, she opened a gate directly in her path and fell through it and back to a place she knew as reality.

CHAPTER FORTY

Kylara reappeared almost exactly where she'd been before she had left. She considered herself lucky in that regard. Given the little she knew about the void that she had taken herself and Boneclaw to, she had been concerned that she might miss the planet Earth entirely.

Pain throbbed in her thigh and she fell to her knees. She looked down, gritted her teeth, and pulled out the black claw that she had denied Boneclaw. After a few deep breaths, the wound began to heal itself. It would hurt for a few days but it was healing. That meant she'd be fine.

Below her, she could see that the battle was over. What skeletons remained lay on the ground, still and lifeless again. The rifts that had marred the skyline were all closed. Already, the plants that had sprung up in the swamp water that had poured out of the pixie realm had begun to brown, wilt, and shrivel entirely. It seemed they weren't very well equipped for life in a realm that wasn't completely suffused with magic.

The young dragon mage was about to fly down when a voice startled her. "Hey."

She turned to look and at first, saw no one. After a moment, in a crevice between a pile of giant boulders, she saw him.

"Galen?"

He nodded, then shook his head and shrugged. "I don't think my family will let me use that name now."

"I'm sure your family will be happy you're alive."

"Not the Stormwings," He stepped from the crevice barely far enough for her to see what he had become. In the battle against Boneclaw, he had seemed to have the best traits of both human and dragon. Now, in the last light of dusk, she could see that this wasn't the case.

He had the claws and wings of dragons and the body shape of humans, but his skin and face were an uncomfortable mixture of both. His mouth extended like a snout, and long jagged teeth protruded from it. His nose was flattened and stretched on the top, but still roughly human in shape. There was only the slightest smattering of scales. His ears were gone, as was some of his hair. But he still had wisps that hung lankily between patches of scales. His eyes were still human, and they held pain that no dragon could feel. It was the pain of knowing he was broken, of knowing that because of a mistake and bad luck, he would never belong anywhere or to anyone ever again.

"Are you okay?" she asked and tried to hide her discomfort at his looks. She could see why he thought his family would disown him. From what she could tell, they hadn't been nice to him when he'd been handsome. Now that he looked like this and couldn't even become a dragon…well, if he valued his life, he wouldn't return home.

"I'm fine. Better than I deserve. Is Cassandra…"

Kylara turned to look down the mountain. The last time she had seen her aunt, Boneclaw had stuck a claw through her. "I don't know. Come on, let's go see if she—"

Galen shook his head. "I think it'd be better if everyone thinks I died here. I can't learn anything in school anymore and my family will probably hunt me if I'm alive simply because I embarrassed them by losing the skeleton power. But please, can you...I wouldn't be here if not for Cassandra. I knew she was wrong about Boneclaw, but she tried to help me. If she's...that is...if she didn't make it, can you send a beam of light into the sky? That way, if it stays dark, I'll know she's all right."

She nodded. "Farewell, Galen."

"You too." He wandered away without looking back.

Kylara picked up the black claw that had caused her so much trouble, admired its insanely sharp crystalline point, then thought she might know someone who could use a weapon like this.

"Hey, Galen?" she turned quickly and said.

"Yes?" He hadn't walked far yet.

"Catch."

She tossed him the claw. He saw it coming and darted forward, his strange form nonetheless faster and more agile than either of hers.

"Why give me this?" he asked. "Is this a joke?"

That claw had originally come from one of the dragons he'd unearthed with his power, she remembered. She should have assumed it would be a touchy subject for him.

"No," she replied. "I merely thought...if you're out here on your own with no backup, it might come in handy. Take care of yourself, okay?"

He stared at her for a few moments, then snapped her a nod and set off again, the claw held close to his chest.

Kylara flew down to rejoin her mom and friends, terrified that while she had been away, something might have happened to them. She knew she wouldn't be able to forgive herself if something had, but she saw that they had all survived.

Sam and Karl flew to meet her and fell into formation behind her while she spiraled to land beside Hester, Tanya, and Jasmine.

Tanya ran over and hugged her. "I take it this means you locked him up in some other dimension or something?"

She shook her head.

"Then what?" Hester asked. She didn't come to hug her daughter. That wasn't her way. She simply looked at the girl she'd raised with pride in her eyes for emerging victorious from a fight she had no right to survive.

"I threw him into the void—like the place where the Steel Dragon was trapped with him."

Her mother smiled wryly. "Mages. Always thinking outside the box."

Kylara hugged her and for once, the woman responded in kind.

"Hey…uh, speaking of the Steel Dragon…" Sam hooked a thumb behind him. An open portal glowed near the Diamantine house construction site. "She showed up when you left."

The dragon mage had time to snap her jaw shut before Kristen came out of the house. It was almost humbling to see her walking over in a uniform with a cup of coffee in her hand. She wasn't a dragon or a steel-skinned warrior woman, not in that moment. She looked like a cop who was damn happy that a missing person had reappeared.

"So?" Kristen asked. "You're here and he's not. What happened?"

Kylara told them about the battle on the mountaintop. She changed nothing and tried to neither embellish nor gloss over any parts of the tale as she was unsure about the rules of the void and didn't want Boneclaw to somehow come back because of some detail she had inadvertently overlooked.

The only part she tweaked was Galen. She told them about how he could take hold of the shadow dragon, of course, but she said that when she'd returned there was no sign of him and she assumed he was probably dead. It was a tiny lie to both sides and she hoped it would make her feel the least uncomfortable in the long run.

Kristen listened while she spoke, neither asking questions nor offering comments. When she finally finished, the Steel Dragon took another sip of coffee and bowed low to her. She was shocked. If she was the one drinking the coffee, it would no doubt have been sprayed all over the woman's black-and-silver uniform.

"I can't believe that Boneclaw came back," Kristen said. "And that you defeated him in what amounts to single combat is very impressive. Only one dragon has ever done that before. Me."

Kylara didn't know what to say to that. Kristen was her hero and had been ever since she started to follow her exploits over the news. Now they shared the same accomplishment? It was almost too much for words.

"Try not to let it go to your head." Kristen winked at her. "It's a shame, honestly. There continue to be entire realms of magic that my team doesn't know enough about. Your aunt would have been able to teach my mages a considerable amount."

"So she's…"

"She's gone," Amy Williams said and skateboarded into the conversation. "I'm so sorry. I tried what I could but by the time we got here…"

Kylara nodded. She knew what had happened and had merely harbored a hope that she had mistaken what she had seen. As the tears welled in her eyes, she kept her promise to Galen and fired a pillar of light skyward. A coyote howled mournfully from the other side of the mountain. At least, it sounded like a coyote to people who weren't from the desert and hadn't been on that mountaintop.

"She would be very proud of you," Amy said quickly. She seemed nervous about Kylara's tears. "I faced Boneclaw and lost. Every mage who has ever faced him has lost. Everyone except you. I know that would have made her proud. She was a little crazy that way."

The young dragon mage couldn't help but laugh at the incredibly inappropriate joke. "Is it all right if I see her?"

"Of course," Kristen said. "And know you have our sympathies and if you need anything going forward, please ask."

Kylara nodded her thanks and moved to Cassandra's body. The mage still rested on the plinth of earth, washed clean by the last actions of the spirits she had kept in this world for years. Laying still like this, without any thoughts to trouble the edges of her eyes or the corners of her mouth, it was almost uncanny how much she resembled her niece.

She sighed. So many answers to so many questions had died with her. Not questions about who she was. She knew that now. Her actions and the people she kept around her would define her, as they had defined everyone else who came before her. But the little things were lost. Had her mom had a particular smell? A favorite food? Had her dad known any jokes? The minutiae that she had heard other students talk about had always made her wonder. Now, she would wonder forever.

"She was a tough bitch, exactly like her niece," Hester said and rested a hand on Kylara's shoulder.

"Mom!" Kylara said at the use of a curse word.

Her mother didn't smile. She rarely did but she squeezed her shoulder a little tighter. "She was. She kidnapped me, gave your entire school a massive headache, and almost defeated Boneclaw. You're lucky to have family like that."

"I'm lucky to have you too." She took the woman's hand off her shoulder and pulled her into a hug. It hurt to have lost Cassandra and any chance of finding out more about her ancestors, but she was thankful that her aunt had died defending her, Hester, and her friends. She had said that she had wanted a good relationship with her niece, and now, she would always honor her memory. It wasn't exactly fair but it was better than many people had.

"What about us, you big jerk?" Karl asked and ruined the moment.

"Ugh. I guess I'm happy to have you guys too," she joked before Tanya squeezed her in a hug again. Sam and Karl jostled to hug her next and the golden dragon eventually bowed out to Karl in an attempt to save face. Jasmine almost bowed but Kylara stopped her. "We're both mages, Jasmine. You need to stop bowing."

The girl bowed. "As you wish."

"Thanks for still being my friend even after I ditched you," Kylara said to her friends. "I don't know what would have happened if you weren't here."

"You'd be dead." Karl laughed.

"Well...he's not wrong," Tanya said. "But seriously, it's cool. Unless you do it again. Then it's not cool. Cool?"

"Cool," Kylara said.

"There won't be any need for Kylara to attempt a mission like this on her own again," Kristen said and joined the conversation. "Your instincts through all this were good. It's a pity we didn't save the kid but trying to do so is the kind of thing we expect from an honorary member of the Steel Guard."

The Steel Dragon tossed a shining silver badge at Kylara, who caught it, shocked by what was in her hand. "You don't mean—"

"That you're a full-fledged member of the Steel Guard?" Amy asked. "No. We do not mean that. You're still only a kid and good Lord, you have some issues with chain of command."

"But as a friend pointed out to me recently, so did I when I was your age," Kristen said with a smile.

"And for a little while after that," Drew added.

Kylara couldn't help but smile at the man. She hadn't seen him come through the portal.

"I hope that if we make you an honorary intern, you'll finally understand to call us first and we can talk about what to do next."

"There's a magical tracker in that badge, huh?" Karl asked.

Kristen gritted her teeth, while Amy reddened and turned away.

"If you ever want to go off the grid, call me, all right?" Drew said and held a business card out. "I'm not a dragon like you, but if you want to cruise around busting the heads of men who don't know how to treat women right…well, who am I to argue with a mage as powerful as yourself?"

"I thought you said you weren't a cop anymore," Kylara reminded him.

"I'm not. Cops can't go around busting heads. That would be terrible." Drew smiled slyly. "But I do sometimes work as a bodyguard. My rates are cheap too, at least for people I like and I know can handle themselves in a fight."

"Thanks, Drew," she said and took the card. "If I ever run away again, I'll be sure to give you a call." She said it like a joke and everyone around her laughed, but the look in his eyes told her that he knew she was serious.

"It's not much, but if anyone wants to stay for dinner, I have beans on the stove," Hester said.

A few minutes later—and a few trips through the portal—they were all seated outside on a flat stone Hester had sliced in half to make into a table for this occasion. They'd added fried chicken and premade sandwiches to the beans, along with every hotdog from the nearest gas station.

Kylara looked around the table and felt warm and safe in the company of her family, her friends, and her…colleagues? She wasn't sure on that last one as she still had school ahead of her, but she knew that whatever happened, she was thankful to have all these people with her along the way. And she was thankful for those who had been left behind or gone on their own path.

Dinner was eaten with the intense gusto and amicable silence of the hungry.

The mages cleared the table, and Hester began to fuss about who could sleep where despite her not having any sheets, beds, or any other creature comforts.

"Oh, Kylara, I forgot to tell you, I spoke to the headmaster," Tanya said over a cup of tea.

"She must be worried sick. Thank you so much for telling her I'm all right."

"Actually, she wasn't worried about you."

"Wait, what? The last time I talked to her she was still obsessed with the cuff. That's changed?"

"I wouldn't go that far." Tanya smiled mischievously. "She said to tell you that you have considerable schoolwork to make up." The girl plopped a thick stack of papers and books on the table. "But if you want any of the work to count, she first wants a ten-thousand-word essay on when it's appropriate for mages and dragons to reduce the powers of others and when people should have their autonomy."

Kylara sagged. "I guess I'll get started."

"It can wait until morning," Kristen said and winked. "I can pull a few strings."

"Like until Monday?" she asked.

The woman looked at her like she was crazy. "You may be all right with being on Amythist's bad side, but not me. Go to bed. You have schoolwork to do."

Everyone laughed and she reddened, but she didn't mind. If this was the price of being a part of this community, she was happy to pay it.

KEVIN'S AUTHOR NOTES
JANUARY 12, 2021

And we've come to the end of Kylara's first story arc. The big bad is gone; although the canny reader might note that Lord Boneclaw isn't actually *dead*, he's at least *gone* for the time being. Of course, we may see the old lizard again someday…or maybe not. Time will tell.

But don't worry; there's still plenty more to come from Kylara. Three more books, in fact, an entire second arc of story. Ky's about to experience a bunch of major changes. Some of them are going to be really cool; others outright terrifying. Can't wait to share book four with you next month!

As I write this, we're at the very beginning of a brand new year. I have high hopes for 2021. Actually, my 2020 wasn't awful, writing-wise. For the first time in my writing career I managed to pen a *million* new words in 2020. That's crazy, right? I've never hit that number before, and it's been a goal for a lot of years.

This year, I'm setting the standard even higher, of course. My aim for 2021 is to hit and maintain 'Pulp Speed Five' as early as I can work up to it and then keep it running as long as I can. My stretch goal is to hit it for the entire year.

What's 'Pulp Speed'? Well, it's a term an author who helped

get me started as a professional writer uses for highly productive writers. Pulp Speed One is a million words a year. Each speed above that adds another 200,000 words, so Pulp Speed Five is one point eight *million* words if it's maintained for a year, and 150,000 words a month.

I don't write that fast, folks, so this is aspirational, not something I'm stepping up to tomorrow. It's a huge goal, a crazy goal, and like the million word target, I might not hit it this first try. That's OK. It took me a few years of trying to make the million words, but I was always moving in the right direction.

OK, why the focus on speed here? Well — it's not actually above writing any faster. For me, it's more about spending more time writing and less on other things, like goofing off playing video games or doom-scrolling on FaceBook. If I was somehow cutting corners on the work, it might damage the quality of the storytelling, and that's not something I *ever* want to do.

But I *do* love these challenges! I enjoy pushing myself to hit that next level, whatever it might be. I've done other bits like this in the past: a book in a month, a book in two weeks, other assorted short challenges. But my biggest struggle isn't so much doing a lot in a short time. I'm pretty awesome at procrastinating something until I have almost no time left and then getting it all done at record speed…

But that's not what I want to be good at, so I make these pushes to improve my consistency.

The result tends to be more stories for you, my reader, and *also* that I get better at this whole storytelling shtick. The more I write, the more my skills improve. I want to maximize that so I can bring you the very best tales I can.

This year is going to be busy! Michael and I have the final three books in this series to release. Then we've got six or so books in a new Children of Tiamat series, featuring a character you've already seen who hasn't had their own tale yet.

I'm wrapping up three of my own series and launching three new ones this year. The new stuff is *cool*, too! I've got:

1) An urban fantasy series with a werewolf who decides to become a Batman-like superhero.

2) A science fiction series about an old warrior who fought for a corrupt empire, escaped, and now must find a ways to atone for the terrible things he did.

3) Another science fiction series set in the near future involving conflict that spans both the real world and a virtual one. Spaceship battles online, and real-world threats offline.

So darned many stories, so little time. I've got at least three other series I really want to write, too. Maybe those will be what I'll work on *next* year…? Time will tell!

Thanks for reading, and I hope you'll explore some of these other adventures with me in the year ahead!

MICHAEL'S AUTHOR NOTES
JANUARY 15, 2021

Thank you for not only reading this story but these *Author Notes* as well!

I am firmly entrenched with high expectations that 2021 is going to be a better year than 2020. The year has gotten off to a rough start, but last year started great and then went south pretty quickly.

Let's hope for the reverse this year.

Total and complete congratulations to Kevin for producing so many words this year! I have watched him go after his goals year after year, and what I find aspirational is his attitude about it.

I've watched him miss his goals, and he just gets up on January 1st, dusts off his pants, and then proceeds to work on beating the goal in the new year.

I've never noticed him beat himself up with attitude or criticize himself (as I might perhaps do, for example) but take the reality and then move ahead.

And in 2020 he beat his goal.

Dogged determination from the man is something I can aspire to, and I appreciate Kevin influencing my life by just living his.

If you get a chance to talk to Kevin at an event, I encourage you to do so. (See how I assume we will get back to events where we meet people again in the future? I'm very optimistic about 2021.)

We both appreciate you reading Kylara's story, and I hope you look forward to completing this series (6 books) and that we can entice you with the NEXT story, as well!

Ad Aeternitatem,

Michael Anderle

BOOKS BY KEVIN MCLAUGHLIN

Steel Dragon Series
(with Michael Anderle)

Steel Dragon 1

Steel Dragon 2

Steel Dragon 3

Steel Dragon 4

Steel Dragon 5

Dragon's Daughter
(with Michael Anderle)

Never A Dragon (Book 1)

Dead Dragon New tricks (Book 2)

Thicker Than Blood (coming soon)

Adventures of the Starship Satori (Space Opera blended with military SF)

Finding Satori - prequel short story, available only to email list fans!

Book 1 - Ad Astra: Book 2 - Stellar Legacy

Book 3 - Deep Waters

Book 4 - No Plan Survives Contact

Book 5 - Liberty

Book 6 - Satori's Destiny

Book 7 - Ashes of War

Book 8 - Embers of War

Book 9 - Dust and Iron

Book 10 - Clad in Steel

Book 11 - Brave New Worlds (2019)
Book 12 - Warrior's Marque (2020)

The Ragnarok Saga (Military SF)

Accord of Fire - Free prequel short story, available only to email list fans!

Book 1 - Accord of Honor
Book 2 - Accord of Mars
Book 3 - Accord of Valor
Book 4 - Ghost Wing
Book 5 - Ghost Squadron
Book 6 - Ghost Fleet (2019)

Valhalla Online Series (A Ragnarok Saga Story)

Book 1 - Valhalla Online
Book 2 - Raiding Jotunheim
Book 3 - Vengeance Over Vanaheim
Book 4 - Hel Hath No Fury

Blackwell Magic Series (Urban Fantasy)

Book 1 - By Darkness Revealed
Book 2 - Ashes Ascendant
Book 3 - Dead In Winter
Book 4 - Claws That Catch
Book 5 - Darkness Awakes
Book 6 - Spellbinding Entanglements
By A Whisker (short story)
The Raven and the Rose - Free novelette for email list fans!

Dead Brittania Series:

Dead Brittania (short prequel story)

Book 1 - King of the Dead
Book 2 - Queen of Demons

Raven's Heart Series (Urban Fantasy)

Book 1 - Stolen Light
Book 2 - Webs in the Dark
Book 3 - Shades of Moonlight

Other Titles:

Over the Moon (SF romance)
Midnight Visitors (Steampunk Cat short story)
Demon Ex Machina (Steampunk Cat short story)
The Coffee Break Novelist (help for writers!)
You Must Write (Heinlein's rules for writers)

BOOKS BY MICHAEL ANDERLE

Sign up for the LMBPN email list to be notified of new releases and special deals!

https://lmbpn.com/email/

For a complete list of books by Michael Anderle, please visit:

www.lmbpn.com/ma-books/

CONNECT WITH THE AUTHORS

Connect with Kevin McLaughlin

Website: http://kevinomclaughlin.com/

Facebook: https://www.facebook.com/kevins.studio

Twitter: https://twitter.com/KOMcLaughlin

Instagram: https://www.instagram.com/kevins.studio/

Connect with Michael Anderle

Website: http://lmbpn.com

Email List: http://lmbpn.com/email/

https://www.facebook.com/LMBPNPublishing

https://twitter.com/MichaelAnderle

https://www.instagram.com/lmbpn_publishing/

https://www.bookbub.com/authors/michael-anderle

www.ingramcontent.com/pod-product-compliance
Lightning Source LLC
LaVergne TN
LVHW011803060526
838200LV00053B/3660